Warsaw

Key
→ Christians
⟹ Turks

Scale

0
0

D0734459

POLES Lvov

Kosice

•Kamenets

Boundary of Ottoman Empire

TARTARS

TRANSYLVANIA

CRIMEA

MOLDAVIA

imisoara

WALLACHIA

River Danube

s •

Sofia Plovdiv

Edirne

•Istanbul

onika •

Children of the Book

Other books by Peter Carter

Madatan
The Black Lamp
The Gates of Paradise
Under Goliath
The Sentinels
Mao

Children of the Book

Peter Carter

OXFORD UNIVERSITY PRESS
Oxford Toronto Melbourne

Oxford University Press, Walton Street, Oxford OX2 6DP

London Glasgow New York Toronto
Delhi Bombay Calcutta Madras Karachi
Nairobi Dar es Salaam Cape Town Harere
Kuala Lumpur Singapore Hong Kong Tokyo
Melbourne Auckland

and associates in
Beirut Berlin Ibadan Mexico City Nicosia

British Library Cataloguing in Publication Data

Carter, Peter, 1929
The children of the book
I. Title
832'.914[J]   PZ7

ISBN 0-19-271456-2

Typeset by Rowland Phototypesetting Ltd
Bury St Edmunds, Suffolk
Printed by Biddles Ltd
Guildford, Surrey

In Memory of
Karl Munichreiter

Contents

Part 1
The Threat

Part 2
The Attack

Part 3
The Siege

Part
1

The Threat
1682

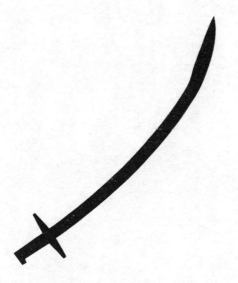

Chapter One

ISTANBUL
6 August 1682

THE crack of dawn. From innumerable minarets the muezzins of Istanbul called to the Faithful of Islam, 'It is better to pray than to sleep!'

Some of the Faithful agreed, rose, and said their prayers, others preferred to stay in bed as the towers and turrets of the enormous city began to quiver in the glaring heat of midsummer, the domes of the great mosques rising above the morning haze like clouds or distant, snow-clad mountains.

At the New Palace, along three miles of wall which stretched from the Golden Horn to the Sea of Marmara, the Sultan's guard was changed. To the clamour of trumpets and drums, swords flashed and scarlet tunics glowed in the sunlight as the Janissaries marched to their posts with the precision of the crack infantry which they were. The night guard tramped thankfully back to their barracks and the new guard, freshly bathed, braced themselves for their morning's duty.

The sun climbed from the dust of Asia; men kept to the shady side of the streets, the sherbert sellers did well, and the more pious Muslims put out trays of water for the despised stray dogs of the city. But, hot though it was, a crowd had gathered by the palace, at the mound outside the Gate of Paradise.

At mid-morning a troop of Sipahi clattered from the gate. The crowd stirred, men at the back standing on tip-toe to see over the heads of those in front, but the squadron of cavalry swung left and trotted down the hill to the Imperial arsenal at Kasimpasha.

The crowd sighed with disappointment and there was a ripple of talk; 'No, not yet . . . no decision . . . nothing . . . no need to push, Brother,' and, in the nature of crowds, some men slipped away to get on with their affairs, others, with a few moments to spare joined in, and a hard knot of idlers stayed put, hoping to be there when The Moment came.

Across the glittering waters of the Golden Horn, in the Christian quarter of Pera, the envoys to the Sultan of the Emperor of Austria were also waiting for The Moment. With their secretary they were sitting around a table of cedar wood sipping coffee. On the desk was a letter. The secretary had already written the salutation and the elegant script flowed across the head of the page;

'To Leopold the First, by God's grace King of Germany, Holy Roman Emperor Elect, King of Bohemia, Hungary, and Croatia, Archduke of Austria, etc; Your Imperial Majesty. . . .'

The rest of the page was blank, waiting to be filled in when The Moment came.

The secretary poured a little more coffee. 'Of course,' he said, 'they may declare for peace. They did last January.'

Count Caprara sighed a yes, but there was no conviction in his voice. He strolled to the window and stared across the Golden Horn at the vast capital of the Ottoman Empire. 'One thing is certain,' he said.

Baron Kunitz, the other envoy, raised an eyebrow. 'What might that be?'

Caprara tapped on the window sill. 'Whatever they tell us will be a lie.'

The sun rose higher; in the city men lingered by the fountains, the water carriers were kept busy and the sherbert sellers edged their price up fractionally. Inside the Sultan's palace, in the courtyard of the Gate of Felicity, a young Circassian slave, carrying a silver cage with two nightingales in it, stepped from a green-tiled kiosk and, shading the birds with his hand, walked through a garden where roses showed their blooms – and their thorns – and by a domed chamber, guarded by a whole company of the Imperial Guard, he stopped and bowed deeply.

The slave was not merely bowing at the soldiers, nor at the room, but at those inside the chamber; for he, and the guards, the eight thousand people who worked in the palace, and the million people of the Istanbul, from the richest man in Eyub down to the poorest beggar in the slums of Yedi Kule, knew that in the chamber, sitting in state, was the King of the Age, the Sword of Islam, the Defender of the Faith – and the Faithful – the Supreme ruler of the Ottoman Empire, the Sultan Mehmed the Fourth, and that sitting with him was the great council of the Empire, the Imperial Divan.

Inside the chamber, on the purple divan which gave the Council its name, Mehmed stirred impatiently. The Council had been in session for five hours. Soon it would be noon and the muezzins would call for midday prayer. It was time for a decision, and, in any case, he was bored. He crooked his little finger and, on his right, the Grand Vizier of the Empire, Kara Mustafa, struck his breast three times.

'Now, let Allah be my judge,' he said, and looked around at the Council. The Aga of the *Janissaries*, who was the Commander of the Ottoman infantry, the Agas of the *Topcu*, the *Lagunci*, the *Sebeci*, and the *Sipahi* – the artillery, the engineers, the armourers, and the cavalry, at the Grand Admiral of the Fleet, the Lesser Viziers of the Empire, and at the *Ulema*, the Council for Law and Religion.

'Let Allah judge me,' he said again. 'Now we should prepare for war against Austria.' He paused, his dark face which gave him his nickname of Kara, the Black, bowed. Seven months before he had stood before the Council, pleaded for the same war, and been rejected. Especially the Ulema had condemned him for proposing war against a kingdom with which the Empire had a peace treaty.

But seven months of persuasion, bribery, and threats had changed that, and now. . . .

He waved his hand towards the north, to Austria, to Europe. 'They, the Christians, are weak and divided. The Austrian king is a fool, his army is pathetic, he has no money to hire more troops, he is at war with the French on the Rhine, and because he is what the Giaours call a catholic, many protestants will join us when we attack him. We can march and take the whole of Hungary.'

Mustafa closed his fingers as if plucking a peach, but there was a languor about the movement, an air, almost, of boredom, for, in the end the issue was decided, the debate a formality. The Empire had to go to war, not because it was threatened by Austria but because the huge army which maintained the Ottoman rule across the enormous Empire had to be used. Idle soldiers meant mutinous soldiers and every man present knew what a mutiny of the army could mean. Mustafa sometimes thought that the Empire was like a great cart being pushed up an endless incline. As long as the cart could be kept moving it would keep moving. Once it stopped it would go, irreversibly, backwards. Sometimes the Grand Vizier thought that he was the only man in the Empire who truly understood that; that he, and he alone, was pushing the cart.

But still there were one or two lingering doubts. 'Poland,' murmured the Aga of the Sipahi, 'Will it not aid Austria?'

Mustafa was dismissive. 'Poland is nothing. A backward, barbarous place. The Poles have enough on their hands with the Russians and the Tartars. Besides, the French will bribe them not to interfere. The French Ambassador has assured me of that.'

Another dissenting voice. 'The German states? Leopold is their Emperor.'

Mustafa smiled. 'In name only. Besides, why should they interfere? What is Hungary to them? No, Austria stands alone, and alone she is nothing. Nothing.'

No more dissent but no assent either as the Council speculated on what a war with Austria really meant. Mustafa played his last card. 'It will be a Holy War,' he said.

There was a click of scandalized disapproval from the Head of the Religious Council and Mustafa made a mental note to have him assassinated at the first possible moment, but no other objection.

The Sultan stroked his red beard. 'A Holy War,' he murmured. 'Let it be so then. *Bismillah*, it is as God wills.'

The Bandmaster of the Imperial Guard raised an ivory baton, trumpets blared and cymbals clashed. The keepers of the Gate of Paradise rushed forward swinging their staves and drove back the crowd. A double file of Janissaries marched out, curved swords over their shoulders and following them, dressed in gold and white, under a green standard, came the Master of the Sultan's horses. Behind him a dozen men staggered under the weight of a huge baulk of gilded timber, decorated with a dozen horse tails. On the mound they heaved up the beam and slid it into a socket.

'Allah is Great,' roared the Master of the Horse, and 'Allah is Great,' the crowd roared back, for at last The Moment had come.

On the edge of the crowd a man who had been lounging by the Gate all morning threw away a half-eaten peach and, disregarding the heat, as if the devil Iblis was at his heels, ran down the hill to the quay of Baghee Kapisi, where, flouting all custom, he paid fifty achmas for a six-oared caique to row him alone across the Golden Horn to Pera, and the house of the Austrian envoys.

A little later the secretary took up his pen and, as Caprara dictated, began to write the letter he had addressed that morning.

'. . . I have the honour to inform you that this day, His Imperial Majesty the Sultan Mehmed the Fourth caused to be erected outside his palace the Tugh, that is twelve horse tails, which means –'

The scratch of the secretary's pen stopped and Caprara stopped speaking with it.

The secretary poured out a little Tokay. 'The horse-tails merely mean that the Sultan intends to leave the city,' he said. 'It is an old Tartar custom.'

Caprara gave the secretary a sceptical glance.

'Yes, I know,' the secretary continued. 'But Ramadan is next month and I can't see the Sultan leaving before then.'

Kunitz also poured himself some wine. 'Why do they do it?' he asked.

'Ramadan? Fast you mean?'

'Yes. Is it like Lent?'

'Not quite.' The secretary shook his head. 'Although the idea might have come from the Bible. Muhammad drew quite a lot of ideas from Christianity. Jesus is a Muslim prophet, you know, second only to Muhammad himself. In fact the Muslims call Christians the People of the Book – the Bible – you know, Jews too come to that. There are special laws for dealing with them. And lots of Muslim names come from the Bible, Yusuf, that's Joseph, Daud is David, Mary is Mariam, Moses is Musa, and Christ himself is Nabi Isa, the prophet Jesus. But Ramadan, it commemorates Muhammad's exile in the desert and the idea is to make every Muslim know what it is like to be poor and hungry and thirsty, so that they will show mercy to the poor.'

'Interesting,' said Caprara.

'Yes, it is a very egalitarian religion. All Muslims are supposed to be equal'– a frown crossed the face of Caprara who most emphatically did not believe in social equality – 'in theory, that is,' the secretary added, hastily.

'In theory,' Kunitz said. 'So this fast of Ramadan. Then?'

The secretary shrugged. 'Then there is the feast of Bahrein and after that the Sultan will almost certainly go hunting. He is quite insane about it.'

'Like our own master,' Kunitz said. 'How long will he hunt for?'

'Oh, two or three months. When the Sultan hunts it is quite a spectacle, believe me. Ten thousand beaters . . .'

'And then?'

'Winter in the north, I should imagine. In Edirne.'

Caprara drummed his fingers on the table. 'I think that we should go with him, don't you?'

The secretary smiled crookedly. 'You will find that you have little choice.'

'What does that mean?'

'Just an old Turkish custom.'

Kunitz leaned forward. 'Are you saying that we will be hostages?'

'Something like that.' The secretary waved a white, diplomatic hand. 'Should we finish?'

'Yes,' Caprara paced across the room. 'Where were we?'

'The horse-tails.'

Caprara shook his head. 'Horse-tails! Utter barbarism. Continue as follows, ''. . . which means that the Sultan will soon leave the city. I must warn your Majesty that the Ottoman Empire has already been placed on a war footing and we are convinced that at a meeting of the Divan which took place this morning the Grand Council has decided to make war upon us. However, as hostilities cannot take place before next spring it would seem that we have time –'' He stopped in mid-sentence as the secretary shook his head.

'Not us,' said the secretary. 'Them. They have the time.'

The sun dipped over Europe. A breeze from the cool waters of the Black Sea brought relief to the sweltering city. Catching the breeze a fleet of ships came down the Bosporus. The city bustled to complete its affairs. In the bazaars the last bargains of the day were struck and in the slave market by the Burnt Pillar a few mediocre captives brought from Russia by Crimean Tartars were sold off at knock-down prices. And, as the Muezzins called for evening prayer, a courier, wearing the white and red of the Royal house of the Habsburgs, drove his horse through the Edirne Gate in the walls of Constantine and flogged his mount north, to Vienna.

Chapter Two

OSIJEK

EIGHT days later, having crossed Thrace, the Austrian courier was in Belgrade in Turkish Hungary. The courier would have very much liked to leave the Turkish possessions by crossing the River Drava over the great military bridge at Osijek, eighty miles to the east, but as the Turks had no intention of allowing an Austrian to take a look at their launching point into Austrian Hungary, he was politely but firmly directed up the east bank of the Danube and provided with an escort of cavalry to make sure that he did not lose his way. Consequently the courier missed the chance of doing some useful spying and young Timur Ven missed the interesting sight of an Imperial Austrian courier.

Timur was a young recruit in the Janissaries, the regular Turkish infantry. He was in the Twenty-eighth Orta of the Janissaries under the command of a Colonel Vasif, and their duty was to guard the bridge, over the Drava River.

There were really two bridges; a huge pontoon bridge over the river itself, and then another, vaster one which ran for six miles across the marshes of the far bank, its enormous timbering and spectacular watch-towers a monument to Turkish engineering skills, its missing planks and rotting beams, a monument to Turkish neglect and apathy.

Not that the ramshackle state of the bridge was entirely due to neglect. If Turkish troops could march north over the bridge to invade Austrian territory, so, too, could Austrian troops march south and invade the Ottoman possessions, and so a little neglect was quite sensible. The bridge could always be repaired if necessary.

But guarding Osijek and the bridge was not the most exciting task in the world and leaning against the parapet of the fortress, Timur yawned deeply. On the gun-platform, fifty feet beneath him, draped across the bronze muzzle of a cannon, a dozing cat opened its green eyes and yawned insolently back.

Timur plucked a pebble from the parapet and held it between his fingers, aiming it at the cat, but then he hurled the pebble away in a wide, safe arc. It would be wrong to hurt the animal. Had not the Prophet himself, Muhammad, peace be on his name, cut away the sleeve of his gown rather than disturb his cat which had fallen asleep on it?

A hundred feet beneath the cat the pebble clicked against a dazzling limestone rock and ricocheted into the river. The splash disturbed a moorhen which scuttled downstream.

A flock of white storks beat their way across the marshes, buzzards and kites soared in slow circles around the town. On the watchtowers of the bridge the guard was changed without fuss but smartly, for Colonel Vasif, the new commander of the garrison, was a great believer in order, discipline, and Islam, in, the men often thought, that sequence, and he could have an extremely short temper.

A drowsy hour passed. Goats bleated, dogs barked in the huddle of white-washed houses which lounged against each other, a bell tolled and was answered by another, which gave a melancholy clank.

In his eyrie Timur leaned forward expectantly. Far below, from the blue shadows of a house came a man. He wore a tall black hat without a brim, rather like a chimney pot.

'The priest Metaxis,' Timur said to himself.

A moment later, from the other end of the lane, another man appeared. He was dressed in black and wore a shallow black hat with a wide brim.

'Pastor Grauen,' Timur thought.

Halfway down the lane the two men met, glared at each other with loathing, then, neither being willing to give way in the narrow lane, elbowed each other, the Pastor Grauen winning the battle and striding off triumphantly. On the bridge two sentries laughed, derisively and slapped their swords.

Timur grinned down, sharing the joke. The little comedy had developed over the past three months. The priest, Metaxis, and his flock of Greek Orthodox Christians had always lived in the town, born under Turkish rule as their fathers, and *their* fathers had before them. The Pastor Grauen and his flock were Protestants, refugees from Catholic persecution in Austrian Hungary. Both groups were Christians but there was no love lost between them. Once there had been a violent clash as the two congregations met on the way to their respective churches. Colonel Vasif had ordered the two ministers to be hauled before him and had suggested that, to avoid meeting, they exchange churches. When this reasonable offer had been indignantly rejected, Vasif had warned them against bringing their disgusting religious squabbles into the land of the Sultan.

'Believe in what you wish,' he had said, 'As long as you believe in God. Learn from Islam! Learn from the Jews! Do they squabble? Pay your taxes and you will be left in peace, but any more trouble and I will have you flogged.'

As Grauen and Metaxis disappeared into their churches Timur shook his head. He had only been in Osijek a few weeks and Christian ways were still strange to him. People of the Book they might be but their behaviour seemed to him merely childish. He shook his head in amazement but he was no longer interested for, far away, on the Belgrade road, there was a plume of dust and a flash of light, as if a mirror was shining. But Timur knew that there were no mirrors on the dusty road to Belgrade. Armed men were coming to Osijek.

An hour or so later, Father Metaxis and his flock heard horsemen coming but, with a lifetime's experience behind them, they did not turn their heads as much as an inch but remained standing, their faces as stiff as the gilded faces of Christ and His mother painted on the Ikon over the altar.

Further up the street Pastor Grauen heard the horses, too. Over the heads of his congregation he saw through the open doors of his chapel a brilliant, sun-splashed dapple of purple and yellow, the flash of a lance head, and a swarthy, triangular face as a rider, bent low in his saddle, peered into the chapel and gave a derisive, piercing whistle.

Not knowing the Turks as Metaxis did, or at any rate not knowing Turkish cavalry, Grauen waved angrily. Fortunately for him the Turk missed the gesture and so Grauen was able to continue his sermon on The One Hundred Certain Proofs of the Damnation of the Pope and the Emperor of Austria, instead of finding himself being given a hundred lashes on the soles of his feet for insulting a messenger of the Bey of Belgrade.

In a cool, airy room, high in the fortress, Colonel Vasif heard the cavalry arrive but he did not stir from his desk where he was going through the Company's returns for the quarter. Sooner or later he would be told who had arrived, although if it was later the guard might find out what a bamboo cane felt like. The garrison had already found out this little habit of Vasif's and so, before the first foot of the first rider had touched the ground, there was a knock on Vasif's door.

'Come.' Vasif peered over the top of his Dutch spectacles.

Timur, who was Vasif's personal servant, slipped into the room and bowed his head. 'Colonel, *Corbaci*, there is a messenger from the Bey of Belgrade.'

Vasif took off his spectacles and gazed benignly on the cropped head bent before him. 'My uniform,' he said, for although he was the master of Osijek, a messenger from the Governor of Belgrade had to be treated with the respect due his master.

Timur laid out Vasif's uniform as the Corbaci slipped off his loose cotton shirt and trousers and bathed. Within ten minutes, resplendent in the red silk of a colonel of the Janissaries, he met the messenger, equally dazzling in yellow and purple livery.

Coffee from Konya, sherbert, spiced sesame cake, polite enquiries after health, and then, etiquette disposed of, a great parchment envelope with the imperial seal handed over. Vasif slit it with a silver knife. After one glance he raised his eyes.

'You know what this is?'

'Yes, Corbaci.'

'So.' Vasif walked to the window and looked down on his domain; the old town with the green dome of the Greek Orthodox church sprouting from red-tiled roofs like a giant onion, the new town, where Grauen and the refugees lived, the elegant minaret of the mosque, kitchen gardens, pastures sloping down to the river, the great bridge striding across the marshes to Christendom, its farthest towers lost in the heat haze. Vasif looked again at the letter;

'You will take all steps . . . force whatever labour you require . . . a company of engineers will arrive within the month' – and, the key phrase – 'The bridge must be repaired.'

'So,' Vasif said, 'it is –' he pointed through the window, across the river and the bridge and the marshes to where, on the distant horizon, blue hills smudged the sky.

'Yes, Corbaci.' The messenger bowed. 'It is war with Austria. We march in the spring.'

The messenger left and Vasif sent Timur for the captain of the company, the *Odabasi* Osman and gave him certain instructions. Then he sent for the cook and gave *him* certain instructions. As the cook listened his eyes opened wide but his mouth remained shut, for it was not wise to question an order from Corbaci Vasif.

Afterwards Vasif slept for a while. When he woke he gave Timur a Koran. 'Read to me,' he said. 'Read the Sura of the Cataclysm.'

Timur squatted before his colonel, opened the holy book, and read that chapter which tells of the Day of Judgement when every man will stand alone before Allah and every soul will know what it has done, and what it has failed to do. When he had finished Vasif nodded approval. 'You read well.'

'If the Corbaci says so.' Timur was pleased by the compliment, although he had recited the Sura by heart, the script meaning little to him.

Vasif paced to the window, Timur at his heels. 'How is your father?' Vasif asked.

'Well, Corbaci.' Timur thought of his father, an ex-janissary, now running a mildly prosperous coffee house in Istanbul.

'Good.' Vasif folded his arms. 'He was always strong. A man among men, real men who knew that Allah gave them life so that He might take it from them when it pleased Him. Yes.'

In the courtyard below them a file of men came from the barracks, casual, slipshod, talking and laughing. Vasif jerked his small, square chin.

'They think that they are men. Janissaries! They are no more than dogs. They idle away their service here and they see the Christians, the men drinking, and the women unveiled walking the streets like harlots, and they forget Allah and His laws. They whine because they have to turn out for a night watch. Bismillah! I will take the fat off them. I remember when I was in the Ninth Orta, thirty years ago on the Dniester. Fifty miles non-stop we marched and the cold so bitter our eyelids froze together. Aye, fifty miles through the snow with the Poles and the Cossacks on our heels and our bellies empty but not one whimper – not even from me and I was only a lad then, your age. The last of the Devshirme.'

'Corbaci.' Timur bowed. Every man in the garrison knew that Vasif was a *Devshirme*, perhaps the last of the Christian children who, in the old days, the Turks had taken from Christian families to be brought up as Muslims and Janissaries, knowing no father but the Sultan, no family but the army, and no fear except the fear of Allah. It was that which, perhaps accounted for the very un-Turkish blue eyes which glittered in Vasif's weatherbeaten face.

'Yes,' Vasif's voice was musing. 'Fifty miles through the snow and ice and the Corbaci and the Odabasis dead. It was your father who led us. He was the Bayrakdar and he carried the standard every inch of the way. A real man. Yes.'

Vasif paused and Timur had a vision of the Ninth Orta struggling through a Polish blizzard and his father carrying the forked red and yellow standard. 'Corbaci.' Timur placed his hand on his breast.

With grave courtesy Vasif touched his own breast. 'You know of the camels of Allah?'

Yes, Timur knew of them. Some Muslims believed that if a Believer died and was buried among infidels then his soul could be stolen and damned to Hell forever, and so Allah, in his infinite mercy had provided seventy-two thousand ghostly camels who wandered the Earth taking the dead back to Islam.

'So.' Vasif returned to his desk. 'Next year will find work for the camels.'

Sunset. Vasif put on his best uniform, buckled on his sword, picked up his hat, and went down the spiral stairs into the courtyard. As he arrived, Janissary Tedeki, who had the loudest voice in the entire garrison, took a breath and threw his head back;

'Allah is most great,' he called. 'Allah is most great. There is no God but Allah, no God but Allah. Come to prayer, come to prayer. Come to salvation, come to salvation. There is no God but Allah.'

Vasif placed his hat on a stone bench, put on a white skull cap, and removed his shoes. Three white lines were painted across the yard. Vasif toed the middle of the first line and stood facing south-east, towards Mecca. The yard filled with the men of the Orta who fell in beside him. This evening there were no gaps in the lines for every man had got the message; no missing prayers this evening. Even four defaulters had been brought up from an entirely unpleasant dungeon so that they might join in.

The sun touched the horizon and the men knelt and touched the ground with their heads, abasing themselves before Allah.

'In the name of Allah,' Vasif chanted, 'In the name of Allah the merciful, the compassionate, praise be to Allah, Lord of the worlds, the merciful, the compassionate, King of the Day of Judgement. It is You we worship, You we ask for help. Lead us to the path of the righteous, the path of those on whom You have poured down Your mercy, not the path of those against whom You are angry, nor those who have strayed.'

Vasif struck the ground again with deep veneration and his men knelt with him. Three times they struck the ground, united in the equality of Islam. Then Vasif clicked his fingers and, like a shadow, Timur ran and brought Vasif his hat.

It was a curious hat. A tall cylinder of white felt with long flaps which flowed over Vasif's shoulders and, oddly, pinned to the front was a silver spoon. But although the spoon looked odd it was a symbol of great importance. Once, when Vasif as a young Janissary had been stationed at Sidon on the Mediterranean, a Dutchman, trading in wool, had laughed at the spoon and Vasif had slashed his head off his shoulders before the Dutchman had finished laughing. Now Vasif was about to show what the spoon symbolized.

'Let us eat,' he said.

The men put on their hats, identical to Vasif's and sat, cross-legged, in a circle around a fire. Vasif and his captains, the *Odabasis* brought from the kitchen a huge brass tray piled high with rice and lamb and served each man in turn, without distinction of rank.

The men ate in silence, for this was no ordinary meal. When the Janissaries had first been formed the common meal had bound the corps together like a family, just as the common meal had bound together the Tartar nomads who had founded the Ottoman Empire four hundred years earlier. Indeed, every name in the Janissaries was a reminder of that. The *ojak* – the corps – meant hearth, the fire around which the men ate. Corbaci – Colonel – meant Ladler of soup; and that was why the Janissaries wore a spoon on their tall hats – and that was why it was unwise to laugh at them.

The men ate and the fire glowed like a baleful eye, lighting here and there on a high cheekbone, a hooked nose, a knife. Shadows danced and flickered on the walls, grotesque humpbacked shapes swaying to and fro. Sitting next to his Corbaci, Timur thought that the shadows were like camels, the ghostly camels which in His infinite mercy Allah had created to save the souls of poor, fallen Muslims. The camels were wandering the Earth now, he thought, at that very minute, from Buda in the north to Cairo in the south, from Kaffa in the Crimea to Berat in Albania, seventy-two thousand camels wandering through sand-storms and blizzards . . .

The simple meal came to an end and Vasif stood up. 'Janissaries,' he said, in his dry, clipped voice. 'Today the Bey of Belgrade sent me orders. The bridge is to be repaired.'

There was a little growl from the men, a menacing, sullen murmur. Every soldier present knowing as well as Vasif did that repairing the bridge meant only one thing. Vasif looked around the circle. Was the growl one of pleasure or displeasure? Soldiers were not always overjoyed at the prospect of going to war and having their brains blown out, no matter what loot there might be in prospect, besides which, many of them were, quite illegally, married and some actually had small farms and shops. Not that Vasif was unduly worried about what his men thought. Any man who did not obey his orders would lose his head and, if necessary, he, Vasif, would remove it. He had done it before.

'Now,' Vasif clapped his hands sharply. 'Let the band play.'

The band marched forward, blasting on the long Turkish trumpets and its drummers hammering on the great brass cooking pots which doubled as the Janissaries' drums. In Osijek, in tiny oil-lit rooms, men and women heard the thunder of the drums and looked at each other fearfully. Pastor Grauen glanced up testily from his copy of 'The Sufferings of the Hungarian Calvinists at the Hands of the Catholic Leopold, Arch-Duke of Austria.' Father Metaxis fell on his knees and prayed for the intercession of Saints Cyril and Methodius. A Turkish blacksmith, a retired Janissary, grinned across his forge at his mate, drew his finger across his throat, and laughed, a jolly, infectious, Turkish laugh, and his mate laughed with him. On the edge of the marshes on the far side of the river, a party of Hungarian horsemen, raiding into Turkish territory for cattle and general mayhem heard the drums too, saw the glare of the fire above the walls of the citadel, and, for that night, turned their horses away.

The drums of the Janissaries were sounding not only in Osijek but all along the border, in Romania, Hungary, Transylvania, Slovakia; from Jassy to Satu Mare to Koscice to Zagreb, in every fort on that vague, ill-defined frontier where Christ and Muhammad met, where cultures clashed and recoiled from each other, and where men and women walked their days in fear and cursed impartially both the crescent moon of Islam and the bloody cross of Christianity.

Chapter Three

VIENNA

THE clock on the little church of St. Luke's in Ottostrasse whirred and rattled in a rusty, ramshackle way. Beneath it a small door creaked open and a wooden knight, rather in need of a coat of paint and flourishing a broken sword, rode out on a pop-eyed horse, made a brief, shaky appearance over the narrow street, and retreated into his tower as the clock struck seven. Other clocks across Vienna were striking too; some tolling six, some seven, some the half hour or the quarter, but as the door closed on the knight the great clock in the cathedral of St. Stephen's ended the jangling argument by striking, authoritatively, nine o'clock on a bright August morning.

In his poky bakery under the shadow of St. Luke's, Herr Jacob Vogel made the last of a batch of rolls and slammed them into the oven. He wiped his face with a dusty apron and took a huge gulp of water from a jug. Behind him, in the open window of the bakery, a long face appeared with a longer nose protruding from it.

'Morning, Herr Vogel,' said the face.

'Morning.' Vogel was brusque not because he disliked the owner of the face, Herr Haller, although he did dislike him, but because he was always brusque with every one.

'Working?' asked Herr Haller.

'No.' Vogel mopped his brow. 'I'm fishing in the Danube.'

'Ha, ha, ha. Very good. Very good.' Haller leaned companionably on the window sill. 'How are the family?'

Vogel swung a mass of dough onto his table and tore it in half with deceptive ease. 'The family. Very well, thank you. No change since you saw them at Mass this morning.'

'Ah!' Quite unperturbed, Haller smiled. 'You're a sharp one, Herr Vogel. Yes, I did see them in church. I was there with my lad Kaspar. He's a fine young fellow, you know.'

'Yes.' Vogel rammed a piece of wood under the oven with one hand while with the other he grasped a razor-sharp knife and slashed the dough into amazingly exact squares. 'Yes. He's a fine lad.'

'You're right,' Haller cried, as if Vogel had just announced a new and astonishing truth. 'And he's a good carpenter, too. One of the best.' He scratched his nose. 'Like your Anna. She's a fine young woman.'

Vogel stared at Haller. 'Anna?'

Haller tapped his forehead. 'Worth a thought, isn't it?'

'A thought?'

Haller nodded knowingly. 'My Kaspar, your Anna. Two fine young people. What's wrong with that?'

Vogel splashed water on his squares of dough. 'Herr Haller, I haven't the faintest idea what you are talking about.'

'Ah well.' Haller winked ferociously. 'I'll leave it with you, Herr Vogel. In fact I'm *happy* to leave it with you because I know that you see things straight. A good, honest man, Herr Vogel is. I've always said that, yes, *and I always will*! Anyway'– briskly – 'Change the subject. He's gone. Went last night.'

Vogel sprinkled sun flower seeds over his squares. 'Who's gone?'

'Him,' Haller jerked his head. 'The All Highest. The Emperor. He's gone to Laxenburg. They're all there.'

'They!' The squares were banged into the oven. 'And who are they?'

'All of them.' Haller cupped his chin in his hands. 'All the bigwigs. They're having a council of state.'

'Council?'

'It's about *them*.' Haller hissed.

Vogel clapped his hands to his head. '*Them*,' he shouted. '*Them – They – Him*! Why can't you talk like a normal human being?'

'Ah,' Haller was undisturbed. 'It's the Turks, see. A courier came in last night with a letter from Istanbul. That's why they're having the Council. The letter says that the Turks are going to start a war with us.'

Vogel took a deep breath.' Herr Haller, I've been hearing that tale for the last nine years.'

Haller nodded solemnly. 'I know, but this time it's true. The Turks are going to break the treaty.'

Vogel poured water over his exasperated head. 'How can you say such things? How can you? How does a carpenter come to know about state affairs? Does the Emperor send you little notes?'

Haller smiled artfully. 'I hear things. My cousin works at the Palace, you know.'

Vogel sighed. 'Herr Haller, your cousin is a doorkeeper!'

'It's true though.' The long nose twitched. 'The Turks are coming.'

Vogel dusted his hands. 'Herr Haller, do you have any work to do?'

The face vanished. A moment later Frau Vogel came into the bakery. 'Rolls,' she said.

Vogel opened the oven and took out a batch of fresh rolls.

'Who were you talking to?' asked Frau Vogel.

'Haller.'

'What about?'

'Nothing. Gossip.' Vogel was as brusque with his wife as he was with everyone else. Perhaps it was because he spent most of his life in the roaring heat of the bakery, or, perhaps, it was just the way he was made. Not that it bothered his wife. She merely raised a blond eyebrow over a pale blue eye set in a plump, white face very suitable for a baker's wife.

'Gossip?'

'Rubbish.' Vogel threw the rolls into a basket. 'Take these. The customers are waiting.'

Frau Vogel did not move. 'What gossip?'
Vogel sighed. 'About the Turks starting a war.'
'That's what the women in the shop are saying,' said his wife.

At noon, as the clocks of Vienna rang out their various times, the Vogel family sat down to their midday meal. Four of them gathered around the table in the little parlour. Herr Vogel, his wife, their daughter, Anna, and their young son, Rudi. Another son, Johann, was a gilder, working on a new church at Amstetten, up the Danube. The first born, Wenzel, a baker of genius, had died of the plague two years before.

The family bowed their heads and crossed themselves as Herr Vogel said the grace; '*Unser Lieber Gott*, Our Dear God, for this good food before us, and for all the good things in life, we thank Thee. Bless us and our Emperor, and *keep us from idle gossip*. Amen.'

'And save us from the wicked Turks,' added Frau Vogel, immune to her husband's exasperation.

She ladled out beetroot soup. Rudi, standing on tip-toe at the table, spooned up a mouthful of the soup. 'It's hot,' he said.

'Of course it's hot,' Vogel said. 'It is always hot in August.'

Anna smiled. She was an ordinary-looking girl, neither beautiful nor ugly, but she had fine violet eyes and her smile illuminated her face like a jewelled capital letter in a dull manuscript. 'He means the soup, Father.'

Vogel took a large bite from his roll. 'Blow on your spoon,' he said, indistinctly. He swallowed the roll with a mouthful of beer and looked sternly at Rudi. 'What have you learned at school this morning?'

Rudi blew vigorously on his spoon and shrugged.

Vogel rolled his eyes. 'Is that what the monks teach you? Do I pay them so that you can learn shrugging?' He rapped Rudi smartly on the head with his spoon. 'Now, answer properly.'

Rudi rubbed his head. 'The Catechism.'

'And?' the spoon waved threateningly.

'And arithmetic –' hastily.

'Better.' The spoon came down. 'Arithmetic is good. When you own this bakery you will need it. Learn all the arithmetics you can. What is eighty-nine kreuzer take away fifty-six?'

'Seventy-two,' Rudi hazarded a guess in the hope of avoiding another crack on the head but getting one just the same, although his father was vague as to the answer himself.

To avoid another question, and another crack on the head, Rudi said, 'Peter Schreyer says that the Turks are coming.'

'There!' Frau Vogel nodded solemnly as if Peter Schreyer, aged eight, had exact and secret sources of information. 'And the Emperor has gone to Laxenburg. Frau Haller told me.'

Vogel sighed. 'The All Highest always goes to Laxenburg in the summer. It is cooler there. Anyway, he is afraid of –'

He bit the rest of the sentence off but Rudi innocently finished it. 'Of the plague.' And Vogel felt his heart twist within him at the thought of Wenzel in his grave.

There was silence in the room broken by a knock at the door which, without an answer from Vogel, swung open to reveal the lodger from two floors up, the Grafin Elizabeth von Schwarzbach, a faded relic of the aristocracy, remote connections with the Hofburg, the Emperor's palace, living, like many of the minor nobility in over crowded Vienna, cheek by jowl with lesser mortals, and not making a social call either, but complaining about the lodgers above *her*; a gang of candle-makers and, Vogel strongly suspected, part-time thieves, who, it appeared were keeping the Grafin awake at night with singing and fighting.

Vogel banged his spoon down and explained, for the hundredth time, that he did not own the house and that all complaints should be made to the owners, the Augustinian Friars.

The Grafin sniffed, departed, Rudi gobbled a plum, asked if he might go, and darted out. The plates rattled as Anna collected them, and Vogel stretched his short, stout arms and yawned.

'Time for my nap,' he said, as he did every day at that time. With a little 'puff' he eased himself up. From the street came the clear chant of Rudi and the precocious Peter Schreyer.

'Dum, dum, dum,
'The Turkishmen will come.
'Beating on their drum
'The Janissaries will come.'

At the sink, her plump arms bare to the elbow, Anna spoke, a slight tremor in her voice. 'Will they come, Pappa?'

Vogel gazed fondly on his daughter. She was very dear to his kind, testy heart. In the terrible Plague Year of two years previously, when Wenzel had died and Frau Vogel had collapsed with grief, Anna, just fifteen then, had run the house with calm efficiency, and when the pestilence had breathed its sickening breath on Rudi it was she who had nursed the lad and brought him back from the edge of the plague pit. He coughed, a long, dusty, baker's cough, and patted Anna on the cheek.

'No, no,' he said. 'Don't worry, my dear.'

Anna held a plate to her breast. 'But they say something bad is going to happen.'

'They!' Vogel slapped his forehead. 'I know who *they* are. The Hallers.'

'Not just the Hallers,' Frau Vogel said, sharply. 'Everyone says so. And Father Marco said the same thing in Saint Stephen's last Sunday. He said we will be punished because we have been wicked and disobeyed God's Holy Laws.'

'Disobeyed –' Vogel blinked. 'What laws of God have *we* disobeyed?'

'All of them,' Frau Vogel said comprehensively. 'And look at the Hungarians and the Bohemians, saying that the Pope is wrong and rebelling against the Emperor. And anyway, what about the comet last year. Why did it come if the Turks aren't coming?'

Vogel did not try to follow this logic. He turned to Anna. 'Believe me,' he said, 'the Turks won't come to Vienna. Never, never, never.'

'They came before,' said his wife.

Ten miles away, among the Vienna woods, in the old moated castle of Laxenburg, Anna's question had also been asked, although by a more exalted personage, for, proving Herr Haller quite correct, the Emperor Leopold the First had called his Imperial Council of State and framed his query. Now, as dusk crept in and the scent of pine needles filled the air, the Council waited in the trophy room to give its answer.

On the walls of the room the heads of deer, wolves, bears and boars killed by the All Highest looked down, glassy-eyed and gloomy, but even their depressing faces were more cheerful than the faces of the Councillors. There was no talk. Enough had already been said during a long, exhausting, and sultry day.

A little after seven a door opened and the Emperor entered. With the other Councillors, the President of the Imperial Council, Count Wilhelm von Konigsegg, bowed deeply but, as always when he saw Leopold, the faintly treasonous thought crossed his mind that the All Highest did not look quite the part of an Emperor. There was something about Leopold's skinny legs in their red stockings, and the pendulous lower lip which drooped over a skimpy beard, which suggested a half-witted sausage-seller rather than the monarch of ten million people. Konigsegg averted his eyes and found himself staring at the head of an elk whose lower lip also drooped alarmingly, and looked instead at his feet.

Leopold took a seat and gazed at his council through fine brown, intelligent eyes. 'Well?' he asked.

Konigsegg bowed again. 'Sire, to clarify our problem. We have to say that we believe this new Turkish threat is one of three major problems your Highness is faced with. First there is the conflict with the French over your right to the Spanish throne. Second there is the matter of the rebellion of the traitor Imre Thokoly in your kingdom of Hungary. Third there is this business of the Turks.'

He paused and looked at Leopold who motioned with his finger. 'Continue.'

'Thank you, Sire.' Konigsegg dabbed at his brow. 'Now, as

your Majesty knows, there are some in the Council who believe that we should settle with the French, with His Majesty Louis the Fourteenth on *his* terms, and then launch a great crusade against the Turks in the Balkans. But that,' he tapped the table, 'that is not the majority view. The majority of your Council believe that the future of the House of Habsburg lies in Europe proper. We also believe that the Ottoman threat is grotesquely exaggerated. Of course we can expect that the Turks will raid our borders and make ridiculous demands and they will aid Thokoly, but they have been doing that for many years, anyway. We should also remember that all we have had so far from Istanbul are veiled threats and vague demands. They have not declared war. Our peace treaty with them still has two years to go and the Turks have never before broken a treaty with us. In any case there can be no conceivable threat until next year. To bring our troops down now from the Rhine and the Netherlands will only give Louis the chance to impose his will on your rightful and sacred authority over Austria and the Spanish possessions.'

Konigsegg paused and looked again at his emperor, but Leopold's face was as impassive as ever. For all the emotion it showed he might have been listening to his bailiff telling him how many eggs his hens had laid that morning instead of vast strategies encompassing Europe from Madrid to Vienna itself. Only a long finger twitched as a sign that the Chancellor might continue.

Count Konigsegg tugged at the band of his collar. 'All Highest, our conclusions are this; we should stave off the Turks. We can haggle with the Sultan and the Grand Vizier, make some slight concessions of territory, and no doubt, bribery will help us. Then, with our southern boundaries safe we can deal with the French. In the meantime we should appeal to the German states of the Holy Roman Empire for help and we must make every effort to sign a self-help treaty with Poland. We are sure that King John Sobieski will sign a mutual defence treaty because they are threatened by the Turks too. By the way, his Holiness Pope Innocent the Eleventh is ready to pay for Polish troops. Then we can turn and smash the Hungarian rebels and all our borders will be safe. This is our advice, given to the best of our abilities. Thank you, Sire.'

'And thank you, sirs,' Leopold said with his invariable courtesy. He paused for a moment. What complications there were in the intricate web of politics which had to be weaved in order to maintain not only his, Leopold's rule, but those of his descendants. And where did his duty truly lie? In battling with a French, Catholic monarch, in crushing the detestable protestant heretics of Hungary and Bohemia, or in facing the Islamic threat from the south? He paused, hesitating for a moment, but knowing that, in the end, the fortunes of his own house were supreme; after all, the triumph of the Habsburgs meant, anyway, the triumph of Catholicism and the triumph of the rule of those born, and blessed by God in doing so, to rule. He nodded assent.

'We think that your advice is good. Act upon it.'

Somewhere in the castle a bell tinkled three times. 'Mass,' said the Emperor. 'It is the day of Saint Susanna. Let us kneel and pray for her intercession with almighty God for our Kingdoms, and our Empire, and His Holy Church.

Chapter Four

POLAND

AUTUMN slanted across the land. Elms and lime trees were tinged with a melancholy yellow, willows were shedding their narrow leaves, and the cranes were stretching their wings for the long flight south. From Gdansk on the Baltic to Zhuravno on the River Dniester the Polish harvest was almost home; rye and millet in the north, wheat in the south, the land had turned from green to gold to bronze and now, shaved by sickle and scythe, it lay brown and bristly, waiting for winter.

Deep in the south-west, on the edge of the vast steppe lands where dust devils flickered, and where the wild Tartars roamed, the serfs of the *Schlacta* Ladislau Zabruski were reaping the last of his harvest; every man woman and child stooped like black question marks under the September sun. All but one.

His hands tied to an ox-cart he was being flogged by Zabruski's bailiff in a steady, methodical way; six, eight, a dozen blows. The serf's eyes closed and his back turned blue. The bailiff looked up at Zabruski.

'Another dozen next week,' Zabruski said, and drove his horse forward. Following his father, Stefan Zabruski kicked his horse into a canter, whistling a light, airy tune. He felt no compunction about the beating. The man had not bowed when his lord and master the Schlacta had passed, now the bruises on his back would remind him to do so in future.

As they cantered around the cornfield Stefan glanced sideways at his father. 'The Wild Boar' they called him. It was the right name, too, for Zabruski looked like a boar, short and massive, with a thick neck and a massive, thrusting jaw. He was pale like a boar, too, with white bristly hair through which pink skin glowed. Even his teeth were like a boar's, yellow and tusklike. Only Zabruski's one pale blue eye spoiled the picture. Stefan grinned. 'Pig, he should be called,' he thought. 'Not a boar but a pig.'

He thought that again in a cottage on the edge of the forest as his father grunted and slobbered over a rough dinner, downed a quart of vodka, then lurched off to wallow in the serf's bed. A pig, but a brave one, that there was no denying. His father was as brave as any boar that charged you blindly in the forest with froth swinging from its wicked mouth. At the battle of Podhaje, fifteen years before, when the Poles had broken the invasion of the Volga cossacks, his horse down, his lance shattered, and with an arrow sticking in one eye, Zabruski had stood his ground, mowing down the cossacks with his battle-axe. For that he had been given his nickname, and for that he had been given his estates by King John Sobieski. And he was loyal, too, in a blind, unreasoning way. In Cracow, once, he had killed a Swedish free lance for saying that Poland was no true kingdom, and that John Sobieski was no true King. 'But still,' Stefan thought, as he listened to his father snoring, 'still a pig.' Not that he minded.

The next day they rode to Zabruski's home village of Ostrova. The village was nothing. A few mud cottages stared depressingly at each other across a dusty lane, and that was all. There was no shop, or even an inn, and there would have been no point in having either since none of the serfs had any money.

At the top of the lane, on a bluff overlooking a stream, was a stockade and inside the stockade was the Zabruski home. It was large and rambling, built of massive timbers plastered with clay so that it was difficult to set it on fire, as a band of wandering Tartars had found out two years before. There was also a threshing yard, barns, stables, byres, a smithy and a well. It was a self-contained frontier outpost which was appropriate because it was on an extremely wild and savage frontier.

Wolfhounds bayed as Zabruski and Stefan rode through the gates, grovelling servants ran forward and took the horses, hens squawked and fluttered and pigs grunted, as if welcoming the return of one of their own kind. On the verandah Madame Zabruski, her daughters Maria and Teresa, and Stefan's younger brother Kasimir appeared.

Maria and Teresa, both as fat and pink as piglets squealed as Zabruski lurched up onto the verandah. 'The Jew is coming,' they squealed, 'the Jew is coming.'

Zabruski stared down on the girls not as if they were his daughters or even human beings, but as he stared at everything, as if he was making only one judgement – harmful, or harmless. Madame Zabruski drew the girls to her as if she thought that her husband had decided the former.

'Pyotr Chelmnitz saw the Jew last night,' she said. 'In Velbo. He is coming here today.'

Zabruski shrugged and went into the house, kicking a dog out of the way. 'Food,' he said.

In the afternoon, as Zabruski snored off his pork and cabbage, Stefan went swimming in the stream behind the bluff. Cool and naked he floated in the shade of the willows. In the fields serfs called to each other, the bull-like voice of the bailiff, Pyotr Chelmnitz, roared, carts rumbled up to the threshing yard, somewhere girls laughed. Stefan thought of the girl in Velbo who had teased him for being so pale-faced and white-haired. A candle, she had called him, and his face had burned red like one. He lay on the bank and thought of her as the sun dried his body.

When he returned to the house his mother was on the verandah with the girls and Kasimir, a year younger than Stefan but already taking after his father in his sullen moroseness. They had tea in the Russian way, with lemon, sprawled on wicker chairs. Carts piled high with glistening wheat ground into the enclosure, serfs, sore-eyed with chaff flailed away on the threshing yard, girls milked the cows, and then a figure leading a donkey came up the village lane and stood at the gateway, hat in hand, as the dogs growled at his ankles.

'The Jew, the Jew,' Teresa and Maria squealed, but their mother shook her head.

'Wait for your father,' she said.

A half-hour's fidgety wait with the patient figure of the Jew and his donkey standing by the gate, then Zabruski shambling onto the verandah, grunting his consent, Stefan waving a lordly hand, and the Jewish pedlar crossing the yard, laying out his wares and stepping back, his eyes cast down.

The girls squeaked and chattered, tugging at ribbons and silks, ivory combs, mirrors, simple picture books; 'The True Story of a Christian Slave in the Hands of the Turks.' 'Stenka Razin, how God Punished him for Leading the Don Cossacks against the Czar of Russia.' 'The Suffering of The Hungarian Catholics at the Hands of the Heretic and Traitor, Imre Thokoly . . .'

'I want this,' cried the girls, 'I want that, this, that . . .' Zabruski took six packs of playing cards, Kasimir a knife, Stefan a scarf. Madame Zabruski picked up a shawl.

'How much?' she demanded.

The Jew stepped humbly forward. 'Ah, your Ladyship. That is pure silk, brought all the way from China –'

'How much?'

The Jew spread his hands, 'Twelve zloty, your Ladyship.'

'Twelve zloty! Twelve zloty for a shawl?' Madame Zabruski threw the shawl down. 'And how much did you pay for it, hey? Tell me that.'

'He probably stole it,' Kasimir cried. 'He stole it in Velbo.'

'On my mother's grave!' The Jew struck his breast. 'I paid eleven zloty for it.' He glanced up slyly. 'I thought that your Ladyship would like it . . .'

Madame Zabruski shook her head. 'Buy for eleven and sell for twelve,' she squawked. 'No wonder you Jews are rich.'

'Rich Jews,' Kasimir spat over the verandah rail. 'That's what you are, aren't you? A dirty, rich Jew.'

40

'Not rich.' Nathan shook his head. 'But as your Honour says.' His head bent in submission.

Stefan leaned back, sipping his tea, looking at the Jew, Nathan he was called, and for as long as anyone could remember he had come on his round twice a year, in spring and autumn, enduring abuse and vilification as a stone endures the rain which falls upon it. A familiar figure, despised but tolerated, even; as today, his visits looked forward to, bringing novelty and news and yet always remote and, in queer way, untouchable. And Nathan always brought with him in his pack a book or two – he had one now, a real book that was, bound in leather and stuffed with long, incomprehensible words. Why was that? Stefan wondered. Never once had Stefan seen one bought.

The squabbling ended and a pile of goods were gathered and placed on one side. 'Thirty-two zloty, your Honour,' Nathan said.

Zabruski grunted. 'What news?' he asked.

'Ah, changes, your Honour. Great changes, The Sultan has ordered the Tartars in the Crimea to be ready for war.'

Zabruski's eye glittered. 'Against us?'

Nathan spread his hands. 'Against Poland, against the Cossacks, the Russians . . . Austria. Who knows what the Turks will do?'

'Aye.' Zabruski nodded and threw some coins into the dust. 'The rest next year.'

'Thank you, your Honour.' Nathan picked up the coins and bowed. 'Your Lordship has a long memory. He will not forget.'

'Yes!' Kasimir stood up, his face flushed with invincible ignorance. 'We have got long memories,' he bawled. 'Who killed Christ?'

Nathan paled. 'They say we did, your Honour.'

'And are you sorry?' Kasimir yelled.

'I am sorry for all our sins,' Nathan said.

Kasimir took a step forward but at a growl from Zabruski sank back like a dog at his master's command.

'Next year,' Zabruski said.

'Thank you.' Nathan picked up his pack. 'If your Honour will allow – some water? For the donkey?'

'Aye.' Zabruski left the verandah, followed by his family, all except Stefan who, on a casual impulse, followed Nathan to the well.

'You,' he called. 'Jew.'

Nathan turned warily. 'Yes, your Honour.'

'That book. The one in your pack.'

Nathan's hand was already sliding into his pannier. 'Your Honour wishes to buy it?'

Stefan, who needed a book like he needed a Tartar arrow in his throat shook his head. 'No. But why do you bring them . . . books? Nobody wants them, nobody buys them.'

Something rippled across Nathan's face; not a smile but not far from one. 'Why, your Honour, who knows? One day someone might.'

Stefan frowned. 'What is it? A story? A history?'

'No, your Honour. Not a story. Not a history.'

'Show me.' Stefan held out his hand.

Nathan slid the book from his pack. 'See,' he said, 'It is a fine book. Does your Honour see the leather? It is the finest kid, from Morocco. The book was made in Amsterdam. Does your Honour know that city?'

Stefan had a vague notion of Amsterdam. Was it in Low Germany, where the French were fighting the Austrians, or was it the Spanish fighting the Hollanders? He took the book. 'What is in this?'

'Ah,' Nathan looked up, his eyes dark, enigmatic pools, but this time there was a smile on his lips. 'Your Honour, it says that the earth goes round the sun.'

Stefan blinked. 'What?'

'That is what the book says, your Honour.'

Stefan threw back his head and laughed. 'Is it a joke?'

'No, your Honour.'

Stefan stopped laughing and went red, trembling with rage,

trembling at the sheer, grotesque absurdity of the notion. 'Who wrote this?' he growled. 'A Jew?'

Nathan's smile vanished and the dark pools were hidden behind long eyelashes . . . 'No your Honour. No indeed. It was written by a priest. A Catholic priest.' He turned a page. 'Does your Honour see? Here is his name, Nicholas Copernicus. He was Polish, your Honour. A Polish priest.'

Stefan stared at the page, utterly incredulous. Nathan ran his finger across it.

'Your Honour sees that it is in Latin. Here is the title, *De Revolutionibus Orbium Coelestium*. And does your Honour see here – 'Nihil Obstat . . .'

'Nihil. . . .' Stefan groped for the smattering of Latin he had been taught, 'Nothing . . . ?'

'Nothing in the way,' said Nathan. 'It means that the Pope in Rome allows it to be read.'

'The Pope? And it was written by a Pole?'

'Yes, your Honour. A hundred years ago –' Was there a tinge of mockery in the Jew's voice? 'There were many things written in Poland then. It was –'

'Was what?' Stefan scowled.

'Nothing, your Honour.'

'And . . . and . . . ?' Stefan was incoherent. He pointed to the sky.

'Yes, your Honour.' Nathan's voice was neutral, his face a blank mask. 'It is only a book, Pan. May I go now?'

'Yes. Yes, get out, get out,' Stefan threw the book into Nathan's face. 'Get out and don't bring any more books here or I'll burn them – and you – you dirty Jew.'

Evening came with the sun sinking on a sullen, incredulous Stefan who observed it going round the earth with his own eyes. The last carts lumbered in from the fields, the serfs shambled off to their lousy beds, and, as the evening meal was being laid out,

Zabruski's neighbour, the Schlacta Potocki came riding in with two armed men.

The Zabruskis and Potocki sat around the huge, crude table. Zabruski's priest stumbled in from his obscure retreat and mumbled a prayer which was almost as incomprehensible to him as it was to the others. At the head of the table Zabruski gobbled eel soup and stared at Potocki.

'Lvov?' He demanded.

'Yes,' Potocki downed a tumbler of vodka. 'Money.'

Zabruski nodded. The Schlactas were always short of money. They were virtually self-sufficient, growing their own food and with fuel in plenty in the forest, but there were always things, needs, luxuries – the spinet which no one could play and which had been dragged three hundred miles from Warsaw, the French clock which did not work and never would because no one had the skill to mend it, tea, lemons, sugar, gambling debts, weapons, gunpowder, the land-tax – all of which could only be bought for cash, borrowed against the harvest from the money-lenders of the towns.

'Get it?' Zabruski asked.

Potocki crammed down a mouthful of pike. 'Yes. The Jew, Solomon.'

Stefan looked up from his plate, his eyes red with anger. 'The Jew, today. He said that the earth went round the sun!'

An outraged howl went up. The priest rolled his eyes, crossed himself, and mumbled at the thought of the Jew and his Christ-denying ways.

Zabruski scowled. 'I'll have him flogged. I'll send Pyotr Chelmnitz to whip him, spreading his dirty lies.'

Absolute assent. That was the thing to do, have the Jew flogged for spreading his dirty lies which went against all nature and the Laws of God.

More vodka, pork, cabbage, pickles, the last of the wild strawberries, more vodka. Madame Zabruski and the girls left the room. Zabruski swung his feet onto the table and undid his belt.

'What's this about the Turks?'

Potocki picked at his rotten teeth with a knife. 'A lot of talk in Lvov,' he said. 'The Turks are howling again. The King has made a pact with the Austrians. If the Turks attack Austria we help them, if they attack Poland they help us. The French don't like it.'

'They wouldn't,' Zabruski belched. '–––– the French! I've seen them. When we elected Sobieski king. There they were in their silks and satins and their Messieur this, and Messieur that, kissing their hands at you and laughing up their sleeves.'

He stared at the table, gorged and half drunk but as cunning, as savage as ever. 'They tried to buy my vote,' he cried. 'Tak! It was Schlacta this and Schlacta that; what a fine man you are, how strong you are, come to Paris and meet our women, but all the time they were sneering at us, Poles barbarians, savages. I told one, I told him, come to the Dniester, face the Tartars, face the Turks, face the Russ – then bow and kiss your hand. Tak! I took his money though, and voted the other way.'

The men laughed and Zabruski threw a gobbet of pork onto the floor for the dogs. He wiped his mouth on his sleeve.

'So there will be a vote on the pact.'

'Yes.' Potocki said. 'The nobles will vote in Warsaw this winter and we'll vote next spring.' He laughed. 'There will be plenty of money about. The French will try to bribe us, and the Austrians. How will you vote?'

Zabruski lurched to his feet, his eyes glazed with drink. 'How?' he bellowed. He slapped his thigh where, in battle, his sword hung. 'With my King. With John Sobieski.' He staggered forward. 'Cards.'

Stefan lay in the bed he shared with Kasimir. His brother moved restlessly, sweating and mumbling in his sleep. Downstairs Zabruski and Potocki cursed and quarrelled as they played cards. Stefan slipped from the bed and stood by the window looking out on the night and in the enormous wilderness which stretched before him there were no lights. Not one lantern or candle shone in the vastness of wood and forest and steppe.

Stefan rubbed his chest. 'So,' he thought, 'there might be a war; a real war, not a mere skirmish with the Tartars but a war with the Tartars' masters, the Turks. Yes, a real war with great armies, shining in armour and bright with banners, marching across the earth and making it groan beneath its tread.'

Something 'yipped' in the forest, a young wolf, perhaps, trying out its voice before winter came. A nightjar whirred, owls hooted, the new moon rose. Stefan spat through the window, remembering the pedlar. The earth going round the sun! He hoped Pyotr Chelmnitz had caught the Jew and flogged him. Yes. He yawned and went back to bed, next to Kasimir's sweating hulk.

Eight miles away, in a charcoal-burner's hut, Nathan ben Israel, having been flogged by Chelmnitz, fed his donkey and then himself, and said his prayers, chanting the one hundred and thirty seventh psalm of David, the minstrel, and reaching the eighth verse;

> 'Oh daughter of Babylon, that art to
> be destroyed;
> 'Happy shall he be that rewardeth
> Thee
> As thou has served us.

Rocking to and fro, with deep, vulnerable feeling, he struck his breast.

> 'Happy shall he be that taketh and
> Dasheth thy little ones
> Against the stones . . .'

'Let it be so,' Nathan whispered. 'Oh Lord Jehovah, let it be so. Let the Turks come and destroy the Goyim. Let them do to the Goyim what they do to us. Amen, amen, amen.'

And west of Nathan, across the dark wilderness, Kings and Princes took council with their advisers and wondered how to take advantage of the Turkish menace; and in France Pierre Bayle had completed his essay against the Superstitions of Comets, and in Cambridge, England, Isaac Newton was working on his book, On the Theory of Tides Under the Gravitational Influence, of Sun, Moon, and Earth, and west even of Europe, the first German immigrants to North America, were being sea-sick on the rollers of the North Atlantic.

And in Istanbul, on the Tower of Fatima in the mosque of Suleiman the Magnificent, the senior Imam of the city saw the New Moon rise;

'God is great,' he cried. 'There is only one God . . .'

On the north gate of the Sultan's palace the Aga of the Artillery heard the long call and dropped his outstretched hand. 'Dok,' he roared and along the walls his cannon thundered and belched out flame.

Across the waters of the Golden Horn, Kunitz, Caprara and their secretary heard the cannon and the cheerful din of a celebrating city. A little pale about his mouth Caprara said,

'So. The fast of Ramadan is over. Now the Sultan will leave the city.'

The Secretary shrugged. 'As I have said, he may merely be going hunting.'

'Yes.' Caprara took a little wine. 'But hunting what?'

Chapter Five

EDIRNE

THE Keeper of the Grand Vizier's Zoo was a worried man. He was peering at an ostrich which lay in an untidy, collapsed heap, its bare, scaly neck stretched out on the floor like a dead snake.

The Keeper shook his head and the ostrich rolled a dull, half-opened eye at him. 'Give it rose-water,' the Keeper said. 'With gold leaf in it.'

'Yes, Effendi.' The slave who looked after the ostrich bowed.

'And music!' The Keeper had an inspiration. 'Music might help. Yes. Sing to it. Have a boy play the lute. Sing love songs.'

'And keep it warm. Very warm. Do not forget that.'

'No, Effendi.'

'And pray for it.'

'Yes, Effendi.'

'And if it does not recover, pray for yourself.'

'Yes, Effendi,' with deep feeling.

'On your head be it.' said the Keeper. He left the tent, shivering as an icy wind tugged at his cloak. 'And my head, too,' he thought, sickeningly.

He walked through the Zoo which accompanied the Sultan and the Grand Vizier on their travels. A leopard snarled and deer-hounds bayed in response. The Keeper licked his lips and hurried to his tent. Inside, by a charcoal brazier, Kara Mustafa's Falconer was drinking coffee. He raised an inquiring eyebrow.

48

The Keeper stood by the stove, rubbing his hands and shaking his head. 'Not good,' he said. 'Not good at all.'

'What can you expect?' said the Falconer.

'Yes.' The Keeper agreed, in despair. What could one expect? It was a long journey from Istanbul to Edirne in the bitter winter but when Kara Mustafa had left the capital to join the Sultan two weeks previously he had insisted on bringing his zoo with him. No wonder the ostrich was ill.

'Perhaps it will recover,' the Falconer said, without conviction.

'Ah yes. Yes. Certainly it will recover.' The Keeper felt his neck as if he could already feel a noose tightening around it.

'Of course –' the Falconer stretched his arms in the easy, relaxed gesture of a man knowing that all *his* birds were pefectly fit and well and for whom strangulation was an academic proposition. 'Of course, it is as Allah wills.'

'As you say.' The Keeper gave a ghastly smile. 'It is all as Allah wills.' But as he stood for evening prayers he wondered if that pious proposition could really be true. Would it be – could it be – the will of Allah that he should find a bow-string around his neck because the Grand Vizier's ostrich died?

The east wind blew across the plain, a few, thin snow-flakes spun down from the starry sky, the sound of a lute floated from the tent of the ostrich. Inside his palace in Edirne, the Sultan lay on a divan, having his feet massaged by a page-boy.

He, too, was thinking of the will of Allah. Was it truly the will of God that the Ottoman Empire should break its treaty with Austria and go to war? Or was it merely the implacable will of Kara Mustafa? Outside the city, on the dark plain, campfires glowed and sparked like the eyes of a multitude of dangerous animals. Was it, the Sultan thought, was it the will of the soldiers camping around those fires? Possibly. As the Grand Vizier had said, something had to be done with the army – the troops simply could not be allowed to sit around eating their heads off and fomenting mutinies.

The Sultan sighed. Sometimes he was not very clear what was going on. He felt like a sleepwalker, stumbling forward in darkness, or like a spar on the open sea, taken into unknown waters by unseen currents. Perhaps, he thought vaguely, perhaps that was what the will of Allah meant and that true Islamic virtue lay in surrendering oneself to the mysterious forces of *Kismet*, of fate, destiny – whatever that might mean, or be.

The page rubbed a little more sesame oil between the Sultan's imperial toes. Mehmed gazed fondly down on the boy's unformed features. For a moment the thought crossed his mind to let the boy decide whether or not to declare war on Austria. Why not? After all, if he did then that would have been what Allah willed.

Mehmed yawned. All he really wanted to do was to hunt; to hunt, make money, and avoid being assassinated, or, worse still, blinded and left to rot in some dungeon as so many Sultans before him had been. He closed his eyes; pleasant images flickered across his mind; deer leaping, slavering dogs on their heels, golden hawks swinging from his gloved fist, the whistle of arrows on a frosty morning . . . the Emperor of Austria loved hunting, too . . . war . . . peace . . . what was Kara Mustafa doing? The Sword of the Age slept.

In fact Kara Mustafa was giving the Austrian envoys an intimate supper. It was an excellent meal; venison, quail, mutton, rice, everything but wine which the Austrians were missing badly.

But still, the Grand Vizier was at his most cordial. His swarthy face which, as well as his ferocious temper, had given him the nickname 'The Black', was gleaming with good humour as he pressed a little more of this and a little more of that on his guests. Indeed, Caprara and Kunitz were beginning to feel rather like two geese being force-fed before being killed, plucked, gutted, roasted – and eaten.

For most of the meal Mustafa had been talking of his own career; his rise in the bureaucracy of the Ottoman Empire, his warlike experiences fighting the Poles, his capture of Kamenets, and, the ultimate prize, his elevation to Grand Vizier. But as the coffee was brought in he changed towards another subject.

'The blessings of plenty,' he said. 'Peace and plenty. They are worth any price, are they not?'

'Well,' Caprara was cautious. 'As to *anything* . . .'

Mustafa smiled, a dangerous, flashing smile. 'Practically anything. I was saying so to the envoy of the Russian Czar not long ago.'

'Were you?' Caprara shook his head as though this was amazing news, although bribes had brought him every word which had passed between the Grand Vizier and the Russians.

'Yes,' Mustafa nodded. 'And the Czar has been glad to make some concessions to us in order to preserve peace.'

'How very interesting?' Kunitz said.

'Yes, isn't it.' Mustafa pressed cake and coffee onto his guests. 'It is all in the cause of peace. In fact it is surprising how many people are ready to support us in our just demands. Prince Michael Apafi of Transylvania, for example. And he is a Christian, as your Excellencies well know.'

'And by the way,' Mustafa was elaborately casual, 'Prince Thokoly and the Hungarians are of the same mind. Is that not amazing?'

'It is,' Caprara said. 'And it is even more amazing since Prince Thokoly is a subject of the Emperor of Austria.'

'Ha, ha. There seems to be a difference of opinion on that. But still,' Thokoly and the rebel Magyars dismissed with a wave of the hand – for the moment. 'Still, as you can see, Christendom is . . . divided, whereas the Empire – the Ottomon Empire, that is, is strong, and absolutely united.'

'I am delighted to hear it,' Kunitz said, insincerely. 'But are there not disturbances – a rebellion, one might say, in Persia?'

'Persia!' Mustafa laughed heartily. He was a truly fine actor, Caprara thought. 'Persia is nothing. A handful of dogs. Believe me, they will be put down in a month.' He leaned forward a little, confidentially, 'In fact I feel a certain pity for them. When they are defeated I am afraid that unpleasant things will happen to them. It is the soldiers, you know. When they fight against heretics and infidels they become . . . inflamed and there is no stopping them. It happened in Transylvania a few years ago. You may remember.'

The Austrians did remember. Sickening slaughter as the Turks swept into Transylvania on the Polish border. Three thousand Christian heads carried on pikes through Istanbul.

Mustafa sighed. 'Such things happen in war, do they not? Especially where religion is involved. I hear your own troops do terrible things to the Protestants. Perhaps that is why the Protestants support us! Ha, ha. It all goes to show how difficult it is to rule, to govern. Take your own country. What problems it faces. War with France, all your possessions in danger, your allies deserting you. I feel a deep sympathy for your Imperial master,' he added, quite untruthfully.

'Thank you,' Kunitz said, equally untruthfully. 'But I am afraid that your Excellency is misinformed. The German states are absolutely loyal to the Emperor, and Holland and England will certainly declare war on France this year, and Poland will come to our aid if there should be any unfortunate misunderstandings between our two countries.'

Mustafa shook his head sadly. 'The English and the Dutch. What are they? Tiny countries far away, and as to Poland what is it? A mere straggle of villages – barbarians actually. Besides, the French envoy has assured me that the Polish parliament will never ratify your treaty. The French are spending a great deal of money to assure that.'

'I am afraid that the French are ready to say anything,' Kunitz said. 'They are a most frivolous people.'

'If you say so.' Having made his point that Austria would have to fight a war on two fronts, Mustafa was ready to agree. 'But let us not squabble over that disagreeable nation. Let us talk about our own countries. Now, as your Excellencies well know, we wish merely to live in peace with you, but that requires some small concessions.'

Kunitz sighed. 'We have been negotiating for months, now and the Emperor has agreed to many concessions. He has agreed to give up territory. He has agreed that you can build new fortresses on the border. He has even agreed that you may tax Austrian subjects, but every time we make an offer you demand more.'

'Ah,' Mustafa patted Kunitz on the knee. 'Come now, that is mere bargaining; an offer here, an offer there, a little give and take . . .'

'You will forgive me,' Kunitz said, 'But we have yet to hear an offer from you. We have heard demands, certainly, endless demands, but nothing has been offered in return.'

'Yes, yes, understood.' Mustafa leaned back. 'But that is because of disputes in our Grand Council. Some of the military leaders . . . their demands have been quite outrageous. You know what soldiers are – mad for war – and the entire army of the Empire will be here in spring. I have had great difficulty in restraining them. But now I have managed to make them see reason and we have agreed on one, final request.'

Kunitz raised his hand. 'If it is the question of Gyor again.'

Mustafa struck his knee, and there was no smile on his face now. 'But it is,' he said. 'Inshallah, and we will have it. The audience is over.'

'So it is Gyor?' The secretary poured out much needed glasses of wine for Kunitz and Caprara. 'Then that means war.'

There was no answer. Indeed there was no need for one. The great fortress of Gyor on the Danube, a hundred miles below Vienna was the chief defence of Austria against attack from the south, which meant against the Ottomans. For Kara Mustafa to ask for it was to ask Austria to throw away its shield.

'They can't be serious,' the secretary said. 'They will settle for something else in the end.'

'Perhaps.' Kunitz drank his wine, his hand shaking a little. He peered through the window at the fires on the plain. There were no stars shining now and the snow was falling thicker. 'Perhaps,' he said.

The snow drifted down on Europe. It dusted the great bridge across the Drava, it fell, heavier, on Vienna where the knight of St. Luke's, his little doorway choked with snow had to stay inside his tower, and, driven by a howling wind, it poured across Poland in a torrent so thick that a man could not see his hand before him.

No movement possible. A hundred thousand wretched villages sealed in upon themselves, cities, far apart, remote and distant, like islands in a white sea; in Osijek, young Timur Ven stamping frozen feet; in Vienna, Herr Vogel baking his rolls, Frau Vogel gossiping by the fire with Frau Haller, Rudi crying with chilblains, Anna wondering why she blushed so when she saw young Kasper Haller, the Emperor at another Mass; Stefan idling in Ostrova, hoping for a war, wolves howling in the night, and the Ottoman host somnolent by its firesides on the plain of Edirne. 1682 dying, and the year of decision waiting to be born.

Part
2

The Attack
Spring 1683

Chapter Six

OSIJEK

ALTHOUGH Stefan Zabruski would have taken some convincing that it was doing so, the earth swung on its slow journey round the sun. The snow melted and the spring rain came in an interminable, drenching downpour. The swollen Danube spread its arms and embraced its vast valley in a sodden embrace, scarcely less miserable than winter's grip. But still, the cranes, which six months before had flown south, returned, whooping and spreading their silver wings over the Ottoman horde which rose from its camp in Edirne and, following the cranes, marched north, to Hungary, and the Austrian frontier.

Plovdiv, Pazarjik, Sofia, one by one the bastions of Ottoman power were reached and passed; three thousand Janissaries led the way, twenty thousand cavalry followed, forty thousand more infantry, engineers, baggage carts, huge flocks of sheep and cattle, dragging their way across the Balkans.

Week by week the army increased in size; troops from Asia, from the Turkish plateau, from Syria, Persia, Arabia, moved up behind the main column and at Nis, Caprara and Kunitz saw cavalry from Egypt and Nubia join the camp.

A Major in the Sipahi, the elite Ottoman cavalry, grinned at the Austrians, and waved a swarthy hand. 'Now you see greatness,' he said. 'See how, under God, Islam binds the world together. All brothers, all equal. *Sayf al-Islam*, the sword of Islam, forged by

Allah.' He laughed with pride, although curiously without malice and drew his finger across his throat. 'For you, and your Emperor, Sayf al-Islam.' Kunitz was gloomy but, surprisingly, Caprara was not impressed. 'There are plenty of them,' he admitted, 'But they are a rabble. Sayf al-Islam; more like a rusty dagger to me.'

But bright sword of Islam or rusty dagger, it cut a swathe of destruction among conquerors and conquered alike. For forty miles on either side the land was raided, plundered, pillaged, stripped down to its bare bones, and the peasants, Christians and Muslims alike, stood in the rain and stared helplessly at their desolated farms and empty granaries.

However, the point of the sword was still locked in its scabbard, for, three hundred miles to the north, the bridge over the Drava, the entrance to the Austrian possessions was still not ready for the army slouching towards it.

There, in a grey, tippling rain, a Major of the Turkish Engineering Corps was peering over the parapet of the bridge into the swollen waters of the river. From under the bridge came muffled voices and the thudding of hammers. The Major shouted a question. A youthful Captain's face appeared, upside down, and shouted an answer with a volley of oaths tacked on. The Major straightened and turned to Corbaci Vasif with a resigned shrug.

'We should have been here before winter,' he said. 'The struts should have been strengthened against the ice.'

There was a note of accusation in his voice and Vasif shrugged moodily in return. He pulled from his pocket a sheaf of letters he had written to the Governor's office in Buda, all pleading for a company of engineers to be sent before winter set in. He had the answers, too, dozens of them; all helpful, polite, expressing deep concern and promising full and immediate action.

'Slackness,' Vasif barked. 'Sheer slackness.'

The engineer smiled ruefully. 'I know,' he said. 'I could show you my letters, too. I need four thousand feet of timber and what do I get? Two waggon-loads of firewood. Our masters seem to think that war is just a matter of fine words and waggling swords.

They have forgotten what real war is all about. But we know better, eh, Corbaci?'

He turned away to his task and Vasif nodded approvingly. 'There is a man with sense. A real campaigner.'

Hovering at Vasif's heels, Timur Ven said, mechanically, 'Yes, Corbaci.' But he was not truly convinced. Surely war *was* to do with flashing trumpets and the thunder of kettle drums, and not this dreary business of poking about under bridges and writing endless letters for timber and bags of nails. Indeed Timur had already seen some of what he considered the glittering panoply of war, for a squadron of light cavalry had moved into Osijek ready to make the first, scouring raids across the river. He was brought back to reality by a bang on the ear, delivered by Vasif.

'Corbaci.' He stood, ramrod straight.

An intimidating stare from Vasif. 'No day-dreaming,' he said in his most icy voice. 'You are on duty.'

'Dok!'

Vasif jabbed his finger over the bridge. 'The engineers,' he said, as if, in his uncanny way, he was reading Timur's mind. 'Don't despise them. One day your life may depend on them. Understood?'

'Dok!'

An ear which tingled for the next two days, but compensation on the third, for Vasif rode to Belgrade, taking Timur with him, to meet old Ibrahim Pasha, the Beylerbeyi of Buda, who had come down from the north to rendezvous with the main army, bringing with him his own forces, ten, fifteen thousand light cavalry, camped across the river at Zemun, the men, hardened by years of guerilla warfare on the frontier, hawklike, predatory, merciless.

Timur admired them, too, but Vasif was dismissive. 'They have their part to play,' he admitted, in his just, professional way, 'But it is the infantry which win wars. The infantry. Us.'

At the gate of the palace of the Bey of Belgrade Vasif dismissed Timur. Meet me in an hour,' he said.

With the confidence of youth, Timur swaggered into the Janissaries' barracks, and with the appetite of youth found the kitchens. As Timur was a Janissary, too, an affable cook gave him soup and rice, listened good-naturedly as Timur talked of the coming war and its glories, and the undoubted cowardice of the Christian army they were going to meet, and destroy, as his mate clattered among the pots and pans.

'Have some coffee,' he said, as Timur finished his meal and his oratory. He pushed a coffee pot at Timur, sat down at the table, and leaned forward in an easy, companiable way. 'How old are you, sonny?' he asked.

Timur, not too pleased at being addressed as 'sonny' said firmly, 'Sixteen,' adding, hastily, 'Two years a Janissary.'

'Two years, hey?' The cook whistled in admiration and behind him, his mate, a broad red face looming from the steam like the sun from fog, whistled too.

'And how did you get into this lot?' asked the cook.

'My father was a Janissary,' Timur said. 'Forty years.'

'A real old sweat,' the cook poured out more coffee. 'What's he doing now?'

'He's got a coffee-house, in Istanbul.'

'Good for him. Istanbul hey? Not bad. Not bad at all. I wouldn't mind ending up there myself. What about you?' he asked over his shoulder.

'Too true,' came from the steam.

'And he put you in the force?' the cook went on.

'Yes,' Timur took a cake offered him. 'He knows Corbaci Vasif.'

'Vasif?' The cook looked up shrewdly. 'The Devshirme? I've heard of him. A ramrod isn't he? Orders is orders, shut up and obey them. I know the type . . . so, you're a Janissary and all ready to go and be a hero.' He paused for a moment. 'Well you don't seem a bad lad at that – and you know your manners,' he commented as Timur thanked him for another cake. 'You looking forward to this war?'

'Yes.' Timur was emphatic. In fact he was looking forward to the war more than anything in his life before.

'Good. Nice to have something to look forward to. Breaks the monotony, like.'

There was a muffled laugh from the steam and the cook himself gave a crooked, ill-concealed grin.

'And what would you say a Janissary's first duty is, sonny?'

Timur sat up. 'To die bravely.'

In the steam the cook's mate laughed again although the cook kept his face straight, perhaps a little too straight to be natural.

'Now who told you that?' he asked.

'My Corbaci.'

The cook gazed at Timur for a moment then said, 'You listen to me, two-year Janissary, let *me* tell you what a soldier's first duty is. His first, his *very* first duty, is to keep his belly full –' he held up a brawny fist as Timur opened his mouth to protest. 'Wait. The second duty is to keep himself dry, and the third duty is to get as much loot as he can. Right?' he asked over his shoulder.

'Right,' said his mate. 'Too right.'

'Of course,' the cook went on, reasonably, 'If you *are* called on to fight then do your duty, but, but try *not* to be called on. Get yourself a nice little number in an office and keep your head down.'

Timur was pallid. With intense seriousness he asked, 'Is this the talk of a Janissary?'

'It is that,' said the cook. 'A thirty-year Janissary. And another thing, you forget all this rubbish about Christians being cowards. See this?' He pointed to his head. A massive scar ran across his greying hair. 'Take a good look. I got that at the battle of St. Gotthard twenty years ago. The Austrians jumped us there, up in Hungary, and I'll tell you something, laddy; they fought like demons and we ran like rabbits. Right?'

'Right,' from the steam.

Timur stood up, his mouth quivering. 'This is treason,' he cried. 'If I report it – by Allah!'

'Report what?' said the cook. 'We've never clapped eyes on you in our lives. Have we – by Allah.'

'Right – by Allah' said his mate, and laughed again as Timur lunged blindly from the treasonous kitchen.

He slouched across a muddy square to the Bey's palace and sat under a coping, brooding as the rain came down. An hour passed, and another. A troop of Bedouin rode past, white hoods hiding their dark faces, followed by a squadron of Circassians from the Caucasus, east of the Black Sea, dark hoods hiding their white faces. A familiar forked pennant led an orta of Janissaries down to the pontoon bridge which crossed the River Sava to Zemun, and, at last Vasif came down the steps of the palace with his light, athletic step, clicked his fingers, and Timur, thankfully, fell in behind him, although, thirty-five years younger, he had to skip to keep up with him.

'Has the Corbaci found wood for the bridge? Timur asked.

Vasif gave a curt laugh. 'That is a problem for the engineers. No, I have other news.' He halted, upright, heedless of the rain. 'No, other news.'

Timur stood patiently, waiting. Lashed on by whips, a file of Christians trudged through the mud, forced labour on their way to the river to build a dock for the siege guns coming up from Istanbul. Behind them hobbled a priest who gave Vasif a deep, respectful, and fearful bow. The rain trickled down Timur's hat and onto his neck.

'Corbaci?' he prompted.

'Ah' Vasif half-turned. 'I saw the Beylerbeyi, Ibrahim Pasha. I knew him in the old days, in Transylvania. I asked him a favour, for old times sake, for the sake of the days when we were men.'

He paused, lost in those days of long ago. The rain found its way down Timur's neck and under his collar. He coughed respectfully, carefully turning his head away. 'Yes, Corbaci?'

Vasif looked at him, his eyes glittering with a luminous, fanatic's gleam. 'We are leaving the bridge. When the army marches, we march with it. That is the news. Good news. A soldier's news.'

Trumpets sounded somewhere, a drum rattled, the rain fell harder. Timur sneezed, blew his nose through his fingers, and had a sudden, fleeting vision of the steaming kitchen and the brawny cook and his mate, companionable among the pots and pans and the steam.

'Corbaci,' he said, almost without thinking. 'What is a soldier's duty?'

Like two gun barrels Vasif's eyes sighted unnervingly on Timur. 'Why do you ask that?'

For a moment Timur felt an urge to tell Vasif of the cooks, but the thought of the rice and the coffee – and the cakes – offered without question to another Janissary, a fellow *voyolan* – wayfarer, stopped him. Almost at random he pointed across the river, to the vast military camp. 'It is just that . . . I mean . . .'

'I understand.' Vasif's eyes altered their range. 'Now we are to go into battle a man might wonder about his duty, let alone a lad. Well, it is simple enough. My duty is to do as I am ordered, and your duty is to do as I order you.'

Simple answers. Orders, obedience, and prayer. All doubts set at rest. But back in Osijek, Timur yearned for more. After his evening meal he stood at a window in the fort, peering into the sodden night, north to Austria. 'Were there Christians there,' he wondered, 'peering south? And what were they really like, those Giaours who so obstinately refused to heed the message of Muhammad, peace be on his name? Were they trembling with fear at the thought of the Sword of Islam poised over their necks or were they, as the treasonous cooks had said, demons in battle, as fearless as the warriors of Islam?'

Of course Timur saw Christians daily, but they were the dejected subjects of the Sultan, little better than serfs, miserable, downtrodden, fearful. But across the river, in *their* strongholds, in the great and populous cities, what were they like there? Well, he touched his curved sword and shook his head in wonderment, then went to his bed as the Sword of Islam pushed steadily north towards him.

Chapter Seven

VIENNA

As if in retreat from the Ottoman army, spring edged slowly north, although in Vienna it would have taken an optimistic heart to believe it.

From his palace, the Hofburg, the Emperor Leopold looked down gloomily on his city. Under the shadows of the tall houses and the innumerable churches the snow was slowly melting, but as the grimy mounds slipped away they revealed all the debris of the winter; dead cats and dogs, rotting cabbage stalks, ashes, ordure, broken pots, household rubbish of every sort which, in defiance of all the city's laws, the incorrigible citizens of Vienna had chucked out during the long winter nights.

In the cramped garden of the Hofburg two men wandered, pushing a wheelbarrow with shovels in it, and ambled into the maze. The maze was clever, designed on the best French model, and, once you were in it, extremely difficult to find your way out. Sometimes Leopold felt that he was living in a maze; but one made of threats and counter threats, treaties and pacts, wars of aggression and defence. In Germany alone, in the Holy Roman Empire of which he was the elected Head, there were more than six hundred states; Electorates, Kingdoms, Dukedoms, Principalities, Palatinates, all locked together in a fantastic system of interlocking alliances and all of them committed, in theory, to defend their Emperor to death, but none of them, it seemed, as death drew near, in fact prepared to lift a finger to his defence.

The two men in the maze began to work, but in an idle, inept way, merely shifting the snow from one side of the path to the other. The Emperor shook his head; *Schlamperei* – slovenliness, typical Viennese slovenliness – and it was everywhere, even now, seven months after the warning from Kunitz in Istanbul, and three months after the Ottoman army had begun to march, the city walls were not in proper repair, vital stores, ammunition and gunpowder from Amsterdam were still delayed on the Rhine . . . and the French were preparing to attack in the Netherlands . . .

There was a rustle of skirts behind him. The Empress Eleanor – Magdalene, sitting in a gilt arm-chair. Leopold turned, dragging his mind from imperial problems;

'You are well? Quite well?'

The Empress inclined her head. 'Quite well.'

'You have seen your physicians today?'

'Yes.' The Empress ran her fingers lightly over her black bodice. 'God willing I shall have the child in four months.' She picked up a piece of embroidery, an altar cloth, and selected a strand of red silk from her work-basket. Over her needle she peered short-sightedly at Leopold. 'Is it true?'

'Is what true?' Leopold was mild, tender.

'About the Tartars?'

'Yes. Yes, I'm afraid that it is.' Leopold looked at the ceiling where a swarm of plump cherubs hovered around a stout Virgin Mary. The news had arrived that morning. Thirty thousand Tartars had answered the Sultan's summons. Now they were riding across Podolia. Podolia! Leopold felt like clutching his head at the thought; Crimean Tartars, thirty thousand of them! And the Ottoman main army was steadily moving north – he had a vision of it munching its way up the Balkans like some huge green caterpillar . . .

'And Thokoly?' There was venom in the Empress's voice.

'That is also true. Our envoys are quite positive. The Grand Vizier is going to offer Thokoly the crown of Hungary, and he is going to accept it.'

'And the others?'

There was no need for Leopold to ask who the others were. Prince Serban of Wallachia, Prince George of Moldavia, Michael Apafi of Transylvania; the Turks were calling in all their allies and vassals.

'Christians!' The Empress's horsy face was twisted with anger. 'They call themselves Christians and yet they are ready to join Muslims in a war against a Christian Emperor – *their* lawful Emperor. Heretics!' She stitched a drop of blood falling from a thorn. 'You should have put them to the sword long ago.'

'We did, my dear.' Leopold wandered restlessly about the room. 'We did and now they are marching with the Turks.'

There was a silence, sullen, disapproving; then, 'A priest was stoned in the streets today, at the Carinthian Gate.'

'Yes. I was told.' Leopold breathed on the window-pane and drew a cross. There had been other attacks on priests in the past few weeks. The people believing that the Church and its policy of ferocious repression of Protestantism, had driven the Hungarians into the arms of the Turks; which indeed was the case.

Leopold returned to the window. The workmen had gone, leaving their wheelbarrow and spades behind them. Beyond the garden, on the Hofplatz, torches glowed and bonfires shot sparks into the night. Shadowy figures flickered across the flames and Leopold raised an approving finger. At least work was going on to strengthen the city walls. Late, of course, but better late than never. Leopold wondered if there had ever been a city whose walls *were* in repair. It was understandable, of course; to keep a city's walls in repair was an expensive business. Leopold only hoped that Rimpler, the Italian engineer, and Herman of Baden, the President of the Imperial Council of War knew their business. At any rate, the fact that work was being done at all showed that even the vast Austrian bureaucracy was capable of movement.

'I must go.' Leopold turned from the window. 'I have to meet the War Council and the Burgomaster.'

'The Burgomaster!' There was surprise and disdain in the Empress's voice.

'It is necessary. The Council will not demolish the houses outside the walls although Signor Rimpler insists on it. We must have a clear field of fire for the cannon.'

The Empress jabbed at the altar-cloth. 'Then why not tell the soldiers to blow them up? You are the Emperor.'

A ghost of a smile crossed Leopold's lips. 'It is not quite so simple.'

'Why isn't it?' Another drop of blood appeared on the cloth. 'In Pfalz-Neuburg my father would have had the burghers on their knees before him. Commoners! You are their Lord – their absolute ruler. *Order* them to do as you wish.'

Leopold tugged at his red stockings. 'The City has its own rights, its own laws. If I interfere too much, well, the City Council tightens the purse strings, and we need the money.'

'Then tell Count Abele if you need money. He is the President of the Treasury.'

The smile retraced itself across the Emperor's lips. 'He is an expert at spending money, not making it. For that we need the merchants.'

The needle flashed dangerously in the Empress's fingers. 'Merchants! They are the source of all trouble. My father always says so. Allow trade and what happens? Heresy creeps in from the Netherlands and England . . .'

'Yes.' Leopold agreed with every word, trade and heresy did go together, but what could be done? Countries could not live without money – especially a country like Austria.

'In any case,' The Empress's harsh voice broke into Leopold's thoughts. 'Surely all this money we are spending is wasted. The Turks can't be mad enough to attack Vienna. It is preposterous.'

Leopold agreed with that, too. 'It is merely a precaution,' he murmured.

The great clock in the Hofburg rang seven times. 'Now I must go,' Leopold said. 'I must not keep the Council waiting.' At the door he paused. 'Let us remember that God is with us.'

'Yes, indeed.' The Empress as pious and devout as the Emperor.

'And there are signs.'

'Signs?'

'Signs from Heaven, from Almighty God. Remember the Sultan's turban.'

'Turban?' There was bewilderment in the Empress's voice.

'It blew off, when the Sultan left Istanbul last year. Let us not take that sign too lightly.'

Full night came. In the Golden Eagle the Landlord lit his lamps and the customers were able, although it was forbidden by law, to play *skat* without ruining their eyesight. Herr Vogel, who enjoyed a game of cards with his beer, threw down an ace with an enormous flourish. 'Mine!' he shouted, raked in his winnings, and shuffled the cards, ready to deal and then saw Herr Haller enter the inn.

Haller sat in his usual place, underneath a portrait of the Emperor. The picture had the odd effect that wherever you sat in the inn Leopold seemed to be staring dolefully at you. Haller was having the same effect on Herr Vogel. Every time the little baker peeped over his cards, Haller had his eyes fixed on him. Vogel sighed. Sooner or later he would have to talk to Haller. The cabinet maker's eyes were like two lodestones, drawing him irresistably forward. Vogel threw down his cards. 'Deal me out,' he said bitterly, the more so because he was on a winning streak.

He went across the room to Haller who, with great solemnity, bought him a drink.

'Herr Vogel.'

'Herr Haller.'

Both men raised their steins and drank. 'Time goes on,' Haller said.

'Yes.' Vogel nodded his head five times, slowly. 'It often does. I've noticed that.'

'Spring,' said Haller, 'is almost here.'

'Yes.' Vogel agreed again. 'It usually does come about now.'

'There is hardly any ice left on the Danube.' Haller pointed through the window, in case Vogel thought that the river flowed down Ottostrasse.'

'True. True.' Vogel rolled his eyes. 'It is because the weather is warmer,' he added, with heavy irony.

Haller was impervious to irony. 'Quite correct,' he said. He stared meaningfully at Vogel. 'Well?'

Vogel shook his head. 'I don't know. I just don't know. It is a big decision. To give your daughter away . . .' He sighed and peered gloomily into his beer.

Haller was vigorous. 'Not such a big decision. What's a marriage after all? My Kaspar and your Anna. My Kaspar is a fine young man, you know.'

'Yes.' Vogel was quite ready to agree with that. Kaspar was a fine, decent lad. But it was not the thought of having Kaspar as a son-in-law which depressed him but the thought of having Haller as an in-law. He stirred uneasily. 'Anna is still young.'

'Not *young*.' Haller spoke as though Vogel had suggested that Anna was three years old. 'She is eighteen, isn't she?'

'Seventeen,' Vogel murmured.

'Well there you are.' Haller slapped the table triumphantly. 'Just the age my Gertrude was when I married her.' He sipped some beer and looked sideways at Vogel. 'It would all work out very nicely. That land of yours outside the walls. Kaspar could build a house there –'

'Herr Haller –' Vogel slapped the table. 'They are going to pull the houses outside the walls *down*.'

'Ach!' Haller smiled his knowing, maddening smile. 'Don't worry about that. It's just rubbish, pulling down good houses just in case the Turks get here. No, no. The aristocrats want them pulled down but the burghers will never allow it. They've got too many houses of their own there. Anyway, I know for a fact that the Turks are just going to do some looting in Hungary and then go back. They would never get past Gyor, anyway. No, don't you worry about the Turks, Herr Vogel.'

Vogel slapped the table again, although he would have preferred to slap his companion. 'Herr Haller, it was you who said the Turks were definitely coming. You have been saying so for months.'

'Ah, yes.' Haller had the grace to blush a little. He poked his long nose into his stein. 'That was then. It's different now. Anyway – just think, a nice house in the suburbs, Kaspar and Anna could live in part of it and rent the rest. That would bring in a nice little sum every quarter. A house is a very good hedge against inflation, you know, and the way prices keep rising. . . .'

'You don't have to tell *me* about rising prices,' Vogel said, gloomily.

'Well, there you are then. It's a thought, isn't it? Oh, and by the way, I should say that I don't want Kaspar hanging around for ever. He's twenty-one now and Herr Breitner, the violin-maker, has got a very nice daughter. Think about it.'

Herr Vogel did think about it as he slipped his way back home. He could not deny the truth of what Haller had said. Two young people marrying, what was wrong with that? And Kaspar was a nice young man, unlike his hideously tedious father, and the land beyond the Burg bastion could be developed and the rent would be useful. . . .

He let himself into the house. Anna was sitting by the fire, sewing. She raised her open, kind face. 'Can I get you anything, Father?'

'No.' Vogel sat down heavily. 'Where is your mother?'

'Down the street, with Frau Haller.'

Vogel's heart sank. So, the women were talking together. He knew what that meant. But! He clenched his chubby fist. Nothing would be done without the free and willing consent of his daughter. He watched her as she bent over her needlework. His daughter, his only daughter, his patient, kind, and uncomplaining girl. He coughed, as if he was clearing his throat of flour.

'Anna,' he said.

'Yes, father?'

Vogel felt unaccountably hot. He tugged at his collar. 'I . . . I was in the Golden Eagle tonight.'

Since her father was in the Golden Eagle every night this was no surprise to Anna.

'Yes.' Vogel felt that he was actually on fire. 'I . . . I played Skat.'

Since Vogel played Skat every time he went into the inn this, too, was equally unsurprising to Anna. She picked at a stitch.

'Did you win father?'

'Yes.' Vogel jumped to his feet, charged to the water tub and gulped a ladleful of water. 'Oh yes, I won. I won all right. And . . . and I talked to Herr Haller.'

Anna's head sank deeper over her needlework so that her face was hidden, but a pink flush spread across the back of her neck.

Vogel was flushed, too. In fact he was redder than a beetroot. 'He . . . you . . . I mean . . .' He took a deep breath. 'He says Kaspar wants to marry you,' he bellowed.

'Yes, father,' a barely audible whisper from Anna.

'But do you want to marry him?' Vogel roared, as if he was having a terrible argument with his worst enemy.

Anna dropped her needlework and clapped her hands over her face. 'As you say, father.'

'No.' Vogel's face was purple. 'Not as I say.' He charged across the room like a small bull and held Anna's shoulder. 'It's as you think best. You! No one will ever make you do anything you don't want to do. Never, never, never! Do you hear me?'

He bent down and peered into Anna's face. Her violet eyes shone through her entwined fingers. 'I like Kaspar,' she said.

'You do? You're sure?'

Anna dropped her hands. She was smiling. 'Mother says August.'

'August!' Vogel stared accusingly at his wife.

'August,' said his wife with her night gown on.

'But – but –' Vogel grasped at a straw. 'The Turks will be here then.'

His wife lumbered onto a groaning bed. 'Don't be a bigger fool than you can help,' she said.

Vogel struck his forehead. 'Me a fool? Me? It's you and Haller who have been going on about the Turks coming.'

'Pooh!' Frau Vogel pulled the goose-feather counterpane up to her chin. 'What does that matter? Do you think that the world has to stop because of those madmen. Anyway, they aren't coming to Vienna. The Poles are going to stop them.'

'The Poles?' Vogel flapped his arms in despair. 'Who told you that?'

'Frau Haller.'

'And who,' Vogel said, 'Who told Frau Haller, if I might ask.'

'Herr Haller. Blow out the candle.'

An hour later Vogel stood in his bakery preparing for his night's work. Everything was ready; flour, yeast, lard, salt, butter, water, the oven glowing and a neat stack of firewood. The familiar jangle of church bells clanged across the dark city followed by the great clock of the Hofburg tolling eleven. Vogel leaned on the window-sill for a moment. Lights were on in the palace and from within its walls a trumpet sounded shrilly. Probably a signal that the Emperor was going to bed, Vogel sighed. He was a modest man, content to be a baker – a good baker – and a good citizen, respected by his neighbours and his Guild. Happy, for all his irascibility, to be a good, loyal Viennese; yes, happy with his shop and his children, even happy with his wife. But, just for once he wished he was someone else. Leopold, for instance. To be sure, the All Highest had his problems, what with all the talk of the French wars and rebellion in Hungary and now the Turks making trouble, but at least he wasn't going to have Herr Haller as a relative.

'August,' he sighed, and heaved a sack of flour onto the table.

Chapter Eight

POLAND

Two weary oxen dragging a cart through the spring mud of Poland. Four lousy, tattered serfs trudging beside them, goading the beasts forward. On the cart, Pyotr Chelmnitz, flogger of Jews and serfs, inside the cart, Stefan Zabruski.

Rain swept across the drab wastes of the plain, soaking the men and the beasts, and drumming on the canvas of the cart. But under the awning, sprawled across sacks of wheat, next to his father's battle armour, Stefan was content. He rubbed the massive helmet with his sleeve. In the burnished steel he could see the reflection of his face, oddly elongated and with two black holes for eyes. It looked like a skull, but that deathly and deadly image did not disturb Stefan. He began to sing, a light Cossack air;

'It is good to have a house,
It is good to have a roof and a fire
When winter is here.
But when spring comes,
A good horse is better than a
Roof or a fire.'

Plodding through the mud the serfs heard the song. They glanced furtively at each other as Chelmnitz spat and cracked his whip viciously over the sad, patient backs of the oxen.

At dusk they came to a village, a sodden straggle of mud huts with rotten thatch spilling from them, and a hovel which passed for an inn. The innkeeper doled out soup made from mouldy potatoes and gobbets of yellow fat, and, like the family, which in a bizarre kind of way they were, Stefan, Chelmnitz, and the serfs ate together, gaped at by a handful of depressed peasants.

At the end of the meal the innkeeper sidled furtively forward and took away the dishes. 'It was good, your Honour?'

Stefan glared balefully at the man. 'Is this what you live on here?'

'Yes, Pan.'

'Then what –' Stefan spat out a twist of half-chewed gristle. 'Then what do you give to the pigs?'

Pyotr Chelmnitz burst into loud, meaningless laughter. 'Ha ha ha, that's a good one, by Christ,' and although the serfs had thought the meal better than the ones they got in Zabruski's village, they joined in the laughter.

'That *is* a good one,' they yowled. 'What a lad our master is, haw, haw, haw.'

Stefan was pleased by the laughter. He wanted to make another joke and hear more, rapturous applause. 'God help you,' he roared. 'You would be better off in the hands of the Tartars!'

For a moment there was a shocked silence. Even amongst men used to the lash, and for whom kicks and blows were a daily fare, the remark evoked an image of horror too sinister to contemplate. Then Chelmnitz smashed his fist onto the table.

'By Jesus,' he shouted, 'By Christ! Another good one, ho, ho, ho.'

The serfs joined in the baying. Like so many wolves they bared their rotten teeth at the peasants, and like so many sheep the peasants bleated with them.

Stefan tossed a mugful of vodka down his throat. Ah! he thought, how pleasant it was to be a Schlacta's son, to sit at the head of a table with loyal serfs, to make jokes and to have men laugh at them. 'Drink up, lads,' he cried. 'Drink up.'

The rain drummed on the thatch, the peasants sat in their dark corners, the innkeeper scuttled backwards and forwards with vodka. On one foray, misled by Stefan's drunken grin, he asked whether his Honour was going to Cracow. On the instant Stefan's grin vanished.

'What is that to you?'

The innkeeper cringed and backed away. 'Nothing, Pan. I beg your Honour's pardon.'

'Aagh!' Stefan swigged more of the treacherous vodka and raised his flushed, drunken face. 'Tak, we are going to Cracow to declare war on the Turks.' The room was spinning slowly and Stefan tried to focus on a dim oil lamp. 'Tak! Sobieski against the Turks. Poland against the world!'

'Tak, Pan, Tak.' The serfs grinned in drunken, loyal agreement. Vodka dribbling from his mouth, Chelmnitz leaned forward. 'War, Pan. It's good. Plenty of loot . . . gold . . . women –'

'*Nie!*' Stefan scowled. 'No, by Christ and his wounds. The war – for Poland's honour, and the King's.'

The oil lamp was beginning to spin now, also. Stefan tried to stand and reeled backwards against the dank wall. Vague, blurred images were crossing his fuddled mind; the Polish cavalry, invincible in their winged armour crashing into an enemy – any enemy – battle-axes flashing in the sun, lances splintering; 'Tak,' he mumbled, 'The Madonna will lead us, the Black Virgin of Czestochowa! Turks . . . Russians . . . Tartars . . . dirty foreigners. Eiee – Poland against the world!' With a last belching hiccough he fell down and was violently sick.

Laughing, and reeling themselves, the serfs dragged Stefan to the innkeeper's bedroom, kicked out the innkeeper's wife and five children, threw Stefan onto the bed, then lurched to the stables where they collapsed on the straw litter.

'Pyotr,' Grigor, one of the serfs mumbled. 'What is Cracow?'

Chelmnitz scratched himself. 'A town. A big town.'

'Like Velbo?'

'No.' Chelmnitz was disgusted. 'It's a real town. Churches, monasteries, taverns, hundreds of them.'

Grigor gave a long sigh. 'Ah, we'll see some marvels.' A stifled yawn, then, 'Why are we going to Cracow, Pyotr?'

'To vote whether to fight the Turks. But it's all settled, anyway.'

Another serf raised a matted head from the straw. 'How's that, Pyotr?'

'Ah, the King and the nobles settled that in Warsaw at Christmas. Anyway, we're taking the Schlacta's armour aren't we? What are we doing that for, if he isn't going to fight?'

A last drowsy voice. 'Where are these Turks?'

Chelmnitz burrowed into the straw. 'Them? Why' – not knowing where they were he waved his hand in a wide, drunken gesture – 'Over there, somewhere . . . everywhere.'

Snores, belches, groans and grunts; the rats coming out, and the cockroaches. The rain drumming on the thatch. Silence.

Two days later they reached Cracow, that city of marvels and wonders. Zabruski was staying in a ramshackle town-house, part of his wife's dowry. There Stefan found him, surrounded by a horde of uncles, aunts, and cousins. Greetings, waves, embraces, sentimental Polish tears tasting of salt and vodka, and Zabruski grunting as Stefan handed over the priceless armour. But Zabruski's grunts were genial, like a boar with its belly full of acorns, which was not far from the literal truth, for his pockets were stuffed with money.

'Bribes,' he laughed. 'Every voter in the council. The French stuffing money in our pockets, and the Austrians, throwing money about like madmen.' He laughed again. 'And it's all for nothing. The matter is settled. Tak! No one here is going to vote against the Diet but the foreigners can't believe it.'

Stefan nodded. He understood perfectly the situation. The Diet, the Parliament in Warsaw, had accepted the treaty with Austria but the provincial Diets had to ratify the Treaty with Austria, too, hence the bribery. He sniggered artificially and Zabruski noticed that at once.

'You don't like it,' he said. 'You want some sort of Holy War, a Crusade. But we won't be voting for their dirty schemes but for us, for Poland and the King.'

Stefan was satisfied, almost. Poland, King John; King John and Poland and damn all foreigners, and whatever lingering doubts he might have had melted away as, with French and Austrian gold, he was bought a blue velvet suit, fine white silk stockings, and a small-sword of genuine Toledo steel, the price of which would have kept a peasant family in comfort for three years, and which looked stingingly elegant against his blue coat. He had one disappointment, though. His father would not buy him a horse.

'No,' Zabruski growled. 'What is the point in buying a horse and having it eating its head off for months. When we go to war – *if* we go, I will buy you a good horse, but not till then.'

Stefan was slightly bewildered. 'But I thought, well, I thought that the war had started. I thought that the Austrians and the Turks were . . .'

'No, no.' Zabruski shook his massive head, and in his new, mellow, debt-free mood actually took the trouble to explain the situation. 'It's like this; the Turks haven't declared war on anyone – yet. That's their way, cat and mouse. They've got their army together but who knows where it is going? They are making all sorts of demands on the Austrians, frightening them – but the army is at Belgrade, three hundred miles from Vienna. Suppose the Austrians give them what they want? They might turn on us, hey? Cut across the mountains in Bohemia and before you know it they're knocking on the gates of Warsaw. So that's the agreement; if the Turks attack Warsaw the Austrians help us, and if they attack Vienna, then we help them.'

'But if they don't attack either?' Stefan asked.

Zabruski shrugged. 'They'll roam around Hungary, but what's that to us?' He slapped his pocket. 'We've got our money.'

'So we just wait?' Stefan was deeply disappointed.

'Just wait.' Zabruski gave his son a bearish push in the chest. 'Go and enjoy yourself.'

And despite the prickle of discontent, Stefan did enjoy himself, lounging about the city meeting relatives and friends, and friends of friends, and the smart disappeared completely when he found that on the eve of the provincial Diet, the greatest landowner in

Southern Poland, Prince Lubomirski, was to give a ball.

A real ball, too; not a dreary country dance with two drunken fiddlers sawing away and the schlactas' sons and daughters lurching around a splintered floor like young carthorses, but a genuine, elegant dance. Stefan imagined it, grace and beauty, music from a real orchestra, light spilling into the dusky evening, girls. . . .

And for once reality lived up to expectation; a brilliant ball, Lubomirski's Hall filled with the nobility of southern Poland; Counts who owned thousands of acres and hundreds of serfs, their women with necks glittering with diamonds – Schlactas with clumsy sons and tittering daughters, lords of perhaps five hundred acres of wilderness, but marked by the magic wand of their class, all greeted by the great Count Lubomirski himself as his clan gathered.

The first dance; the Master of Ceremonies arranged the dancers in long lines – a gap – a man required. The Master of Ceremonies placed his white-gloved hand to his mouth and glanced around the ballroom; his worldly eyes resting on Stefan, a finger beckoning him and a voice which brooked no refusal informing him that the Demoiselle did him the honour of the dance.

Red faced, Stefan walked forward and found himself facing, not the chiffon-clad, lissom creature of his dreams but a great, beefy girl, a schlacta's daughter with a huge pink face and meaty powdered shoulders on which sweat was already making milky runnels. Stefan stared disdainfully at her and she stared disdainfully at him as the orchestra struck the opening bars of a minuet.

The minuet was not much danced in Ostrova. Stefan had half-learned it from a wandering dancing-master but he could not remember the long, intricate movements of the dance and the next fifteen minutes were the worst in his entire life. He blundered here and there, bowing to the wrong partner at the wrong time and once, having completely lost the thread of the dance, bowing to no one at all and straightening to find himself staring at his country cousins who grinned at him with utter and complete delight. On and on went the dance until it seemed to Stefan that it would last until Doomsday but, just as he was about to dash from the Hall, from Cracow and, if possible, from Poland, the orchestra gave a final flourish and to applause, and a little laughter, the dance ended.

Stefan's partner stared at him with loathing as he stumbled back to his grinning friends. 'Haw, haw,' they cried, 'Haw, haw, haw. The dancing-master of Cracow! When's the wedding, Stefan? She looks like a barrel of lard.'

More music and another dance announced. Stefan started as if a horsefly had bitten him and, convinced every eye in the room was on him, fled the Hall and found himself in a drawing room lined with an enormous buffet. He downed a glass of wine, and another, and then a third, his mood changing from embarrassment to truculence. He took another glass of wine, looked up, and saw a man beckon him.

The man was called Soprona, an uncle, Stefan's mother's brother, dark, huge moustache, flea bites on his thick wrists, fierce but good natured, and quite fond of Stefan.

Wobbling slightly, Stefan joined his uncle who grinned sympathetically, 'Never mind,' he said. 'I'd sooner face a dozen Tartars than do that dance. Let me introduce you – Monsieur Du Bois, a . . . a French visitor.'

A smooth bow from the Frenchman, a lurching one in return from Stefan. Groggily, but with intense curiosity, Stefan stared at Du Bois. Elegant, crisp, crimson and gold, discreet jewels, a smooth face turned away as Stefan, voteless was politely ignored. In good Polish Du Bois spoke to Soprana of Poland's real interests; the need to protect her southern borders against the Tartars, the need to guard her eastern frontier against the Czar of the Russ, and the north against Sweden and Brandenburg, her need not to become involved with that feeble bankrupt the Emperor of Austria; to remember His Majesty, Louis the Fourteenth of France, the Sun King – Le Roi Soleil – and to be sure that if Monsieur Soprona did remember the Sun King then the Sun King would remember him . . .

Smoothly Du Bois went on and drunkenly Stefan listened.

Some of the talk he understood – clearly Du Bois was trying to bribe Soprona – and a great deal of the talk he didn't understand, but through the fuddle of wine he heard the repeated references to the Sun King. It reminded him of something . . . the sun . . . the sun . . . money and the sun – and then he remembered clearly and vividly, Nathan the pedlar and the book. He staggered forward, bumping into Du Bois.

'There was a Jew in Ostrova last year,' he shouted. 'He said that the world went round the sun!'

Soprona stared with amazement at Stefan, and Du Bois raised an eyebrow 'I beg Monsieur's pardon?'

'A Jew,' Stefan said. 'He had a book.'

'Ah!' Du Bois smiled. 'A book.'

'Yes,' Stefan felt that he was being laughed at in a subtle way. 'Yes,' he said, defiantly. 'The book said that the world went round the sun.'

'Well,' Du Bois smiled. 'I can assure Monsieur that there is one sun convinced that the earth goes around him.'

'Him?' Stefan was confused, gaping.

'My master, King Louis, the Sun King.'

Du Bois smiled again, a superior smile. Stefan did not like it. His face sullen he pushed forward but Soprona planted his massive body in the way.

'Go back to the dance,' he said.

'Listen –'

'Go and dance.' Soprona was sharp. 'Go. Now.' There was authority in Soprona's voice and he gave Stefan a push. 'Now.'

Stefan yielded and, his pale face burning, went back to the ballroom. The dance was continuing but there was a change in the atmosphere. The early formality was visibly fraying; voices were louder, more strident, faces were flushed with wine, collars and jackets were being loosened, and the dresses of the women were slipping lower on their shoulders. The Master of Ceremonies was tapping with his ivory cane but less attention was being paid to him; less, lesser, little, none. And then as he announced another stately, formal dance, a voice cried, 'Mazurka!'

Someone yelled, 'Huzza!' More voices joined in. 'Mazurka! Mazurka!' Yes, a dance without these tiresome rules and regulations, a dance with fire and excitement, and a *Polish* dance. 'Mazurka! Mazurka!' The demands and the cheering grew. The Master of Ceremonies turned to Count Lubomirski who flicked his finger. Disapproval in every line of his face the Master of Ceremonies bowed. 'Messieurs et Mesdames,' he began but his voice was drowned by wild, unchallenged whoops and war-cries, the orchestra, more at home with a folk dance than a minuet struck up with a will and the dancers charged the floor, Stefan with them, his arm around a girl, a lithe, pretty girl and, catching sight of Du Bois' scornful face shouting, 'Poland! For ever and itself!'

Morning, a few frowsty heads and dry throats, and a resigned shrug from Du Bois as he learned that, to a man, the Poles had voted for the Austrian treaty.

And in Belgrade the Sultan was handing over to Kara Mustafa the Sacred Standard of Islam and with it the supreme and unchallenged mastery of the army. 'Go with God,' he said, but as the vast army broke camp and marched to Osijek and the great bridge he wondered just where the army was going to, and why, and what hidden and incomprehensible purpose had gathered it together.

Chapter Nine

OSIJEK

J UNE the Fifteenth in the Year of Our Lord, 1683. For Timur, his orta and officers, and all the army and for all Islam, the Nineteenth day of the First month of Jumada, one thousand and ninety-four years after the Prophet had escaped from Mecca and fled to Medina, where the sword of Islam was first forged, sharpened, and raised.

In the rain, as the Drava flowed sullenly against the struts of the bridge, the first troop of cavalry thundered across the river into the Austrian possessions. Watching them go, the Twenty-eighth Orta of the Janissaries, in full marching kit.

But it was a long wait in the rain for the Twenty-eighth as the vanguard crossed the bridge. Resigned, ironic grumbles from the men; Thev, 'Those mysterious beings who controlled the army – 'They couldn't run a sherbert stall, couldn't make a living selling water in a desert, couldn't hit the floor if they fell down.' But at last, a staff-officer cantered up to Vasif and waved a lordly hand. Vasif barked a brief order, the standard bearer raised the Orta's pennant, and with an easy, mile devouring stride, Vasif led his men forward.

A thrill for Timur to march forward at last; a thrill to hear the band of the Grand Vizier crashing out its martial message, and an even greater thrill to stamp past Kara Mustafa himself and to raise a fist and to cry, '*Allah Akbar*! God is Great!'

It was a little less thrilling later, after various inexplicable halts,

82

to leave the second bridge and to plough your way through a muddy slough left by thousands of horses and men, but Vasif never faltered, nor his men and, as Janissary Tedeki, roared, 'It's a change, lads, and now that we're moving Allah will smile on us.' Which Allah duly did. By later afternoon the sky had cleared, and as the army reached higher land the ground was drier and firmer and so the first bivouac was quite tolerable; kitchens ready, hot coffee and soup, and even an Imam waiting, ready to lead the evening prayer.

'Not bad,' said Tedeki, stretching out on the ground. 'If it's like this all the way it won't be too bad.'

Next to him Janissary Ghazi agreed. 'But all the way to where?' he asked.

Tedeki guffawed. 'That's a point,' he agreed. He looked across the camp fire where a shadowy figure was going to Vasif's tent. 'Hey,' he called, 'Timur, Timur, here a moment.'

Timur, a bowl in his hands hesitated – then joined Tedeki. 'What is it?' he whispered, 'I'm getting the Corbaci's coffee.'

'All right,' Tedeki said, 'A minute won't hurt, will it? Listen, you hear all the news. Where *are* we going?'

Timur could not refuse the bait. He squatted, glanced over his shoulder, and whispered, 'Gyor. We are going to Gyor.'

'Oh,' Tedeki brooded for a moment then looked up. 'And where is Gyor?'

'Er . . .' Timur felt his face go warm with embarrassment because in fact he had no idea where Gyor was, and only a vague notion of what it was, but he was saved by Janissary Emre, an old campaigner, thirty years on various parts of the frontier, but a quiet, thoughtful man, devout, pious even, and by the standards of the Janissaries, learned in his religion.

'It's a fortress,' he said, 'Two hundred miles to the north.'

'Ours?' Tedeki asked.

'No,' Emre kicked the fire, idly. 'Austrian. But I was at Neuhausel years ago. That's one of our forts, not far from Gyor.'

'Aye? What's it like up there?' Janissary Ghazi spoke from the gloom.

'Like? Hills, rivers, marshes. A real tangle.'

'A tangle?' Tedeki spat into the fire. 'And the Austrians, what are they like?'

Emre paused, thinking. 'Didn't see much of them,' he said. 'They've got two legs and two arms, just like us.'

'Just like us, hey?' Tedeki grunted. 'And we're going to blow their brains out.'

'If they don't blow ours out first,' Emre said.

The next day Allah was still smiling. The sun blazed down from a clear sky and ahead of the infantry clouds of dust rose where the cavalry swept the countryside. At noon the army stopped, briefly, and ate; a sparse meal; bread, goat-cheese, a couple of rock-hard dates, water. Timur ate his meal looking south towards the bridge twenty miles away. The plain glittered with sparks, gleams, glints where the sun struck armour; banners and pennants dipped and swayed like a huge field of exotic flowers and there was a strange, muted, confused noise, the sound of a vast army on the move. Timur shook an awe-struck head but a lieutenant from the orta, *Vekilharc* Niyazi merely grinned. 'Half the army is still waiting to cross the river,' he said, as a trumpet sounded the call to march on.

Forward again on to a bare limestone plateau; scanty grass, white rocks, ravens croaking and buzzards soaring across a pale sky. Good ground for marching but on the third day the Aga of the Janissaries called his Corbacis to a meeting. Vasif returning, addressing the orta. 'Water,' his clipped voice drier than usual. 'Rationed from now on. No rivers here and the Christians have poisoned the wells.'

On again and Allah still smiling – His will, of course, and not to be challenged – but a feeling that perhaps a frown in the shape of a rainstorm would be acceptable. One pint of water a day; half a pint for the next five days, then a quarter. Ten days march; twenty miles a day, cracked lips, sore eyes, blistered feet, the never-ending longing for water, but a change was taking place in the orta; fat dissolving, muscle forming, the men hardening in the burning sun, Vasif watching with grim satisfaction. On the ninth day of the march, as Timur brought him a few dates and a little cheese, he smiled, a bitter, thin-lipped smile. 'They are changing,' he said. 'Inshallah, they are beginning to look like men. Like soldiers of the Sultan and of Islam. Yes. Soon they will be ready for what awaits them.'

Something in that, as Janissary Ghazi said, pulling boots over blistered feet, 'By Allah, I'd sooner fight ten Christians with my bare hands than go on with this much longer.'

But not much longer to go. The plateau dipping, tilting towards green fields spangled with flowers and dappled with tents, a river gleaming like the path to Paradise, a town, Szekesfehervar. The final rendezvous of the Ottoman army.

The orta camped, bathed, drank, and drank, and drank, under Vasif's sardonic eye.

'A little stroll,' he told a not completely convinced Timur. 'Just a little stroll.'

During the next few days the rest of the army came in; the triumphal procession of races and nations from half the world, and, from the east, dust plumes heralding their arrival like the finger of the God of Wrath, coveys of horsemen with slant Tartar eyes, carrying wicked and deadly Tartar bows, and who had ridden on their wiry ponies seven hundred miles from the Crimea. And on the seventh day Kara Mustafa arrived.

All men were equal in Islam, but not in the Ottoman army; however, even Mustafa, the Serasker – supreme commander of the Horde, thought it diplomatic to call a council of war especially since, quite like the humble Janissaries Tedeki and Ghazi, the High Commanders were not quite sure why they were where they were, or where they were going now they had arrived.

In his sumptuous tent, a palace of silk, Kara Mustafa looked at the circle of faces around him; the Governors of Syria, Egypt, Anatolia, the Princes of Transylvania, Moldavia, Wallachia, the Agas of the army, and the Khan of the Tartars; able men, all of them, shrewd, ruthless, and determined, but, today, apprehen-sive, watchful, guarded.

The obligatory coffee taken away, Mustafa dabbed his lips. *He* had brought these men together. *His* will had driven the army this far, to the edge and beyond of the Sultan's domains. But their obedience depended on his success; one slip and they would be on him like a pack of wolves. He clapped his hands gently.

'Decision day.'

No dissent. Time to decide what to do with the enormous army gathered outside the tent.

Mustafa nodded. 'Good, The aims of the campaign. First we take Gyor and Komarom.'

A murmur of agreement. The two Austrian fortresses on the Danube taken and Ottoman fingers would be around Austria's throat forever, disgorging bribes, subsidies, taxes. A pleasant prospect.

'Yes,' Murad Ghiraj, the Tartar Khan placed his finger tips together. 'We can take those, ravage Austria, and winter in Hungary.'

'*Ravage* Austria?' Michael Apafi, Prince of Transylvania, his face pallid.

'Why yes.' Ghiraj's triangular face split in a charming smile. 'That is why we are here, is it not?'

Mustafa leaned forward, 'Austria, Prince Michael. Austria, not Transylvania. Your country will remain . . . unravaged – as far as possible, of course. The Khan's suggestion is a most excellent one. However, I have something else in mind.'

'Something else?' Sari Hussain of Syria raised a polite eyebrow.

'Yes.' Mustafa stroked his beard. 'Merely to take Gyor and Komarom is not, I think, sufficient.'

A puzzled silence, broken by Hussain. 'But Excellency, what else is there?'

'Ah,' Mustafa sighed. Now his moment had come. Now was the time to reveal the secret he had nursed in his breast since that day, eleven months ago, when he had persuaded the Divan to send the army north. 'There is,' he said, 'there is Vienna.'

Utter silence, shock, incredulity. 'Vienna?' whispered Apafi.
Mustafa gave Apafi a dangerous, sideways glance. 'Yes.'

There was a flutter of unease as it dawned on the Council that
Mustafa was serious. Ghiraj Khan looked gloomily at his finger
nails. 'That would mean a siege.'

'Yes,' Mustafa smiled. 'I understand. Your people, they are not
equipped for siege warfare, but I had thought that you might raid
to the north of Vienna, create . . . diversions.'

A tempting bait, taken and swallowed. The Tartar Khan and
his horse happy to create diversions – that is, plunder and loot –
until Doomsday.

Ahmed Bey, the Governor of Timisoara pulled a gloomy face.
'A siege needs artillery.'

'We have artillery,' Mustafa snapped. 'The finest in the world.'

Ahmed Bey was still dubious. 'But the big siege guns . . . they
are in Istanbul. . . .'

'What we have is sufficient.' There was a touch of impatience in
Mustafa's voice, but he was still ready to persuade, conciliate. 'I
have gone into this very carefully. The walls of Vienna are weak,
especially in front of the Emperor's palace. Believe me, Vienna
cannot withstand a siege.'

A long, thoughtful silence. Outside the tent the clamour of the
army; drums, trumpets, commands. The Bey of Egypt raised an
elegant hand.

'Forgive me Excellency. It is not merely a question of besieging
the city. First we have to get there.'

'Of course we must get there.' Mustafa was becoming irritable.
'That is a mere detail. One hundred and fifty-miles. What is to
stop us?'

'The Austrian field-army?'

'Tcha,' Mustafa was contemptuous. 'A rabble. At Neuhausel
they ran away at the mere sight of the Tartars. Is that not so?'
Turning to Ghiraj Khan.

'Yes,' the Khan nodded, although, indeed, every man present
knew that at the mere sight of the Tartars the Austrian troops had
panicked.

'So,' Mustafa concluded. 'The army is a rabble and their commanders, this General Leslie and the Duke of Lorraine – they are old men, quite worn out. For the past four weeks they have been marching up and down the Danube like dogs at a fair. No, we will brush them aside and then, and then – Vienna! The Golden Apple, ours for the plucking.'

There was a collective sigh as the thought began to sink in. To take the Golden Apple, as Vienna had been known to the Ottomans for hundreds of years – ah! – that would be something. Yes, the Golden Apple, tempting them as the first apple tempted Eve . . .

'Serasker.' Sari Hussain of Syria, a power in his own right, handsome, dazzling in white silk. 'Serasker, what are the views of Ibrahim Pasha?'

There was a little murmur of agreement and Mustafa frowned, although he had been expecting the question. It was natural that the Council would want the views of the Bey of Buda, a man who had spent forty years on the frontier and who knew the Austrians, and Austria, like the back of his old hand. The trouble was that Ibrahim had flatly told his Serasker that the plan was lunatic folly and had been sent back to the rearguard to organize the supplies, where, in due course, Kara Mustafa intended to have him strangled. Mustafa congratulated himself on his insight in sending the old dog away with his ominous growls that Europe would not stand by and see Vienna in Ottoman hands. But now there was the Council. 'I have no confidence in Ibrahim Pasha,' he said. 'He is half senile. I put the question to you. Do we go to Vienna?'

He stared challengingly around the Council but found only impassive faces; after all, Kara Mustafa was the Grand Vizier, the Sultan's Vice-Regent, the Serasker and the Bearer of the Standard. On his head would rest the crown of glory if Vienna fell – and around his neck would go the bow-string if it did not.

'So.' In accordance with Islamic law Mustafa put the question twice more. 'Then we march,' said Mustafa. 'Tomorrow.'

Chapter Ten

VIENNA

A BEAST was coming to Vienna, dragging its slow, menacing way through the Schutt, the marshy island to the south of the city. The beast was grunting and slobbering and there was a sickening stench as it dragged its legs through the ooze. A voice thundered from a purple sky. 'Wickedness! God has sent this beast to punish Austria because of your sins, Anna Vogel!'

Anna opened her eyes. A grey gleam of light was probing through a crack in the shutter. Bells chimed, dogs barked, there was a clatter on the stair as the candle-makers from the attics went to their vaguely sinister pursuits, and from downstairs there were bangs and clanks as her father pulled hot rolls from the ovens of the bakery.

For a moment Anna stared at the ceiling. The dream about the beast had been a dream about the Turks. But that was silly. To get to the Schutt the Turks would have to beat the noble Duke of Lorraine and his army at Gyor, and they could never do that. Everyone said so. But perhaps the voice was not so silly. Anna had recognised it. It was the voice of the priest in St. Luke's who, last Sunday, had said that the Turks were God's punishment for the wickedness of the Austrians. Anna was not sure what the wicked ways of the Austrians were but, her cheeks burned, she had been wicked thinking of Kasper Haller during the service – and she was certainly being wicked lying in bed when there was work to be done.

She jumped out of bed, washed her face in the basin, dressed hurriedly, and opened the shutters. Ottostrasse was already awake and bustling. Across the narrow street Herr Breitner, the violin maker, had opened his shop and was testing a fiddle and his wife had draped the bedding from an upstairs window. Frau Seligmann, the innkeeper's wife was bustling down the street with a basket over her arm, and Frau Kappel, the tailor's wife was throwing out a bucket of slops while her little dog, Saky, barked at a passerby.

Anna threw her bedclothes over the window-sill to show the nosey neighbours that the Vogels, too, were up and about, then, her dream quite forgotten, she pulled Rudi from his bed in a cupboard, scrubbed his face vigorously, then ran down the stairs and laid the table for breakfast. Her father came in, bringing with him the smell of fresh rolls, and her mother came from the shop, bringing a sour smell of criticism.

'Didn't you hear me calling you?' she demanded. 'Lying in bed until half past-five! Wait till you're married, you won't be able to dawdle in bed half the day, then.'

'Ach!' Vogel snorted. 'Leave the girl alone. Why make marriage sound like a punishment?'

Anna blushed and lowered her head as Frau Vogel tossed her head as if to say, 'Well, isn't it?'

A normal start to the day. Mild bickering, Rudi spilling his weak ale and being made to stand, mutinously, in a corner, Frau Vogel complaining about the price of vegetables and Herr Vogel hoping that he had made it clear that although he had, finally, agreed to Anna's marriage to Kaspar – and God bless them both – under no circumstances was he going to allow Herr Haller to address him, Herr Vogel, as Jakob and if he, Herr Haller, that is, thought that he, himself, Herr Jakob Vogel was going to give him, Herr Haller, free rolls for the rest of his life then he had another think coming and – and having lost the thread of the pronouns – beaming on Anna and saying that of course she could have all the bread and rolls she could ever possibly want or need.

A normal morning except that as Frau Vogel was insisting that her husband make Herr Breitner pay his overdue bill, the great bell of St. Stephen's began to toll with a solemn, funereal knell, and all the bells of the city tolled with it.

Anna crumbled a roll between nervous fingers. 'The Turkenglocken,' she whispered. The Turkish bell.

Rudi was summoned from his corner and, around the table, the family bowed their heads. 'Dear God, our Heavenly Father,' said Herr Vogel. 'Forgive us our sins against you, the Holy Catholic Church, and our Emperor. Deliver us from the hands of the Turks and grant your servant, the Duke of Lorraine and his brave army victory over our enemy and yours. In the name of the Father, the Son, and the Holy Ghost, Amen.'

All over Austria the same scene was being repeated as, by Imperial decree, the Turkish bell was rung and the Empire prayed for forgiveness. Prayers and supplications, intermingled with sudden, terrible images of the savage Janissaries, the merciless Sipahis, and, worst of all, the barbaric Tartars – as alien as men from the stars.

The bells stopped and Frau Vogel raised her head and stared accusingly at her husband as if he, personally, was responsible for the approach of the terrible Turks.

In the afternoon, as Herr Vogel had his nap, Frau Vogel told Anna to go out. 'Buy some fish,' she said. 'And take Rudi with you. Frau Haller is coming *to have a talk*.'

Anna knew perfectly well that this meant yet another talk about the wedding. What these talks were about Anna knew vaguely from mysterious hints about money, furniture, bedding and – and always with an air of menace – *wifely duties*. Anna would have been very glad to take part in these talks about her future but like a good Viennese daughter she said, 'Yes mother,' took a basket, a purse, and Rudi and set out for the Rotenturm Gate on the Danube where the fishermen had their market.

They cut their way through side streets and across the High Market to Rotenturmstrasse which led to the fish market. In the dank shade of the tall houses the citizens of Vienna were going about their business, buying and selling, chinking away at their crafts; housewives busy shopping, men dropping into taverns for a drink, children playing, all the normal cheery bustle of a great city at work, and yet the city did not seem its normal self; the streets were tense, there was an air of suppressed, nervous excitement – or fear. The people looked withdrawn, as if they were carrying with them some private grief, or they were over-exuberant, laughing loudly, raucously over tiny incidents – a woman slipping and spilling milk, a drover dropping his whip, a lost dog running aimlessly in circles. And there was violence. Two men, surrounded by a bawling mob, having a vicious fist fight down a side-street, a group of women in a furious row outside a butcher's shop, smashed windows in a church. . . .

Anna took Rudi firmly by the hand and with Maria hurried on, followed by lewd comments from half-drunken idlers lounging outside a rough inn, but the journey was in vain for there was no fish at the market.

'No,' a cheerful fishwife said. 'Nothing until tonight. The Fisherman's Guild had to go to Mass this morning to pray against those God-damned Turks.'

'Ach!' An indignant house wife shook her head. 'Why today?'

'Well, dearie,' the fish-wife laughed. 'All the other days except Friday are full up, and you couldn't ask the men to go to Mass then, could you?'

No. Quite reasonable. Friday a fish day for all catholics and all the Guilds of Vienna being ordered to take their turn praying for Divine intercession; the clock-makers on Monday, the bakers on Tuesday, the carpenters on Wednesday . . .

The girls and Rudi wandered away, along the city wall which zig-zagged in a stony girdle around Vienna. On the Danube the pine-covered islands looked cool and inviting and in the Vienna River, the tributary of the Danube which flowed past orchards and cottages, cattle were standing knee-deep and children were bathing.

'I want to go swimming,' Rudi said.

Anna shook her head and disregarding Rudi's half-hearted protests tugged him along as they sauntered along the walls. The sun was high and the heat was sticky, stifling. Anna found herself looking longingly at the river and although she had never been swimming in her life she felt a longing to slide into the water.

She bit her lip and turned away from temptation into a narrow street, accepting its smell in exchange for its shade. At the end of the street, where it entered the Herrengasse, they heard the rattle of drums.

'Soldiers!' Rudi cried, and indeed it was; a regiment of infantry, solid men, in blue and grey, marching to the roll of the drum with a steady confident stride.

As the men marched past a group of idlers applauded. 'Mansfeld's Regiment,' a man said.

'Ja,' a fat, beery butcher wiped his face with a blue apron. 'Let's hope they don't run away when they're needed.'

'What do you mean?' Another lounger, mean faced, hard knuckled, a grating, challenging voice. 'What sort of talk is that?'

There was a sullen murmur of agreement from the crowd. The butcher backed against the wall, his fists up, more than the heat making him sweat as the mob snarled at him; a spy mania already gripping the city.

Anna grabbed Rudi. 'Come along,' she said. 'Let's go and see the soldiers.'

A little bait but enough to lure Rudi away from the fascinating prospect of perhaps seeing a spy caught and beaten to death. Anna hurried Rudi onto the calm and order of the Herrengasse with its great offices of state; the Council House, the Imperial Offices, the vast Augustinian church. 'It is the Turks,' she thought, 'The thought of them is changing the city, sparking off fears and hatreds.' She was suddenly reminded of her dream of the beast dragging its way to the city and, in an inarticulate way, she was aware that, if not the beast itself, then its foul breath was already infecting the city; that accounted for the tremor of hysteria, the laughter and the violence on the streets. . . .

It was a relief then to come out onto the open Burgplatz with its great friendly clock and its three towers with the remains of a

fourth which had fallen down years ago and, in an easy-going
Viennese way, had never been rebuilt.

Lots to see on the great square. The Mansfeld regiment piling
their arms outside the Emperor's wooden theatre, a troop of
dragoons clattering over the cobbles, carts rumbling in through
the Palace Gate, country people coming in to market – but other
carts, too, laden not with wheat or vegetables but beds and
chairs, pots and pans.

'Refugees,' Anna thought, people from the south withdrawing
from the threat of the beast. She felt bewildered. The Turks were
hundreds of miles away so why should people leave their homes
and seek refuge in the city?

Rudi tugged her hand. 'I want to look into the moat,' he
said.

Anna shook her head, not in denial but as if to shake off the pall
of fear. 'All right, but only if I hold you.'

They crossed the square to the city wall. With Anna's firm hand
on his breeches, Rudi heaved himself up and peered down. 'Is
this where the Turks came before?' he asked.

Anna looked down, too. Forty feet into the dank chasm, two
hundred feet to the outer wall and the Burg Ravelin in the middle.
'No,' she said. 'They were at the other side of the city.'

Rudi wriggled forward a little and spat into the moat. 'But they
did come, didn't they?'

'Yes, but it was a long time ago.'

Rudi slid down from the wall. 'When are they coming now?'

'Don't be silly.' Anna smiled her bright anxious smile. 'They
aren't coming here.'

'Then what are they doing?' Rudi pointed an accusing finger at
the Burg, or Palace, Bastion, a huge arrow of stone jutting into the
moat. Scores of men were working on the bastion – 'And there –
and those,' His finger pointed like a pistol at the Lobel Bastion on
the other side of the Burgplatz, 'and there,' the remorseless finger
pointed to the outer wall where a gang of men were planting a
forest of stakes along the rampart.

Anna forced a smile. 'They are just mending the walls.'

'Why are they doing that,' Rudi asked, 'If the Turks aren't coming?'

Anna had no answer to that. She turned away from the omens of war but Rudi suddenly yelled, 'There's Kaspar! There's Kaspar Haller.' He gave an ear-splitting whistle. 'Kaspar! Kaa-aspar!'

Among the men working on the Lobel Bastion Kaspar, with apron on and adze in hand stood up and waved. Rudi darted forward like a cat only to be collared by a soldier who returned him to Anna with a grin.

'No one allowed on the bastions, Fraulein,' he said. 'Orders.'

There was no need for his apology. Anna was only too glad to get away for it would never do for her to be seen near Kaspar without a chaperone. With downcast eyes she walked away but before she had gone a step or two a shadow crossed her path and looking up she saw Herr Haller. Haller grinned down, his face shiny with sweat. 'Ah,' he said, 'Anna' – and added, with less enthusiasm – 'and little Rudi. And what brings you here today. Not –' a knowing grin spread under his long nose as he swivelled it towards the Lobel Bastion.

Anna blushed furiously. 'Of course not,' she stammered. 'Rudi wanted to see the soldiers.'

'Little Rudi!' Haller stretched out a hairy hand and ruffled Rudi's hair at the same time pushing him aside. He stooped and whispered in Anna's ear, 'But was a certain girlie hoping to see a certain young man? Hey?'

Haller reeked of cabbage and beer and Anna stepped backwards. The sentry who had collared Rudi paced by them and looked sharply at Haller who straightened abruptly.

'Ah . . . um . . .' He cleared his throat. 'The soldiers, yes. And Kaspar. They are making sure the walls are in order. Just in case, you know. Just in case.'

'In case of what?' Rudi asked.

A spasm of annoyance crossed Haller's face. 'In case the Turks get here.'

'I'm not afraid,' Rudi cried.

'No.' Haller turned to Anna, blocking Rudi off. 'But if they did come, the sweat was pouring off Haller, 'If they did come . . .'

Anna was confused. Why was Herr Haller gabbling away like this? Talking about the Turks coming . . . sweating and shaking – it suddenly occurred to her that he was shaking with fear; that *he* was afraid. She felt giddy with the sickly heat and the sour whiff of beer and sweat and cabbage. A waggon loaded with stone crashed past, its iron bound wheels ear-splitting on the cobbles. She stepped back and Rudi's head appeared round her skirt.

'You're frightening her!' he shouted. 'You're frightening my sister!' His tough little face set in a determined scowl and he kicked Haller firmly and accurately on the shin.

Haller yelped. 'What the –' He hopped, rubbing his leg. 'You little . . .'

'You're not going to frighten my sister,' Rudi said, sturdily.

There was the rattle of a musket and the sentry moved towards them. 'You all right, Fraülein?' he asked.

'Yes, yes, she's all right,' Haller cried. 'Young lady – frightened of the Turks, just reassuring her. Going to marry my son, ha, ha.'

'I asked the young lady,' the sentry said. 'Fraulein?'

'Yes, thank you,' Anna put her hand to her mouth.

'There, just as I said. A misunderstanding.' Haller bared his long yellow teeth and limped away.

The soldier watched him go and gave a contemptuous shrug. 'Don't you worry, Fraulein.' He tapped his musket. 'If the Turks ever do get here they'll wish they hadn't. Anyway, they'll never get past Gyor. The Duke of Lorraine will stop them in their tracks. *Grüss Gott.*'

He touched his hat and swung away on his beat. Anna looked down on her brother. 'Oh, Rudi,' she said.

'I kicked him, didn't I?' Rudi said. 'I gave him a good kick.'

Despite herself Anna burst out laughing but Rudi was solemn. 'I'll kick the Turks, too, if they come here.'

He turned on his heel and stared south. Anna followed his gaze, beyond the Palace gate, beyond the cottages and pleasure gardens of St. Ulrich, into the damp, misty vistas of the Schutt, down to where the Austrian army was facing the enemy.

She crossed herself and from the depth of her innocent heart and innocent faith, whispered, 'God bless the Duke, and all his men.'

Chapter Eleven

GYOR

THE Duke of Lorraine was in need of Anna's prayers. Indeed he would have been grateful for the prayers of the whole of Christendom for, as the Vogels and the Hallers, and all the citizens of Vienna were drifting into their slumbers, far from presenting a dauntless barrier against the Ottoman attack, he and his army were in full retreat.

For weeks, just as Kara Mustafa had said, Lorraine had been marching his men up and down the tangle of rivers, marshes and islands which the Austrians called the Schutt. He had lunged downstream to the Turkish base at Esztergom, only to be recalled by Leopold who was terrified at the thought of losing the army, then he had marched north to attack Neuhausel but, after bitter wrangles with his officers and appalling transport problems, he had withdrawn from there, too. Finally he had formed a defensive line along the River Raba which flowed from the south-west and joined the Little Danube at Gyor.

There, the Duke felt secure enough. His left wing was guarded by the guns of Gyor and on the right wing the fords across the Raba was defended by loyal Hungarians and a strong Austrian regiment commanded by General Styrum. Lorraine himself had thirteen thousand infantry, ten thousand cavalry, and a battery of artillery to hold the main crossing.

Although only too well aware that the Ottoman army was

coming up from the south the Duke was sure that he had plenty
of time, and that he could hold the Schutt; sure that is until on the
morning of the Second of July, he left his tent and saw across the
river that the enemy had arrived.

Eighty, a hundred thousand, a hundred and fifty thousand
men; a host, a multitude, a forest of pennants, red, green, yellow,
tents, smoke, and scouts already on the opposite bank.

The Duke was stunned. The Ottoman army seemed to have
come from nowhere, like warriors sprung from dragon seed and
the strangeness of the sight was enhanced when, at noon, the
whole vast array fell silent as the muezzins called it to prayer. The
brief prayer over, Turkish scouts began probing for a crossing,
undeterred by the Austrian cannon-fire, and then, in the steamy
heat of early afternoon, horsemen, Tartars, in thousands began
breaking away from the main camp and striking upstream.

But even that sinister sight did not distress the Duke. The fords
were well guarded and, although he had been staggered by the
speed of the advance of the enemy army, he was confident that
they could not force the river.

But at dusk, as swallows skimmed across the water, a courier
on a horse white with sweat galloped into the Austrian camp with
a message from General Styrum. The Tartars, masters of river
crossings, had swum the river far to the west. The Hungarians
had panicked and fled, and now the fords were left unguarded. If
Turkish heavy cavalry and infantry got across, Lorraine's line of
retreat would be cut off and the irreplaceable army lost.

There was only one thing to do and Lorraine did it. Quietly and
without fuss, in his plain grey coat and mounted on a plain grey
horse, Lorraine ordered a retreat. General Leslie, with the infantry, was sent across the River Leitha into the island called the
Great Schutt and, as the first stars twinkled, Lorraine led the
cavalry north.

All through the dewy night the cavalry walked their horses.
There was no panic – no haste even – if the Turks were going to
follow it would take weeks to bring their enormous force forward;
and so a disciplined withdrawal to the musical jingle of the

harnesses of ten thousand horses and, on the right, the murmur of the river Leitha.

A break at dawn, food and water for men and beasts, the sun rising and, coming from woods and burned-out farmhouses, coveys of horsemen, slightly built, dressed in skins and wearing conical fur hats, whistling shrilly and giving high-pitched, taunting yelps as they wheeled around the Austrian cavalry; the musical twang of a bow, the hum of an arrow, a stricken horse whinnying with pain, a trooper coughing blood, and then the Tartars were gone, as stinging and as elusive as gnats.

The gnats stinging all day and the cavalry bearing with them stoically. Nothing to be done, anyway. The heavily armoured cavalry were incapable of chasing the Tartars and, although the horses were vulnerable, a man would be unlucky to be hit. Most of the arrows merely glanced off armour and, anyway, it was all part of the fortune of war, to be accepted with a shrug of broad shoulders, unless, that is, you were the one to get an arrow in the throat.

Weary dusk again and the crossing and the town of Ungarisch-Altenburg. The cavalry crossing the bridge into the safety of the Little Schutt. Lorraine, making his way through the town was satisfied. It took good troops to retreat without panic. He only hoped that the discipline would hold good for he intended to retreat again the next day. As he explained to his senior officers in a room in the Council House.

'I intend to fall back on Berg.'

There was murmur of agreement. At Berg, twenty miles away, hills crowded in on either side of the Danube proper, leaving only a narrow gap, through which any army attacking Vienna would have to pass. And with a solid force there, any attacking army would get a bloody nose.

There was a shuffling as tired officers prepared to get to their beds and snatch a few hours sleep, but one voice spoke out, a Hungarian Colonel;

'Excellency, you will forgive me. Over there –' a gesture, pointing across the river.

'Yes,' Lorraine was kind and understanding. Over there, across the River Leitha, was Hungarian territory which even then, as a glance through the window at innumerable fires showed, was being . . . well . . . ravaged. 'Yes, Colonel, I understand your feelings. I intend to send some cavalry across the river to help your people. But you must understand, it is vital that the army be kept together as a whole. Vienna must be preserved and I have strict orders from the Emperor himself that Austria, the Emperor's hereditary possessions must be preserved. I am risking a severe reprimand by withdrawing so far.'

The Colonel was still sullen, and Lorraine was sharper. 'I am afraid that Hungary has brought this curse upon its own head, Colonel. If all Hungarians were as loyal as Prince Esterhazy this would never have happened.'

End of argument. A few simple orders given; eight hundred men, a token force – to re-cross the river into Hungary, a strong detachment to be left in the town with strict orders to burn the bridge if necessary, not that it would be, of course, since the Turks could not possibly get this far, and then, at dawn, the retreat to Berg.

Compared to the day before this was a mere saunter. No Tartars and the day mild, almost tranquil, but, despite all reassurance, the country people began to fall in behind the cavalry, resentful, fearful peasants driving carts and wagons, sheep, cows, pigs, a solid mass of refugees, choking the road, pressing on the rear of the army and sending before them a growing apprehension; and the unease beginning to spread amongst the troops like the first, mild symptoms of a deadly disease, so that the troopers too began to look over their shoulders.

Lorraine began to feel the unease too, and that night, as the army camped in the town of Deutsch-Jarhndorf, he walked among his men, a plain man speaking the plain truth, as he saw it. 'Not to worry, lads. We'll be at Berg tomorrow and there we stop. We're safe as houses, boys. The Turks aren't coming.'

Which was where he was absolutely wrong for as dawn came, ten thousand Janissaries were drawn up, waiting for the order to cross the Raba.

A long, ullulating cry from the muezzins, the eerie rustle of ten thousand prayer mats being unrolled, and the familiar prayer; *'Bismillah al-Rahman al-Rahim . . .'* In the name of God the merciful, the compassionate, King of the day of Judgement.

A moment for private prayer. Colonel Vasif praying that his orta would not disgrace him, Janissaries Tedeki and Ghazi praying for loot, Major Osman praying for a brave death, Janissary Ven, his eyes tightly closed and his forehead pressed to the ground, praying, with all the passion of his young heart that he might find glory, fame, and that he might kill as many Christians as his sword could find.

Kara Mustafa rode through the ranks. 'God be with you, Allah guide you. Go with God.' The mist swirling, rising like a curtain in a theatre to reveal the green plain of the Schutt. The blare of a trumpet, a great roar of 'Allah Akbar!' and the first orta struck across the river.

A blazing day as the Janissaries marched north. The fat, as Vasif had said, burned off them; four miles an hour, five, as the officers swung their bamboo canes at laggards; in its yellow and red livery the long column looking like a venomous snake, and striking at Ungarisch-Altenburg with the speed and certainty of one.

Merciful night and the next morning the Duke of Lorraine was ahead of his army at Kittsee, just a little south of Berg, at a Council of War with the Vice President of the Imperial War Council and the Commander of Vienna, General Count Starhemberg. The three men were grave, concerned, but not in any way despairing. As Lorraine pointed out, there were great difficulties for the Turks. Gyor and Komarom were holding out, Ungarisch-

The Attack

Altenburg was virtually impregnable, and without control of its bridge the enemy could not break into the Little Schutt, and the Great Schutt was held by General Leslie and the infantry. Of course there was total devastation in Hungary, and the Tartars were also swinging north, around Vienna, but they were, militarily speaking, mere nuisances. So, all in all, although the Emperor's displeasure hung over them like a thunder cloud, the three men were calm. Calm until noon when an officer rode in and told Lorriane that the Turks had captured Altenburg – and the bridge.

Lorraine stared blankly at the man. 'Impossible,' he said flatly. 'That is quite impossible.'

But it was true. The Janissaries had struck and taken the town and the priceless bridge, and ten thousand men were pouring into the Little Schutt, and another twenty-five thousand were coming up fast behind them in a cloud of dust so thick a man could not see the back of the man before him. And there was dust behind Lorraine, too, a vast column rising from *beyond* Berg.

Again there was only one thing to do, and again Lorraine did it. Back up the Danube at a trot, a canter, a gallop – through the gap at Berg, down into Hainburg, the cavalry smashing their way through hordes of refugees. At Petronell, the Tartars making a slashing attack on the baggage-train and its guard openly panicking. Lorraine himself led the counter-attack, rallying his men in what was, after all, a mere skirmish, and, as incongruously, nightingales began to sing, the army, shaken, but still a unity rested at Schwechat, within sight of the tall steeple of St. Stephen's church.

Chapter Twelve

PETRONELL

THE long day had brought growing unease to an already uneasy Vienna. Sharp eyes had seen the columns of dust swaying across the Schutt, on the Burgplatz shrewd eyes had noted the succession of messengers riding in from the Duke, from the dust, a column of refugees was choking the Palace Gate, and on the other side of the city there was a steady trickle of people leaving by the northern gates. Even the idlest loafer could put two and two together and, for once, make four.

Rumours began to spread; from the Palace Gate to the Locksmith's Pillar, from there to the High Market, to the new Market, down the Herrengasse, into churches, monasteries, convents, shops and taverns, through side streets and alleyways, and into Ottostrasse.

A group of fearful housewives were gathered outside Herr Vogel's bakery. Frau Breitner, the violin maker's wife, long-nosed, an unmusical and penetrating voice was speaking; 'They say that the Duke has been beaten! All the soldiers ran away from Gyor!'

Vogel groaned in exasperation as he scraped the last globs of dough from his bench. He groaned again as Frau Haller's voice was raised.

'That's just what my husband said. He always said that the Duke was no good as a general.'

Vogel rolled his eyes as Frau Haller's voice droned unswerv-ingly on.

'That's what he said. He always said so. His cousin works in the Hofburg, you know.'

Oh yes, thought Vogel. The women knew that. The whole of Vienna knew it, the whole of Austria, probably the whole of the world.

'And' – more news from the omniscient cousin – 'he says that the Crown of Hungary has been sent to Linz!'

There was a chorus of 'oohs!' The Crown of Hungary, the sacred crown of St. Stephen, if that had been taken from Press-burg . . .

Frau Seligmann, the innkeeper's wife, her voice trembling, hysteria lurking behind every syllable. 'But they can't be coming, the Turks. They just *can't*. Besides, the Saxons and the Bavarians, they are going to attack the Turks. And the Poles –'

'Pooh!' Frau Haller was utterly contemptuous, almost gloating, as if she longed for her prophecy to come true. 'The Poles won't come here. They took the Emperor's money, right enough' – she sounded as indignant as if it were her money which, in a sense, it was, of course – 'but they aren't going to *fight* for us, so don't you go thinking that, dearie.'

'But . . .' Frau Seligmann, pleading for reassurance. 'But King John Sobieski –'

'Sobieski!' Frau Haller's voice was like a knitting needle being poked down your ear. 'All he does is spend his time lolling about with his wife – and not only his wife!'

The knitting needle was withdrawn as her voice sank to a salacious whisper and then rose again, the knitting needle rampant – 'So you know what to expect from him. But my hus-band has always said that. He said it here, in this very street –' Frau Haller's voice was rising and quickening into a gabble, as if the sound of her own voice could blot out the terror of the inconceivable which was becoming conceivable. 'Didn't he say that, Frau Vogel? And another thing, the Emperor has left!'

Vogel could stand it no longer. He thrust his head through the window. 'Elsa!' he barked.

The women started back as though Vogel's round, red face was a fire grenade. Frau Vogel gave a resigned 'tut', looked at her friends with an air of martyrdom, but obeyed her husband's summons.

Vogel glared at Frau Haller. 'Such talk. Why do you spread such rumours? The Emperor has not gone. He went hunting in the Prater yesterday – and he has come back!'

The window slammed down as if to seal the house from the plague but the infection creeping in just the same. Frau Vogel pottering aimlessly about the house, whispering the Hail Mary, and ending, 'Don't let them come, dear God, don't let them come.' Anna, as she laid the table for lunch dropping, and breaking, a cherished Dresden bowl and stocky, stout-hearted Vogel slapping her in a flash of rage which, even as the blow landed, he knew came from fear.

Throughout the afternoon a great crowd swarmed in the Burgplatz, staring up at the Hofburg, rumours running riot amongst the mob: the Duke had been defeated – he was victorious – the Turks were advancing – retreating, Altenburg, Hainburg, Schwechat, all had been lost, recovered, lost again.

The same rumours ran through the Hofburg itself where the corridors were crammed with a murmuring mass of courtiers, priests, flunkeys, hangers-on, the riff-raff of the Palace. In his state room Leopold was holding continuous session.

The city clocks jangled out six o'clock and another messenger, Colonel Montecuccoli, wild-eyed and sweating, forced his way into the state-room and stammered out a message.

'Leopold stared at him in blank dismay. 'The army shattered? The whole army?'

'Yes, your Majesty. At Petronell.'

'You are sure? Quite sure?'

For a moment the Colonel hesitated, but it was true. Certainly it was true. He had seen it with his own eyes, the Tartars coming through the dust like demons, the Austrian cavalry breaking, fleeing outright – the army scattered. . . . 'Yes Sire,' he said.

There was a stunned silence. The army gone – and at Petronell, not thirty miles away. Leopold shook his head. It was incredible. In two days the army had been driven back from Gyor to the shadow of the city walls and now it did not even exist anymore. How could that have happened?

Finally an emphatic voice broke the silence, Colonel Montecuccoli. 'Your Majesty must leave the city. It is imperative.'

A murmur of agreement from the assembled Councillors. Even if the hive was lost the Queen bee must be preserved for the sake of the next swarm. Leopold looked steadily around the room. How would it look, the Emperor himself fleeing his capital? How the French would crow. And the Poles and the Saxons and the Bavarians, would they come to his aid if Vienna was lost? He rather doubted that. And then there was the Empress, pregnant and near to her time. What would a jolting ride in a carriage do to her? Besides which, as Leopold was very well aware, if he left then so could his Council and the nobility, and if they left then so could the burghers, and what would become of his city then? On the other hand if he left, went north to Germany, he could rally new forces, borrow money, press his case among the circles of the Empire . . . none of which he could do as a prisoner in the hands of the Turks.

'Very well,' he said. 'We shall leave the city.'

The words had barely left his mouth before they were being repeated in the crowded corridors, echoed down the staircases, and passed to the crowd outside. 'The Emperor is leaving! The Turks are at the gates!'

True terror gripping Vienna now; a desperate, tearing scramble to leave the city. The wealthy running in a rabble, fighting for carts and waggons, scattering money as if there was to be no tomorrow. Noblemen mounted on bony nags, priests on donkeys, autocratic ladies scrambling for places in the open carts of the despised peasants, houses deserted with wine still in the cellars and carpets left on the floors.

Night came, bringing with it unimaginable fears; the city gates were choked with half-crazed Viennese fighting their way out and half-crazed refugees fighting their way in. Eight o'clock and the Emperor left, a jumble of coaches and waggons crashing from the Hofburg, down the Herrengasse, the Emperor's bodyguard slashing through the mob, over the Scottish Gate and the Danube, heading north to such safety as that offered.

The terror had reached Ottostrasse, too, and like oxen threatened by wolves, the inhabitants of the street had come together in the Golden Eagle; men, women, and children alike, the Vogels, the Breitners, the Hallers, tearful, fearful, angry and bewildered; 'Should we go – stay – go where to? – God rot the Turks, the Duke of Lorraine, the army, the government, spies and traitors . . .'

From his seat by the door, Herr Vogel stood up. Instantly the racket ceased and a dozen gaping faces stared at him as if from his commonplace figure was going to come the words of their salvation.

Vogel coughed and held out his hand in an awkward, defensive gesture. 'Nothing to say.' he muttered.

'But what are we to do?' a long wailing cry from Frau Breitner.

'Do?' Vogel stared at his feet. 'I . . . well . . . baking, that's all. I'm going to bake bread. Tomorrow – we'll, hear what the Burgomasters say. Maybe think again, er . . . ahem . . .' He made a ducking motion and darted from the inn. He walked rapidly down the street and entered his house and lit a lamp. The familiar objects of his daily life shone around him. The blue and white bowls, copper pans, the green tiles of the stove, a dresser, a chest, a stuffed heron, table and chairs, the crucifix gilded by Johann, the lamp itself brought from a faraway land long ago by some mysterious wandering Vogel. Not much for the labour of generations of Vogels but his and his family's. And was he to leave it all to the mercy of nameless marauders? To thieves, to the rabble? To the Turks, of whom he knew nothing and who knew nothing of him but who, for some mad purpose, they wished to destroy and all he possessed.

His mouth tightened and his jaw jutted forward pugnaciously. He went into the bakery and, like his father, and his father before him, began firing the oven. He swung a sack of flour onto the bench, reached for yeast, salt, fat, looked up and saw, framed in the doorway, his wife, Anna, and the Hallers.

Frau Vogel stared at him through her pale blue eyes. 'Well?' she said.

'Well what?' Vogel heaved up a bucket of water.

'What are you going to do?'

'Do?' The water poured on the flour. 'Bake. People will need bread tomorrow, won't they? Same as they always do.'

Frau Vogel, her face as expressionless as ever; 'And is that all?'

'No.' Vogel expertly flicked the oven door open with his foot. 'If there's going to be a siege there'll be rationing. Make out a list of our customers and what they normally buy.'

'So,' Frau Vogel gave her familiar jerk of her head. 'So we're staying, then.'

'Not we. Me. You and the children get out.'

'Out?'

'Yes.' Vogel began to knead the flour. 'Tomorrow at dawn. Start packing what you want. You can get up to Johann at Amstetten. Kaspar will look after you and'– even then he could not bring himself to address Haller directly –' . . .and *him*! I'll give you money, we'll get a cart somehow.'

'And you're staying?'

'Yes.' Salt in the dough. 'Unless the Burgomaster orders me to leave.'

'You fool!'

'Fool?' Vogel stood upright to the height of his five feet four. 'Fool?'

'Yes.' Frau Vogel took a step into the room. 'Do you think that if you stay I'm leaving? Pah! You always were a fool, Jakob.'

For a moment Vogel wondered who his wife was talking to, and then he remembered. It was himself. He rubbed his eyes.

Thirty years married and he could not remember when his wife had last called him by his Christian name. 'Elsa?' he said.

'Yes.' Frau Vogel took another step forward. 'Do you think that I would leave you? You old fool. I'm staying.'

'And me, father.' The words, the first words Anna had ever said which contradicted her father. She flushed and lowered her head, but not before her violet eyes caught Kaspar's, as he stood tall and upright, his muscular, carpenter's arms folded, and he nodded approvingly.

'I'm staying too.' He gave a bashful smile. 'Needed, you know – to work on the walls.' He gave a strange, strangled cough, sweat pouring from his forehead and glanced sideways at his father who bared his long yellow teeth.

'Yes, well . . .' Haller gave a ghastly imitation of a smile. 'Yes . . . well . . . at any rate, not go tonight . . . wait until tomorrow, hey? Think again . . . stick together, all one family – nearly . . . ha, ha,' a laugh as hollow as a grave.

And then, stranger than any fiction, stranger even than the thought that the Turks were actually going to attack the city, Frau Vogel leaned forward and, in full view of Anna, Rudi, and the Hallers, she kissed her husband on the cheek.

A long, eerie night and the dawn announced by the rattle of a drum in the street and the hammering of a musket butt on the door. An officer of the watch, unshaven and yawning, but backed by two tough looking infantrymen, demanding that all the Guild militiamen must appear on the Burgplatz at one o'clock and that all males, without exception, must meet before the Town Hall at three to listen to an important announcement, adding, as an afterthought, that all good citizens should ignore rumours which were being spread by spies, traitors, cowards and French agents, and fail not at your peril, etc and etc.

A scrambled morning; Vogel absolutely refusing to sell more bread than his customers usually bought, a shambling parade of the militia who were issued with ancient and untrustworthy muskets, some of which looked as if they might last have been used against Suleiman's army, one hundred and fifty years ago, and then, at three, the men of Vienna gathering outside the Town Hall and Nicholas Hoche, the Treasurer, standing on the steps, facing his fellow men.

'Citizens of Vienna,' he cried. 'First let me tell you, on my honour as a Christian, the army is safe. It is true it is retreating, but it is retreating in good order. This city will not be defenceless against the Turks.'

There was a ripple of applause and Hoche breathed a little easier. He had been half-prepared for a barrage of rotten vegetables and dead cats.

'Not defenceless,' he repeated, 'but it is true that it now seems that there might be a siege.'

A murmur from the crowd, sullen and resentful but not, Hoche thought, hopefully, despairing.

'A siege yes,' he shouted, his deep voice echoing across the square. 'But Vienna has seen sieges before, and never once have the walls been breached!'

More applause for that and a voice yelled, 'And won't be this time!'

'Correct,' Hoche bellowed. 'But we must face facts like men. Every one of us must pull together. We need men to work on the walls, but I promise you that every man will be paid. We have plenty of food, and plenty of ammunition, and when the army arrives, plenty of good soldiers. It is true that the Emperor has left the city but that is only so that he can organise aid and help. And aid and help is coming. But although the Emperor has left, that does not mean the city is leaderless. I am here, the Burgomaster and the City Council is here, and the Bishop. And here we are going to stay!'

More applause – cheers even. The crowd heartened by that news.

'Now,' Hoche raised his hand for silence, 'General Starhemberg, is in supreme command of the city. Citizens and friends, obey his orders. Be calm and steady. Do your duty. Be loyal and courageous. Believe me, help is on the way. All Europe will march to our aid. Obey the orders of the War Council, do not listen to idle rumours. Trust in God and the Emperor. Long live Austria! Long live Vienna!'

And then, as if to salute the Treasurer and the crowd, to a flourish of trumpets and drums, Lorraine and his cavalry appeared from the haze of the south, in good order.

Chapter Thirteen

VIENNA

THE lightning had flickered over the Schutt but the thunderbolts were not to strike Vienna for a little while for, although the Janissaries and the Sipahis were a mere stroll from the city, the bulk of the Ottoman army, the artillery, the engineers, the commissariat, had to be dragged, and dragged slowly, forward from Esztergom, the Ottoman base a hundred miles down the Danube.

A day, two days, three, a week, July slipping away, but on the night of the thirteenth, in his camp at Schwechat, Kara Mustafa was satisfied. His forces were filtering around Vienna. Only the islands to the north of the city were in Austrian hands and a few days would see them taken and then the Golden Apple would be firmly in his grip, never to be released. He closed his eyes and breathed a prayer of thanks to Allah, the One and the Almighty who turned all things to His own purpose, to the glory of Islam, the Ottoman Empire, and himself, the Grand Vizier.

He opened his eyes. Outside Vienna flames glowed orange and red as the Austrians burned the houses in the suburbs outside the city wall. He shook his head; incredible that the Christians had waited for so long before taking such a step. Allah must certainly have addled their brains.

He leaned back on his divan feeling contented, virtuous, expansive in the damp heat of the late afternoon. A strange, ungainly shape strutted past his tent, the ostrich being led in from its afternoon stroll. Other shapes followed; cannon, supply wag-gons, a drove of sheep, a long line of captives, and then a disciplined body of men, red and yellow, tall hats, swords and muskets, a pennant dipping in salute. An officer with sharp blue eyes. . . .

Mustafa beckoned an aide, murmured a query and received a whispered answer. 'The Twenty-eighth Orta, Corbaci Vasif . . . a Devshirme . . .'

'A Devshirme?' Mustafa gave a languid order, the aide hurried forward, the orta halted, turned about face, and Vasif strode forward. 'Serasker?'

Mustafa touched his lips with a scented handkerchief and felt a glow of joy at the thought of his power. Here, on the very edge of Islam, he had gathered a hundred thousand men, and by the mere crooking of his finger, each and anyone of them stood forward, ready to do his bidding.

'You are a Devshirme?' he asked.

'Yes, Serasker.'

Mustafa was pleased at the title. Supreme Commander. A soldier's address. 'One of the last,' he said. 'The last of the Devshirme. Hey?'

'So they say, Serasker.'

'Your father and your mother, they were both Christians?'

'So I was told, Serasker.'

Mustafa shook his head. 'Strange,' he said, 'Strange. And tomorrow we may be in their city, hey, Corbaci.'

'*Their* city, Serasker?'

Mustafa was a trifle impatient. 'The Christians' city – Vienna.'

'As Allah wills, Serasker.'

Mustafa's cordial smile ebbed a little, that flinty answer was not what he wished for on the eve of his triumph. Like a cat showing its claws, a touch of malice crept from his disappointment. 'Tell me, Corbaci, do you ever feel divided in your loyalties?'

Under his tall hat Vasif's eyes glinted with a touch of menace. 'I am a Janissary, Serasker. Forty-five years in the service.'

'Ah . . .' The malice drained away from Mustafa. Forty-five

years; about the same time that he, himself, had served the Empire, and yet those years seemed to lie more lightly on this ramrod Corbaci than they did on his own fleshy shoulders. He gazed past Vasif, at the orta standing by their pennant. 'Your men, Corbaci. They are good soldiers?'

'They think so, Serasker.'

'And you – what do you think?'

Vasif made a characteristic gesture, holding out his right hand, palm up. 'I will know when this campaign is over, Serasker.'

Mustafa stirred, impatient again. 'Who is the boy?' he demanded.

'My servant, Serasker. The son of an old comrade.'

'He will go into battle with you?'

'Of course, Serasker. He is a Janissary.'

Mustafa sighed. 'He is young . . . young. He may die.'

'Will die, Serasker.'

'What?' Mustafa heaved himself forward. 'What?'

'We must all die, Serasker, one day.'

All die . . . Mustafa's throat went dry. All die? He stared at the unyielding figure before him, silhouetted against the fires of distant Vienna. A fanatic, he thought, a madman, careless of life and fearless of death, a man whose very presence brought the thought of the bow-string with it. He wanted to do something to that figure, to shatter its unyielding flinty obduracy.

'You, boy,' He beckoned Timur. 'You marched through the Schutt, you were at Ungarisch-Altenburg?'

Timur bowed so deeply he almost toppled over. 'Yes, Serasker.' And of course that was true, although the town had been taken when his orta had arrived, the bridge held and the town in flames, the fight over.

'Then take this.' A fat hand was extended, a gold piece in the palm. A reward for service. Timur took the coin and the hand waved in dismissal.

The orta in turn dismissed and Vasif and Timur marched to their tent. Timur rubbed the coin between his fingers. It was a great honour, to be given a gift from the Serasker himself, from the palm of his almighty hand. But why had he been honoured? For marching through a burning town? If that was the case then why had not Corbaci Vasif been honoured, too? Timur was young but shrewd, and he had noticed the subtle interplay of malice and stubbornness between Vasif and Kara Mustafa, and he had noticed too the contemptuous dismissal. Was the gift to him a way of denigrating his Corbaci? If so, then to keep the coin was to accept that denigration and that was unthinkable. But to return the coin was unthinkable, too. And to throw away a coin which had been exalted by being in the hand of the Serasker was inconceivable.

They had reached their tent; a simple affair, rough canvas, a torch flaming outside, the orta's pennant planted outside it. Timur looked at Vasif – hoping for a sign, but the hard features, harder still in the glare of the torch gave no help.

From the darkness a man lurched forward, a water-carrier, a slave, a mere beast of burden, his face averted so that he might not be caught looking upon his masters. On an impulse Timur caught the man by his ragged sleeve. The man's face twisted in alarm – in terror – and then changed to amazement as Timur slapped the coin in his hand. The man shambled off into the night and Timur turned towards Vasif, uncertain whether he had done right or wrong, or even whether the Corbaci had noticed him at all.

His face as impassive as ever, Vasif looked at Timur for a long moment and then he raised his hand and cut Timur across the back with his cane. Six stinging lashes and then Vasif stopped.

'That was for dishonouring the Serasker,' he said. 'Now go and bring me my food.' But as he turned into the tent he said, over his shoulder drily, 'You might make a Janissary yet.'

The green twilight faded into violet – purple – darkness. Bats came out, and the stars, and fires, as familiar now as the stars, ringed Vienna in a noose of flame.

Inside the noose, Count General Starhemberg made a final tour of the city's defences. Stocky, red-faced moustachioed, he rode around the walls and bastions, the Molker, the Eland, the New-gate, past the Gonzago and the Biber and the Dominican, and finally back to the Burgplatz, facing south, towards the Turkish camp.

His staff around him, Starhemberg clambered a little stiffly from his horse. All in all he was as content as it was possible for a general facing a gigantic enemy to be. The week's delay since the great panic had been priceless, quite priceless. During those days the city had been whipped into shape, in some cases literally for Starhemberg had a hard fist and knew how to use it. The citizens, some at bayonet point, had been driven to work on the walls so that the defences were in some sort of shape. There was enough grain in the city to last for weeks. The city had a stable and capable government, and, above all, Leslie, disobeying his orders, had withdrawn from the Great Schutt so that now thirteen thousand well-armed and well-trained infantry stood on guard along the perimeter, and, thanks to the Bishop of Wiener Neustadt, Kollo-nics, who had forced the clergy to disgorge its wealth, there was enough money to pay the troops – and pay them well.

Starhemberg walked to the edge of the Burg Bastion and looked into the moat. Even now in the glare of a thousand torches men were at work, turning the bed of the moat into a ferocious tangle of obstacles. Rimpler, the engineer, had concentrated on this stretch of the moat; as he had pointed out, the two bastions here, the Burg and the Lobel, were the weakest on the walls, and there was no possible way of flooding the moat here.

Men, officers, came and went, making reports, getting curt orders, the fires of the Turkish camp sparked as ominously as the eyes of a pack of wolves, and to the east and the west, more fires marked the devastation of the Tartars. But Starhemberg scarcely gave a glance to the menace beyond the walls, merely getting on with his own business in a matter-of-fact way, finally finishing, remounting and walking his horse to the Hofburg.

As he crossed the Burgplatz a company of men tramped past

him; civilians, the militia, armed with old muskets, out of step, untidy – butchers, perhaps, or bakers – saluting him with a parody of martial drill, but still men taking up arms to defend themselves and their city although God help them if they met the Janissaries, but worthy of a salute back as they ambled off to their Guild Hall.

Starhemberg was quite right. The men were the militia of the bakers and cobblers. Outside the Guild Hall they grounded their muskets, were given an imitation of a parade and walked off to their various bakeries, Herr Vogel making his way to Ottostrasse where his wife was waiting with soup, pickled cabbage, and bread.

Vogel carefully placed his musket on the top of the dresser, well away from Rudi's inquisitive fingers.

'I saw General Starhemberg just now,' he said. 'On the Burgplatz. He saluted us,' he added with a mild feeling of pride.

'So he should.' There was a little of the old tartness in Frau Vogel's voice. 'You're a soldier, aren't you?'

'Well,' Vogel, without martial illusions, chuckled. 'We carry muskets.' He stretched his shoulders and sat down to eat. 'Where's Anna?'

'Putting Rudi to bed.'

'Ah,' Vogel shuffled some cabbage down. It was late for the child to go to bed but the excitement of the times. . . .

Silence, broken only by Vogel sucking his soup and the squeak of a mouse behind the stove. Frau Vogel sat down and smoothed her skirt over her knees.

'Haller came round earlier on,' she said.

'Did he?' Vogel looked up at his wife. It was interesting that she had dropped the 'Herr' when talking about Haller. Ever since the night of the great panic she had cooled towards him. 'What did he want?'

'He was talking about leaving, while the bridges across the Danube are still open.'

'Tcha!' Vogel clattered his spoon across his plate. For the last week Haller had been in and out of the bakery – 'Should they go?

should they stay? Should *he* go or should he stay?' – his horsy face twitching and sweating and yellower than ever.

'He said he would call back,' Frau Vogel said.

Vogel groaned, without rebuke, but brightened as Anna came into the room and sat down by her mother.

'Is Rudi all right?' he asked.

'Yes,' Anna smiled. 'He's excited but he's gone to sleep.'

Vogel pushed his soup plate away and bit into an apple. It was strange about the children. Of all the inhabitants of the city they were the least afraid. Quite understandable, of course. It was all like a game to them, the school closed, soldiers everywhere, parades, meetings. . . .

Anna picked up her sewing. 'The children have a bet about how many Turks their fathers will shoot. Rudi has bet all his toys that you shoot the most, father.'

Frau Vogel gave an angry 'tut'. 'I'll bet he gets more smacks on the backside than anyone else.'

'Now, now,' Vogel finished his apple and picked up a plum. 'He can't lose, mother.' He spat out the plum-stone neatly. 'None of *us* will shoot any Turks,' he leaned back, smiling, enjoying his little joke. Anna laughed, too, although Frau Vogel, never the first to catch a joke, stared at them both suspiciously.

'I don't see what's so funny,' she said but was interrupted by a knock at the door.

Vogel stopped smiling. 'Haller,' he said, but his face brightened as the door opened and Kaspar came shyly through the door.

'Come in, come in,' Vogel beamed a welcome. 'Sit down, Kaspar. Make yourself at home.'

Kaspar edged awkwardly around the table, narrowly missed the stuffed heron and, self-consciously but firmly, sat down next to Anna. Frau Vogel's eye-brows rocketed upwards and her pale blue eyes stared accusingly at Vogel who determinedly avoided them. It was all part of the change the war had brought; children going to bed late, bakers carrying muskets, young couples, even betrothed young couples, sitting together before the very eyes of their parents. Somewhere at the back of Vogel's shrewd, limited mind a thought glinted like a fragment of broken glass. Perhaps these changes would be irreversible and when the Turks had gone, and he never doubted for one moment that they would go, Vienna would never be the same again – perhaps even Austria – the Empire itself, life . . . he shook his head, as if to rid himself of idle, un-bakerish fancies.

'Well, Kaspar,' he said. 'How are we tonight? I say, how are we?'

Kaspar stared fixedly at his boots. 'Very well, thank you, Herr Vogel.' he mumbled. 'Very well – Father says he can't come tonight.' His voice suddenly boomed out, making the Vogels jump.

'Oh?' Vogel tried to hide his delight at this news. 'Er . . . how is he?'

Kaspar gave his boots even closer attention. 'You know,' his voice sank back to an embarrassed mumble. 'He keeps talking about getting across the river. . . .'

'And what about you, Kaspar? Have you . . . er . . . had any second thoughts?'

Kaspar raised his head and squared his shoulders and with unexpected determination said, 'I'm staying. As long as . . .' – he glanced at Anna – 'as long as . . .' – his voice sank again to a strangled croak.

Vogel put Kaspar out of his misery. 'Good lad,' he said. 'We're staying all right.' He leaned back, nodding approval. Kaspar was a good lad with a mind of his own, no great talker perhaps, but, thinking of Herr Haller, Vogel regarded that as a blessing. He looked fondly on Kaspar and Anna; a fine pair they made, true Viennese, burgherlike and solid. Let them marry, have a fine family – and damn Haller. He jumped to his feet. 'Have a drink.'

Beer for Vogel, Kaspar, wine for Frau Vogel and Anna.

'And what have you been doing, Kaspar?' he asked. 'Working on the walls?'

'Yes. Palisading. Sticking up stakes on the counterscarp.'

'Stakes, hey? That will give the Turks something to think about. Wooden stakes. Pointed I daresay?'

'Oh, yes.' Kaspar supped some beer. 'Sharp points. And there are new forts being built in the moat, and trenches.'

Frau Vogel leaned intently forward. 'I hope that you are getting paid for all this work.'

'Oh yes, Frau Vogel,' Kaspar ducked his head. 'Good pay. General Starhemberg and the Council are making sure of that. Everyone who works gets paid.'

'You don't.' Frau Vogel stared at her husband.

'Of course not, mother. Of course the militia don't get paid. We're just doing our duty as citizens. You don't expect to get paid for that.'

'The soldiers get paid,' Frau Vogel said.

'Yes, yes.' Vogel drowned his exasperation in a swig of beer. 'But they are regular soldiers. It's their living, and they are the ones who will actually fight the Turks.'

'We heard them tonight,' Kaspar said.

'Heard them? Heard who?' Vogel asked.

'The Turks,' Kaspar said. 'Creeping about.'

'Creeping –' Vogel put his stein down. 'Creeping about? Where?'

'On the other side of the counterscarp. Among the ruins. A soldier told me it was a Turkish patrol.'

Creeping about! For all the beer he had drunk, Vogel's throat was dry. It was a horrible thought, the Turks creeping about like so many rats among the debris of what had been a pleasant suburb. And not a quarter of a mile away – not ten minutes walk from his cosy and well-loved parlour, and his wife, his dear Anna, and the stalwart Kaspar. It was incredible. He felt a sense of outrage – violation – and the rage he had felt on the night of the great panic gripped him again.

'So they are coming, are they,' he muttered. 'Well let them try it. Let them just come.'

They came the next morning from the heat haze which shrouded the hamlet of St. Ulrich. A squadron of Sipahi bearing standards of red and gold and green, walking their horses to the wail of a long Turkish trumpet, not hurrying and not dawdling, unconcerned but not casual; their elegance drawing a reluctant sigh of admiration from the thousands of Viennese who lined the city walls.

Nearer, and a little nearer, picking a disdainful way through the smouldering embers of burned out houses; silver and gold gleaming in the sunlight, dark faces becoming clearly visible as they neared the Palace Gate. A mere bowshot away they halted and an officer, tall, slender, arrogant, cantered forward a little way and waited in his turn, statuesque and indifferent to the heretical gaze of the multitude on the walls.

The Turkish officer raised his hand and waved a scroll bound with green tassels. The uncanny silence was broken by the furious barking of a dog and then an Austrian officer rode out from the Gate and took the scroll, the Sipahi bowing courteously in his saddle as he handed it over.

The Austrian officer rode back through the Palace Gate, onto the Burgplatz, and handed the scroll to Starhemberg. Starhemberg unrolled the document; superb parchment, magnificent lettering, the Grand Vizier's seal.

Starhemberg glanced briefly at the message – flowery rhetoric garlanding a simple message; submit to Islam, become Muslims, and live in peace under the Sultan; or remain Christians, pay tribute, and submit to the Sultan. Either way, surrender the city or be taken by storm and be put to the sword.

Starhemberg grunted and tossed the scroll to an aide who passed it on to Count Caplirs. A few moments passed and the Austrian officer stirred uneasily on his horse.

Starhemberg glared at him balefully. 'Well?' he growled.

The officer coughed. 'The . . . the answer, Sir.'

'Answer?' Starhemberg turned his horse away. 'There is no answer.'

The Turkish officer received Starhemberg's reply with a pitying smile, gave a mocking salute to the city, rejoined his escort and, to a last derisive blast on the trumpet – answered by cat-calls from Vienna, rode back to St. Ulrich. Almost immediately a Turkish cannon coughed, a small cannon-ball, clearly visible, arced through the air and shattered on the wall. The great Siege of Vienna had begun. It was July the Fourteenth.

Chapter Fourteen

CRACOW

THE Turkish cannon cracked, the Turkish engineers began, at astonishing speed to drive trenches towards the outer wall of Vienna, and the city's inhabitants began, as it were, to look over their shoulders for the relieving armies which, surely, their Emperor was raising in Christendom; and especially they looked towards Poland and many a girl in Vienna went to sleep dreaming of invincible Polish knights riding to their rescue.

And there were such knights, riding untrammelled across the plains of Poland, drifting to Warsaw and Cracow from the Eastern March, the Ukraine, the Baltic Provinces, and some of them did have the faces Viennese maidens dreamed of, hawk-like under glittering helmets, although the older hawks preferred to wear light straw hats, not wishing to have their brains boiled by the July sun.

But one eyas, Stefan Zabruski, was not among that chivalrous host. Far from fitting an heroic image he was in the garden of his father's town-house nursing a most unromantic black eye.

He had gained that unheroic trophy the night before; a languid, airless night, the heat of the day lingering so that even the moths seemed to flutter to their deaths in candle flame with an air of exhausted resignation.

Around the candles, at a grease-speckled table, Zabruski, Stefan's uncle, Soprona, and a dozen other cronies and relatives had been drinking and playing cards, interminable drinking and interminable cards, both having lasted now since the Provincial Diet had voted the previous May.

Cards and vodka, vodka and cards, the bribes of half Europe thrown casually onto the table, colossal gains and colossal losses incurred and wiped out, night after night, week after week, as the schlactas waited for the word from Warsaw and their King to march.

That night, after a run of losing hands lasting for a week, Zabruski had begun to win and an avalanche of Austrian thalers, French livres, and Papal lire had clattered down to come to rest before his dangerous, menacing bulk. As the evening wore on and his wins mounted, the ferocious sullenness which had marked Zabruski during his losing streak ebbed away to be replaced by his rare, grunting affability.

In a corner of the room Stefan had watched the money pile up before his father, noted the savage ill-humour give way to a savage good-humour, and had begun to wonder whether tonight he might, just conceivably might, tackle his ferocious and unpredictable father once more and ask – beg – plead for . . . for . . .

Stefan swallowed nervously and wiped the sweat from his brow with his sleeve. Strange that he should be so dry inside and so wet outside. There was another bellow from the table as Zabruski won again and his massive fist scooped in more winnings, coins spilling onto the floor unheeded except by a servant who artfully kicked them under a chair as he went to the table with a bowl of pickled herrings.

The vodka glasses chinked, a man cursed, Soprona laughed; Stefan slipped through the door into the garden. It was a little cooler there, the air heavy with the scent of lime trees. In the upper story of the house a spinet tinkled, women laughed. Stefan looked up at the lighted windows. A gowned figure crossed the light; Vera Soprona, the Schlacta Soprona's daughter, Stefan's own age but a creature from another world, brought up in Warsaw, light, delicate, smelling of flowers instead of lard, and the focus of Stefan's dreams.

A huge whoop came from the card room, the racket drowning

the women's laughter and the spinet. A bulky shape lurched into the garden. Zabruski relieving himself. In the shadow of a plum tree Stefan licked his lips. Now, while his father was flush with money, and, even more importantly, flush with victory, was the time to make his request and, of one thing Stefan was certain, if his father granted it then he would keep his word. In that, if in nothing else, he was a knight. Taking a deep breath Stefan moved forward. At once Zabruski swung around, his head thrust forward.

'Who's that?' his voice was thick with menace. 'Who's there?'

Stefan walked from the shadow of the plum tree into the light. 'It's me father.'

'Aagh!' Zabruski waved his hand in dismissal and turned away but Stefan darted in front of him.

'Father,' he cried. 'Can I have a horse?'

'What?' Zabruski's voice was baffled but then, as Stefan's request filtered through the haze of alcohol, enraged. 'What!'

'A horse, father. There is a good one – Pyotr Chelmnitz says so – a good price – cheap –' The words bubbled out almost incoherently. A horse of his own here in Cracow. Stefan longed for that more than he had ever longed for anything in his short life. In Ostrova there were horses in plenty. A word to Chelmnitz and one appeared, but in Cracow he was at the mercy of uncles, cousins, vague relatives, all of whom were ready enough to lend him a horse but less ready to lend him a good one, or even a decent saddle to a country bumpkin from some God-forsaken wilderness where horses were treated nearly as brutally as serfs, and so Stefan had found himself riding on sway-backed wall-eyed nags, on a saddle with stuffing bursting from the seams, jeered at by his friends, sneered at by more lordly gentry, and tittered at by girls.

But there was more to it than that even. For Stefan a horse was not just a convenient method of locomotion – one, indeed to which he had been born as much as any Tartar – it was a mark of his social class. A seat on a horse raised him above his fellow men not only literally but symbolically. From that elevation he looked down on the plodders; the peasants, the labourers, the trudgers through the mud, the infantry of the world, and although Stefan was merely the son of a poor schlacta, on the very bottom rung of the ladder of the nobility, yet he was on that rung and it was of vital importance to him to be *seen* to be on that rung, and only a good horse of his own could show that. And it was because of that Stefan had steeled himself to ask his father for a horse of his own.

But had Stefan tried to, he could not have chosen a worse possible moment to ask his father for anything, because the whoop he had heard a moment or two earlier had not been another win for Zabruski, but a crashing defeat as the ambiguous cards had turned losing faces upwards and the gold and silver winking at him had disappeared in one hand.

'A horse,' Zabruski spat. 'You . . .' The figure of his son rocked before his fuddled eyes; indeed he was barely aware that it was his son. The dark, swaying shape might just as well have been some stranger from the night gabbling about buying horses. 'Get out. Get out!' he roared, smashed Stefan back-handed across the face, and stumbled back into the card-room.

And that was why, as the first Turkish cannon coughed at Vienna, Stefan the hero was lounging moodily in a plum orchard, nursing a black eye.

There was movement in the house. A carriage rumbled up the drive, laughter, footsteps, his name called. He moved further into the orchard but there was no escape. A light, teasing voice called his name; Vera Soprona, in pale blue muslin, a basket over her slender arm, her eyes alight, sought him out, laughing as she saw his face and saying, 'A moi! Stefan, vous avez déjà commencé à faire la guerre aux Turcs?'

Stefan shrugged sullenly and turned away. He had the vaguest smattering of French and Vera was fluent; indeed she and her friends spoke little else, using Polish only to speak to servants and other inferior beings, and, sometimes, to Stefan.

He turned his face to one side but, magically, Vera appeared there, peering at his blackened eye, laughing, and repeating her question in Polish;

'Stefan, have you started the war against the Turks already?'

Stefan scowled with one eye, as the other was incapable of movement, and muttered the improbable excuse, used since doors were first invented, that one of them had slammed in his face.

'Ah! Such a wicked door!' Vera placed her white hand on Stefan's none too clean sleeve.

Stefan shrugged away, acutely aware of his grubby blouse. What had he once heard a dirty foreigner say? Poland had plenty of diamonds but was short of clean linen. Next to the scented Vera he felt raw, loutish, crude and sweaty, a peasant. He wished that he was back in Ostrova where he was, if not the master, then at least the master's son and where if a man – or a woman, come to that – laughed at him, or even lifted their eyes as he passed, they would have the lash on their backs.

At the end of the garden, where there was a tangle of thistles, a flock of birds chased each other, beautiful birds, splashed with red and white and gold.

'What are those, Stefan?' Vera asked.

'Birds,' Stefan muttered.

Vera laughed and Stefan rounded on her. 'Well, that's what they are, aren't they, birds? They've got wings haven't they? They're flying, aren't they?'

'Ah yes. Yes Stefan.' The white hand rested on Stefan's arm again. 'I wasn't laughing at you,' mildly reproachful.

'No?' Stefan shook Vera off roughly. 'But you were. You all do, all of you.'

'Us?' Vera's dark eyes were round.

'Tak!' Stefan waved his arm angrily, a circle encompassing quite what he did not know himself, but all those with Frenchified ways, elegants from Warsaw with shirts they changed every day, their mocking smiles, their beliefs that the earth went around the sun and – yes – and their own fine horses. Unconsciously echoing his father's words he shouted, 'What do they know? Look!' He pulled up his sleeve showing a long, ragged scar which he had gained sliding on the ice on the duck pond in

Ostrova a couple of years previously and, lying through his teeth in a bare-faced attempt to impress Vera, he said, 'A Tartar did that! Tak! Yes, a Tartar!'

For a moment he almost believed it himself, and certainly Vera did, or seemed to, for she raised her hand to her mouth as she said, 'A Tartar?'

Stefan opened his mouth but a deep, almost hidden honesty gagged his 'yes' in his throat, and he was saved from both lie and truth, and shame in either case by Vera who touched the scar with a finger – with clean nails.

'They talk of you in Warsaw,' she said.

Stefan blinked in absolute, total amazement. 'Me?'

Vera smiled. 'Of the frontier,' she said. 'Of the schlactas who face the Tartars and the Russ.'

'They do?' Stefan swelled.

'Oh, yes. I have heard King John say so.'

'King John? John Sobieski?'

'Yes, Stefan. John Sobieski. At court.'

Stefan shook his head, not in disbelief but in wonder. King John himself, the King of Poland, actually talking of – well, to be honest – not of Stefan Zabruski but almost, nearly, as good as . . .

'And you've seen him?' he asked. 'Really seen him?'

'Yes, Stefan.'

'What is he like?' Stefan stammered, 'I mean really like?'

'Ah! The King! He is big. Very big and strong. And handsome, with a long moustache.' Vera's fingers twirled in an enormous loop above her upper lip.

Self-consciously, Stefan touched his own, downy lip and Vera laughed, 'But he does not have a Tartar scar on his arm . . . Stefan.'

Stefan went red to the roots of his flaxen hair and down to the collar of his blouse. 'I –' he began, but Vera cut him short.

'I forgot to tell you,' she said. 'You are wanted. Come.'

She ran down the path, Stefan lunging awkwardly after her, but instead of entering the house Vera turned right, left, and right again, and there, in the stable-yard was Pyotr Chelmnitz, and

Chelmnitz was holding a rein, and the rein led to a bridle, and the bridle was on the head of a fine, a superb, a magnificent chestnut colt.

'From the master,' Chelmnitz said, and even his brutal face cracked into a smile.

A horse of Stefan's dreams, a Pegasus, fit not only for the son of a schlacta, but for a prince, a Lubomirski, yes, and by God, Sobieski himself; a horse come from heaven, almost literally, Zabruski having won again at cards and, in his unpredictable way, backing his winnings against the horse and the court cards smiling up at him as benignly as new-crowned monarchs; and so Stefan riding at a canter – the horse beautifully balanced – across the meadows, a Polish hero, fit (overlooking his black eye) for any girl's dreams.

He passed a group of serfs trudging to the mowing. They ducked their heads and their overseer raised his hat. What joy, and who knew what lay ahead; war, fame, glory, aye, love. Who knew what destiny would bring him, or to what fate it would take him?

But at that moment Stefan's fate was being decided not by the workings of an inscrutable and intangible fate, but by the very corporeal, fleshy, mountainous figure of King John Sobieski himself, in his summer estate of Wilanow, just a little south of Warsaw, where he was considering a message just brought to him from the Emperor Leopold. The letter had been brought at amazing speed – three hundred and fifty miles in eleven days – and, if it was to be believed, it was clear that the Ottoman army, against all reason, was attacking Vienna. If that was so, *if* it was so – and who knew what might or might not have happened in eleven days – then Poland's duty was clear. It must march to the aid of the Austrians with all speed.

But . . . Sobieski shifted his bulk uneasily on his chair and looked again at the letter. '. . . desperate situation . . . speed essential . . .' It was all very well but the entire Polish strategy for

1683 had been based on the defence of the southern frontier. To march to Vienna meant a complete realignment of cumbersome and slow moving forces. It could be done, of course; indeed, now, for honour's sake, it had to be done, but how?

Sobieski tugged at his luxuriant moustache and considered. Field Hetman Sienawski was almost at Cracow with seven thousand men. Count Lubomirski with three thousand cavalry were already somewhere on the upper Danube, but the heart of the Polish professional army, was far to the south at Lvov. It would take time to bring it north, and then the great landlords, the true heavy cavalry, the mailed fist of Poland would have to be concentrated at Cracow, too, and they would move at their own speed and their own time. And even when the army was concentrated, to get to Vienna it would have to move through mountainous and little known territory. It would need maps, guides, provisions, and even then enough troops would have to be left behind to guard the passes from Hungary into Poland. Enormous and daunting problems; but still, Sobieski's mind was made up. If Vienna fell then the whole might of the Ottoman Empire could be swung against Poland in the next year. Yes. Poland would be best defended at the gates of Vienna.

Summary orders, scribes scribbling the King's summons and messengers flogging their mounts to death as they carried them, and like some huge, primeval beast the signals moved slowly from the brain to the extremities, and, equally slowly the extremities began to respond. And not only in Poland. Across the whole of Europe Austria's plea was being heard and, however late, responded to. In Saxony and Bavaria, Franconia, Hanover and Westphalia, in the Netherlands and France, and in remote England, Emperors, Kings, Princes and Parliaments beginning to focus on Vienna – where Timur Ven was about to see for himself the bleak and unheroic face of siege warfare.

Part
3

The Siege
Summer 1683

Chapter Fifteen

THE COUNTERSCARP

SEVEN days had passed since Starhemberg had contemptuously rejected the Ottoman demand for the surrender of Vienna, and in the seven days an enormous ring of men and tents had surrounded the walls as the army of the east tightened its grip around the throat of the west. But like an assassin strangling his victim and stabbing him too, the point of Sayf al-Islam – the sword of Islam – was jabbing at the jugular vein of Vienna, the stretch of zig-zagging counterscarp, the outer wall between the Lobel and the Burg Bastions.

But imagery of swords flashing dramatically in the sunlight was, as Timur had found out, far from the reality, unless one counted the flashing swords of Kara Mustafa's executioners beheading Christian captives, for the Twenty-eighth Orta had been held back in reserve at Schwechat, on guard duties as the supply wagons rumbled up from Komarom. Not much drama in that, and not much, so far as Timur could see, in the attack on the city itself.

The walls of Vienna were clearly visible from near Schwechat – the outer wall and looming behind that, the inner wall and bastions – but the only sign of activity was a scribble of trenches, increasing in complexity every day as the Turkish engineers dug their way forward, and the distant mumble of the cannon, the popping of musketry. It was almost inconceivable that a ferocious battle was being fought a mere hour or so's walk away. In fact, with the gaily coloured tents there was something of a carnival atmosphere among the meadows and hamlets around the city.

In his dry, sardonic way, Vasif had enlightened Timur about the actualities of a siege. Outside his tent by a ruined orchard, hacked down for firewood, he had gestured towards Vienna. 'A siege, not a battle. To charge those walls would be suicide. The engineers dig under them – plant a mine – explode it – then we charge. Hope the engineers do their work properly, young Timur Ven. The spade is mightier than the sword. As you will find out.'

Timur did the next day. The orta was assembled, lined up casually, a little conversation; curses on the cook who had burned the bread that morning, heartless laughter at the expense of Janissary Ghazi, flogged on the feet the day before for taking the name of the Prophet in vain, whose bruised feet made it hard for him to walk but who was walking just the same, and more laughter, half envious about Janissaries Rustum and Cirkesi, down with dysentery and so weak that even Vasif had excused them from duty.

The chatter ended abruptly as Vasif, Timur at his heels, strode from the ruined plum trees. The men stiffened as Vasif inspected them, not looking for uniformity but making sure that every man was properly equipped; muskets, powder, ammunition, sword . . . satisfied Vasif addressed them;

'Time to earn our salt. The trenches. Keep your heads down. The Austrians have sharp-shooters. Some fools have been strutting about and been picked off at three hundred yards. If Allah takes me, Odabasi Osman is in command. Remember, the Austrians *may* kill you, but any man who fails to do his duty *will* die. So keep your heads. Understood?'

'Dok, Corbaci.' The men understood Vasif's grim little pun since they knew that any man who did not do his duty would bow his neck to one of Kara Mustafa's one hundred and fifty executioners.

'So.' Vasif nodded. 'At dawn tomorrow the engineers are going to explode a mine. When it goes off, we charge. You follow me, and the Odabasis follow you. Clear?'

That was clear, too. A plain choice. An Austrian pike in your guts or a Turkish bullet in your back.

'So. Allah with us.' Vasif turned on his heels and led his orta forward to the walls of Vienna.

It was a pleasant stroll, in its way. Through St. Marx, and Neue Favorita and into St. Ulrich; market gardens and orchards, roses, birds flitting through the trees and a bustle of men, orderlies, blacksmiths, cooks, armourers, ostlers, imams, slaves, captives and, under the trees, men and women, without heads – but Timur did not look too closely at those.

At the summer-gardens of Count Trautson, where an ostrich stared at them with disdain, and Count Kunitz, still a guest – captive that is – of Kara Mustafa stared at them with interest, a guide met the orta and led them forward to the mouth of the assault trenches.

The trenches were an astonishing warren of dugouts and bunkers, for, as the main trenches led directly to the walls of Vienna, the engineers had hacked out support trenches branching to the right and left where the Janissaries could support them and defend them from counter-attacks as they gnawed their way forward under the shadow of the counterscarp.

The guide led them through the maze, halting every now and then to let working parties through, captives carrying baskets of earth, baulks of timber, stones – and bodies and, finally, pressing back against the walls of the trench to let them out, the orta the Twenty-eighth was relieving; a battered, filthy, blood-spattered company shambling out without so much as a glance at their comrades or a word – that silence, so different from the usual good-natured jibing normal when orta met orta, more sinister than the boom of the cannon, the crackle of musketry, and the screams of a wounded man trapped somewhere beyond the firing line.

But the trench itself was a good one. As Tedeki said, admiringly, 'Well done the Lagunci!' And certainly the trench was wide and deep, half roofed with stout timbers and with a firing step, ladders at intervals, and defended by a parapet of earth and wicker pierced with loop-holes. It was an astonishing construction, especially when one realized that it had been dug under constant fire from the guns behind the jagged palisades on the Austrian counterscarp, and that not fifty paces away.

But it was claustrophobic; stinking like an open sewer since two hundred men had spent three days and nights in it. And there were worse smells, the sour stench of unburied dead, and there were clouds of huge blue-bottles and swarms of gross green flies, landing on the men in sickening clusters. All in all, although men tried to push the thought away, being in the trench was like being in an open grave in a foul cemetery where the grave diggers were doing their best before burying you, to kill you as well.

Dusk turned to night. It rained a little, turning the bottom of the trench into an oozy stinking mire. Swollen rats ran along the parapet, sentries on the firing steps strained their eyes staring into the night, the rats turning into ferocious Austrian infantrymen making a sortie and causing a panicky sentry to open fire, starting waves of musketry which crackled along the trenches to die away as mysteriously as it had started.

Turn and turn about the orta changed duty; men stood down and fell asleep in the filth as flies crawled over them. The night slipped away, the stars swung around the heavens, dawn crept near, and, without orders, the entire orta rose and stood against the scaling ladders, muttering prayers for salvation. Fifty feet beneath them, sweating Turkish engineers sealed the mouth of the mine chamber and backed away from the shaft, unwinding a fuse, followed by a captain of the Lagunci.

The captain straightened, rubbed soil from his face, caught Vasif's eye, nodded, held up his fingers twice, and lit the fuse, its red glow travelling slowly into the darkness of the shaft like the fiery eye of an animal backing into its burrow.

Imperturbably, as if he had all day instead of twenty seconds, Vasif walked down the trench taking his place in the middle of the line, one hand on his sword, the other on an assault ladder. A battery of cannon suddenly opened in the rear of the Turkish lines, on the orta's left a wave of firing crashed against the Austrian Walls, and through all the din Timur could hear the voice of the engineeer calmly counting away the seconds, thirteen, fourteen, fifteen . . .

Timur found himself counting also, but how slowly the seconds seemed to be passing . . . an old memory came back to him. Once his father had beaten him, for what he did not even remember. At the first whack of the cane he had seen a dog trotting across the courtyard of the house. At the sixth and final blow the dog had only just crossed the yard. Under the blows time had seemed to stretch into eternity and yet only seconds had passed; like now, only, incredibly the cannon-fire had stopped, and the engineer's voice had stopped, too.

Down the mine shaft there was a vague, muffled rumble, the trench shook, ahead the earth rose in a large bubble, bursting suddenly, one or two stakes flew through the air, an arm, legs, the trunk of a man, and Vasif roared *'Allah Akhbar'* and led his men over the top, into a shallow crater, and into a withering cross-fire from the palisades. A dozen men went down screaming as the orta slid into the crater and clawed their way up to the palisades. Austrian pikes jabbed through the stakes as Vasif and his men scrabbled at the palisades like terriers. To their right and left other companies of Janissaries were ploughing forward to be blasted by disciplined musketry from the angles of the counterscarp; the Austrian infantry behind the solid timbers perfectly steady, disciplined.

The orta clawed at the palisades but were driven back into the crater, blasted out of there by grenades, and shot back into the trench.

A shattering experience, and shattered men as a result of it, but Vasif lashed them to their feet, posted those capable of standing on the firing step, had the wounded dragged out, the dead thrown over the parapet, and then disappeared on some mysterious errand. Then, more mysterious than the errand, it was quiet. No shooting, no grenades, only somewhere to the left a mortar belched at intervals.

A water carrier came into the trench. Tedeki took a huge gulp and wiped a bloody forehead. 'Bismillah, what a cock-up.' He looked along the trench, counting on his fingers. 'How many missing?'

No one answered. The men slumped, faces twitching, muddy, bloody, filthy, looking, as it suddenly occurred to Timur, just like the men they had relieved – and *they* had been in the trenches for days, not hours.

And that, it seemed was what the Twenty-eighth Orta was going to do. At any rate there were no orders to move and the company sprawled in the bunker as the sun rose higher, the flies swarmed, and what, the night before, had seemed like a grave turned into something remarkably similar to an oven. Timur took his turn on the firing step, peering through the loop-hole. There was nothing to see. A few yards of bare earth leading to the crater, and the wall with its jagged stakes grinning down on him. But no cannon, no flags, no sign of terrible Christians waiting to blow him to Paradise or Gehenna, just the shallow slope leading to a wall and the ferocious palisades. For all that was happening the Janissaries might have been besieging an empty city.

An illusion, for Janissary Plaki, either from curiosity or boredom, heaved himself up a little too high on the firing step and a bullet smacked exactly inthe middle of his hat, a millimetre above his head. The crack was echoed as Odabasi Osman lashed furiously into Plaki with his cane.

'What did the Corbaci tell you?' Osman spat. 'What did he order? Now do as you're told, you dog.'

Tedeki spat 'By Allah,' he said. 'I thought we were here to fight the Giaours not each other,' baring his teeth at Timur in a mirthless grin.

Timur grinned feebly back. He was still trying to make sense of what had happened; the charge to the palisades had been mere confusion; he had strange, vivid memories, Odabasi Osman missing his footing on the assault ladder and being pushed up by a brown hand, a Janissary slipping in the crater and cursing as a rat scampered over his neck, the harsh, choking smoke of Austrian muskets as they fired through the palisades, another Janissary on his knees, jerking in a strange way until Timur realised that his face was blown away . . . it was astonishing to him to realise that he had actually gone over the top, seen battle, fired his musket, shrieked and howled, and the thought gave him a little prickle of pride.

Noon came, no prayers, insufferable heat. Vasif came back from the command bunker – where he had had a blazing row with the Colonel of the Engineers, refusing to accept the excuse that the powder in the mine was of inferior quality and *that* was the fault of the ever-to-be damned commissariat in Buda – took a musket and as an act of mercy shot two dying men on the far side of the crater who had been screaming steadily all morning.

More water came up, bread, a little rice, cannon-balls whistled overhead. On the orta's left, opposite the Lobel Bastion a bitter, futile firefight broke out and died away. And all the long day the Lagunci were at work, driving a new shaft forward for another mine. The orta spent two more days and a night in the trench. Two men were killed by sharpshooters, six men collapsed with dysentery and one man went mad, but, on the whole, it was a quiet time for the orta because, like a boxer jabbing first with his right and then with his left, the main Turkish attacks were taking place on the left; bloody, furious forays, attack and counter attack, and every time the Janissaries beaten back into the trenches.

On the second day Timur saw a sight which disturbed him more than the men lying on the floor of the trench with their brains blown out. The engineers digging the new mine shaft under the covered-way drove themselves ferociously, but they drove their labourers even more so. The labourers were slaves, captives caught up in the sweep across Hungary. Catholics and protestants alike, their religious differences meaningless under the Turkish lash, they staggered up and down the trenches dragging huge burdens of timber and stone, cowed, hopeless, beaten and kicked – indeed Timur himself kicked them, although in a half-hearted way, less from cruelty, or even a desire to make them work harder, but because, vaguely he felt it was expected of him.

But one slave, at least, was not broken. Indeed, looking at him it was hard to believe that anyone – or thing – could break him. He had an unyielding rock-hard face set on unyielding rock-hard shoulders – bleeding from a flogging and swarming with flies – and Timur, lounging at the entry to the assault trench, and half-minded to give him a casual kick, decided not to, wisely as it turned out.

The man was carrying a baulk of timber and as he reached the head of the trench he swung the beam, knocked down two Janissaries from the Eighty-seventh Orta who were on guard, and leaped for the rim of the trench.

He almost made it. Almost. Almost made for himself a few seconds of freedom although a few seconds is all that it would have been. Trapped between the trench and the palisade he would have been shot to pieces before he had gone a yard. Not that it mattered. Another Janissary grabbed him by the legs and slashed at him with a knife, but it was the Janissary's last act on this earth for the slave seized him by the wrist and throat and drove the knife into his chest. And that was the slave's last act on this earth, too. A musket butt crashed against his head, a club thudded down, a sword slashed, boots stamped, and when the enraged guards stepped aside there was something in the trench which might have been connected with something which might once have been a head.

Timur turned aside and delivered his noon meal into a corner. Despite the heat his forehead was clammy, chilled, and he shook like a man in a fever. He had seen men killed by now, and seen them dying slowly if it came to that, but the bestial stamping to death of the slave . . . He raised his head. The slave's body was being thrown, casually, over the parapet and, a little way down the trench, Vasif was watching. Timur half-raised his hand, almost supplicating, but Vasif merely walked forward, kicking the slave's head out of the way as casually as though it was a stone. 'Get back to your duty,' he said. 'And quick.'

A bad moment but worse was to come for Kara Mustafa, enraged at the killing of a Janissary ordered his one hundred and fifty executioners to line up one hundred and fifty prisoners in the Trautson Gardens, and have them decapitated in full view of Vienna.

On the counterscarp, behind the palisades, the Austrian infantry saw the swords flash and the heads roll and knew the sight for what it was, a grisly signal of what lay in wait for Vienna if it fell. A city which refused to surrender would be put to the sword; and that was not merely a figure of speech. Many of the men on the ramparts had done it themselves – and to Christian cities.

News of the executions spread across Vienna; soldier to soldier, a thousand dead; soldier to tavern; five thousand dead; tavern to the streets, ten thousand; Frau Haller to Frau Vogel, fifty thousand;

'And the Turks have crossed the Danube into the Prater,' she added, for good measure. 'All the bridges are closed, and they've burned the Emperor's hunting palace.'

Of that there was no doubt, columns of smoke could be seen rising to the south of the city.

'We're surrounded,' Frau Haller said. 'Absolutely cut off'–with relish as she scuttled down the street, fearful of a Turkish cannon-ball crashing into Ottostrasse.

'Tcha!' Frau Vogel slammed the door. 'Surrounded! Well at least we won't have Haller in here ten times a day with his eternal shall we go or shall we stay.'

Anna looked up from her sewing. 'No mother,' she said.

'Mark you,' Frau Vogel sat in her chair and folded her arms. 'Mark you, these killings . . .'

A little silence; the killings. Never very far from the minds of the Viennese, tales of Turkish butchery creeping around the city like some foul disease, especially Perchtoldsdorf where the little city *had* surrendered. It had all been done according to the laws and customs of war. The keys of the city had been delivered by a maiden with unbound hair. And the entire population had been slaughtered and the heads of its citizens rolled before the feet of Kara Mustafa.

Frau Vogel shook her head. 'Those poor souls today, and in Count Trautson's gardens. What will the Countess think when she hears of it. She'll never be able to rest easy there again. I'm sure I wouldn't.'

Despite herself, Anna smiled. It was incredible. The Turks knocking at the gates of the city, people dying, mortar shells actually landing in the streets, and her mother was worrying about how the Countess Trautson would feel if she got back to Vienna.

'And then there's the Emperor's theatre,' Frau Vogel said indignantly. 'Knocking it down! Why should they do that?'

Anna put her sewing aside. 'Kaspar says that the Friars were afraid that if it were set on fire it would burn the monastery down. It was made of wood, you know.'

Frau Vogel's voice softened. 'Ah, Kaspar,' she said, as if Kaspar himself had given the order to knock down the theatre. 'He says that everything is all right, doesn't he? He says that the Turks won't get through the walls. That's what he says, doesn't he?'

'Yes, mother.' Anna expertly threaded a needle with one hand. It was curious how her mother was changing. Once it had been Herr Haller says this, Herr Haller says that, all the livelong day, but since the night of the panic his role as the oracle of Vienna had dwindled, faded, vanished, and Kaspar had taken over his role. Kaspar the steadfast and the reassuring, comforting in the matter of fact way he went about his work, his ruddy, unimaginative presence an antidote to panic and rumour, very like Herr Vogel himself, come to that.

'He's a good young man,' Frau Vogel said, echoing Anna's thoughts but speaking as though the world, and Anna, denied it. 'When all this is over' – dismissing the Turks, and the siege – 'When all this is over you'll be happy together, won't you?'

'Yes,' Anna blushed, but not furiously as she used to do. It was another change, both in herself, and her mother. Not long ago she would never have been asked whether or not she would be happy married to Kaspar. Such a thought would never have entered into her mother's head. What had happiness to do with marriage? Or Anna's preference to do with whom she was married to? But there was more to the change than that, even. Now there were no more whispered consultations from which she, Anna, was excluded, and Frau Vogel had even, in a virtually incomprehensible way, shuffled into explanations of 'wifely duties'.

In her own shrewd way, Anna knew quite well why this amazing transformation had taken place. The Turkish advance had driven a wedge between the Hallers and her mother, leaving her isolated and fearful, and as she had lost her confidante, so she had turned to her daughter, her husband, and to Kaspar.

There was a clatter on the stairs. Three soldiers, a sergeant and two corporals who had been moved into the upper rooms where the candlemakers had lived, going on to duty.

Frau Vogel shook her head. 'Who would have ever thought it? Soldiers in the house. What will the Emperor think of it all?'

The two soldiers made their way to their assembly point on the Burgplatz. A slightly battered Burgplatz now, as the occasional Turkish cannonball had crashed onto the square. The company, from Scherffenberg's regiment, filed into the passage way which led from the inner wall to the outer wall and, from the shadow of the gallows he had ordered to be erected Count General Starhemberg watched them go, giving a half salute as they went into the shadows.

The men looked resolute. Tired but resolute and resolution was what would be needed during the coming weeks. It was the executions, Starhemberg thought, especially the bloody murder at Perchtoldsdorf. The men knew what would happen if the Turks broke into the city, what would happen to the citizens – and to themselves. No quarter. Not that Starhemberg was too concerned about the executions. Unlike Kara Mustafa, he believed that terror stiffened the will to resist. In fact Starhemberg was more confident now than at any time since the disasters of the Schutt. It was clear that the Turks were going to concentrate their attack on the walls opposite the Burgplatz and so he was able to concentrate his own forces, bringing up artillery from the other bastions, using most of his labour on the moat, which was turning into a formidable barrier which would be needed when the counterscarp was pierced. That, of course, was merely a matter of time. Sooner or later, if the Turks kept up their attack, they would break through into the moat, but then to get to the inner curtain wall, the real defence of the city, they would have to *cross* the moat; only a couple of hundred yards but a couple of hundred yards tangled with trenches, palisades, spikes, pillboxes – everything that the engineer, Signor Rimpler could devise, and all raked with cross-fire from the bastions and the Ravelin – the triangular fort in the middle. Of course, the moat could be crossed, any city's defences could be breached given time, but time, Starhemberg profoundly hoped, time was what the Turks did not have.

Chapter Sixteen

THE GLACIS

ANOTHER dawn; prayers inside Vienna and prayers outside it, the jangle of church bells from Vienna mocking the long cries of the imams in the Ottoman army.

Kara Mustafa raised his forehead from the ground and scowled across at the inviolate city. Nine days, the trenches under the shadow of the palisade, great mounds of earth – almost small hills – thrown up higher than the stakes, men actually shooting down into the covered-way, and still his army had not broken through the outer wall. He had not thought that the Christians could put up so much resistance. Perhaps a little more terror was needed. There were a thousand or so prisoners herded in the rear. The sight of their heads falling might weaken the resolve of those stubborn men behind the barricade. Yes, that was a thought. He turned to give the order and found the Agas of the Janissaries and the Lagunci bowing respectfully before him.

'Excellency,' the Aga of the Lagunci snapped his fingers and two engineers held up a chart. Mustafa spared it a glance; a map of the trenchworks, a bewildering tangle, meaningless to him. The Aga ran his finger across the chart, speaking.

Mustafa listened with half an ear. An attack was being planned that night. A huge mine driven under the counterscarp. A heavy bombardment . . . a charge . . . He waved an impatient hand, these were the technicalities of war, a matter for the Agas. He had done his work bringing the army here to the edge of Islam. All that remained was for him to enter Vienna in triumph and quickly. Not that time was of great importance. The city was surrounded, the Austrian cavalry was safely herded across the Danube in the woods of the Wienerwald, and help – if any help was ever going to come – would be weeks on the way. Yes, the army was as secure as if it was in barracks in Istanbul. The thought pleased him and he smiled one of his rare, brilliant, dazzling genuine smiles.

'Attack,' he said. 'Yes, by all means attack.' Then turned to an aide, gave a clipped order, and watched with satisfaction as his executioners shouldered their curved swords and marched off to the prisoners.

Many eyes watched the butchers as they marched through the camp, including those of Vasif's orta, back amongst their ruined orchard. Tedeki the Bull, leaning against the stump of a pear tree, drew a meaty finger across his throat. 'Zzzk! Goodbye the Giaours.' He laughed heartily. 'Use their heads for cannon-balls, that's the thing to do. Fire them off; fwit! fwit! fwit!'

There were one or two hyena like laughs – but not many. Tedeki caught Timur's eye. 'Cannon-balls, hey?' He bellowed. 'Imagine it,' Tedeki roared. 'An Austrian soldier on that Allah – be – damned wall – just standing there and fwit! A Christian head hits *him* on the head!'

Timur found that genuinely amusing, being hit on the head by a head! He burst out laughing, too. A few of the other men were guffawing but not Janissary Emre. He was looking at Tedeki with a thoughtful expression.

'What are you staring at?' Tedeki said.

'Nothing,' Emre said. 'Only I saw it done once. At Kamenets.'

'Kamenets?' Tedeki was puzzled. 'But . . .'

'That's right.' Emre nodded. 'The Poles were besieging us. They threw Turkish heads at us.' He threw some coffee slops on the ground. 'They had a huge catapult.' He turned away, down to the little stream which served the orta for various purposes.

Tedeki stared at his retreating back with his stupid, good-natured gaze. 'I didn't know he was at Kamenets,' he said. 'Did you?'

The orta shook its collective heads, stretched arms and legs and ambled off to various pursuits, the armourers, the kitchens, to find a shady place to sleep the afternoon away . . .

Timur, unwanted by Vasif for an hour or so, and obedient to the Koran's commandment that cleanliness was part of God-liness, went down to the stream. Emre was there, stripped, his bare feet in the water. Politely, Timur went a little way down-stream and washed himself and then, like Emre, sat in the cool grass as the July heat enshrouded the camp.

On the glacis cannon boomed steadily, muskets popped, a wagtail perched on the opposite bank of the stream, flicking its tail for a moment before flying away. Below the wagtail a group of men from another orta were washing, laughing as they splashed each other, and below them a group of horsemen crossed the stream, Tartars, like bundles of rags on their wiry ponies, with a dozen or so women in tow. From the camp came the long call to prayer. Timur prostrated himself, prayed, rose, and found Emre looking at him.

Emre had a curious expression, thoughtful, and yet penetrat-ing, rather like Vasif's, Timur thought, as if posing an uncanny challenge that demanded an answer without asking a question.

Timur smiled uneasily. 'Emre?'

'You're a devout boy,' Emre said. 'Saying your prayers.'

'Well . . .' Timur shrugged.

'You say them when you think no one can see you, too,' Emre said.

'Allah always sees us,' Timur answered.

'Yes, he does. He hears us too. Even if we don't speak aloud.'

Timur profoundly hoped that was true as he had spent a good deal of his time since the attack in the trenches in praying for his personal safety, without actually saying so, of course.

'Of course,' Emre said. 'Of course Tedeki has a loud voice.'

Timur agreed with that. Tedeki had got a loud voice. He probably had the loudest voice in the army, if not in the whole of

Islam. 'But,' Emre continued, 'But because he's got the loudest voice doesn't mean Allah listens to him, does it?'

'I suppose not,' Timur was puzzled, and he was even more puzzled at Emre's next remark.

'You like a laugh, don't you?'

'Well –' Timur laughed and then put his hand to his mouth as if he had blurted out a secret. 'I don't understand,' he said.

'Well, it's like this.' Emre picked up his blouse and began to put it on. 'We pray to Allah, the most merciful and compassionate, don't we? You know that?'

'Of course I do.' Timur was indignant.

'I'm glad to hear that, really glad,' Emre said. 'But there's nothing very merciful and compassionate about cutting the heads off old men and women, is there?'

'But . . . but they're infidels,' Timur said. 'Dogs.'

'They are *Ahl al-Kitab*,' Emre said. 'People of the Book. They should have been given the chance to convert to Islam.'

'How do you know they weren't?' Timur cried, but Emre merely gave him a look in which contempt and pity were curiously blended, and walked away.

A little later Timur was back at his duties; running errands for Vasif, bringing him coffee, taking messages, more coffee and, at three in the afternoon, being so bold as to take in a tray with two cups on it.

Vasif looked thoughtfully at the tray. 'Two cups?' he said.

Timur bowed. 'I thought that the Corbaci might be having company,' he lied.

'Did you?' Vasif lifted his cup and smelt the delicate aroma of the coffee. 'A word of advice, Janissary Ven. Don't think *too* much.'

'No Corbaci.'

'Thinking can damage your brains.'

'Yes, Corbaci.'

'And if a soldier thinks too much he might need to have an

operation. His head might need to be cut off.'

Sincerely hoping that Vasif was joking, Timur mustered a smile. 'Yes, Corbaci. But . . .'

'But what?'

Timur took a deep breath. 'Corbaci . . . could I ask the Corbaci a question?'

Vasif put his cup down. 'That is not forbidden.'

'Well . . .' Timur plunged forward. 'Corbaci, the . . . these executions.' He paused, half expecting a blistering rebuke, but Vasif merely leaned back and stroked his small, square chin. When he spoke it was unexpected.

'Have you been ordered to execute anyone?'

'No, Corbaci.'

'And has anyone in this orta been ordered to execute anyone?'

'No, Corbaci.'

'Nor will they.' Vasif sipped his coffee. 'What goes on up there –' He nodded towards the killing ground of the trenches. '– that is a different matter. No quarter, no prisoners, understood – both sides. As to the rest –' He paused, picking his words with some care. 'We are soldiers. We have our own honour. As to the rest . . . look the other way. Now bring my officers.'

The officers brought, the orta assembled, told that there was to be a huge attack, a vast mine to be exploded, but that the orta was to be in a reserve trench – a noticeable lightening of spirits at that heartening news – and then the familiar march through the Trautson Garden as the cannons' bombardment increased in fury.

Dusk, the sun dipping, blinking a bloody au revoir to Vienna. Fire-flies gleaming in the Trautson Gardens and a thousand sweating men in the assault trenches. Clouds covered the moon and men licked their lips and wondered whether that was good or bad, and, as men about to face battle do, clutching at straws, assured themselves that it was good most assuredly good – a good omen and excellent for surprise. Yes, by Allah, since the Austrians would not see them as they attacked, and surprise was half the battle, was it not?

Beyond the stakes, inside the covered-way, the Austrian infantry were waiting, too, for, contrary to the Janissaries' fond illusions, there was to be no surprise. None at all since, passing through the Transylvanian lines, one Jacob Heider, a servant of Kunitz, had brought the Turkish plan in that very morning, and so, as the Corbacis of the Janissaries shuffled along the trenches, steadying their men, so, the colonels of the Austrian regiments moved along the angles of the covered-way steadying their men;

'Stand by your posts, lads, earn your wages, remember Perchtoldsdorf, you're in good cover' – rapping swords against the stout timbering of the palisades; which was all very well, and all very true except, as Private Brandt of the Scherffenberg Regiment said to Private Perutz, 'It isn't the *verdammt* Turks coming over the stakes that worries me, it's them coming under us.'

Quite right, too, and the prayer on every man's lips was, if the mine goes off, let it go off under somebody else. And not only the infantry of the line were thinking of the mine. The whole of Vienna was too, for the news of the attack had spread across the city and, in a Viennese sort of way, had gained supernatural proportions. It was under the counterscarp, the moat, the Hofburg and, although that did take a certain stretch of imagination, under St. Stephen's, although even Herr Haller was a little sceptical about the Turks digging a tunnel a mile long in nine days. But still, Ottostrasse was not a mile away from the counterscarp, it was, at the most half a mile and the fact that Starhemberg had ordered every cellar to be searched had added fuel to the rumour that Janissaries were liable to pop up everywhere like demon kings throughout the whole of the city; quite enough fuel, anyway, to fire Frau Vogel's imagination for she, with the Hallers whose cellar was permanently flooded, was in the basement, their ears pressed against the stones, and, although Herr Vogel no more believed in the tunnel than he did in fairy godmothers, he had made no objection; the cellar was, in any case, the safest place to be as the Turkish bombardment increased in fury; there was always the chance of a cannon-ball hitting Ottostrasse.

In the meantime, Vogel was happy to get on with his work.

Indeed, he was more than happy, he was proud for that very day, as his company of the militia had been stood down, the Master of the Bakers Guild had taken him by the elbow and led him aside. As Vogel pounded at his dough he felt a flush of pride at what the Master had said to him;

'Herr Vogel, you are a stalwart. Never missed a parade and your bread is as good as any in Vienna. When all this is over, maybe a place on the Guild Council . . .'

The Guild Council! Vogel's heart beat faster at the thought. Never in his life had he considered such a thought. That he, a mere, simple baker could be considered worthy of such an honour! He had, at times, dreamed that Wenzel might become a Council member, but then the plague . . . at the thought of his dead son his pleasure ebbed, drained away. What were earthly rewards, anyway? It was true what the Church said, true happiness was only to be found in Heaven; all else perished, rusted, turned to dust.

He frowned at himself. What was he doing in this melancholy mood? After all, although he did not know a great deal about the Bible there was one text he did know, and approve of. 'Whatsoever your hand finds to do, then do it with all your might.' Yes, a good text, and his hand could make bread. Good bread, not adulterated but good, wholesome bread which would nourish a new generation of Viennese. And then, his thoughts strayed on, then there was Rudi. Who knew what he might become? He shook himself, shaking off his gloom and turned to his work as the door opened and Kaspar came in.

Vogel looked up with real pleasure. Kaspar was another sign of the future. In a year or so, after the marriage, there would be a new generation of – well Hallers, really, but Vogels, too. That was a thought worth thinking about. And Kaspar was a good lad and, like Anna, he had changed during the past months. There was a new confidence about him, a manliness and poise. It was to do with the Turks, Vogel thought, the Turks and war and the siege, because of events and decisions taken by men who were as far above him as the steeple-cock on St. Stephen's.

But the new confidence had not affected Kaspar's manners. 'Excuse me calling this late, Herr Vogel,' he said. 'I've been on duty with the militia and I knew my parents were coming round.'

'Yes,' Vogel poured out two steins of beer, giving Kaspar a special, Bavarian stein, kept, although Kaspar did not know it, particularly for him. 'They're downstairs,' he said, 'In the cellar. All of them.'

Kaspar grinned. 'Most of Vienna seem to be in their cellars.'

'It's rubbish.' Vogel was as emphatic as ever. 'The Turks are men, not moles.'

Kaspar agreed, 'But they are very good at mining, Herr Vogel. A soldier was telling me the other day.'

'That may be so, and I don't deny it.' Vogel drank some beer. 'But they can mine until they are blue in the face. A city like Vienna won't fall easily. And if they ever do break in we'll fight them street by street – yes, and house by house. If that Suleiman the Great or whatever he was couldn't take Vienna then nobody can.'

He stared challengingly at Kaspar who held up his hands in mock surrender. 'I agree, Herr Vogel.'

Vogel laughed, his round face creased with good-humour. 'Aye, and you'll do your part, Kaspar, that's for certain.'

Kaspar smiled back then, a little uncertainly, gestured to the cellar. 'May I . . .'

'Ach!' Vogel smacked him on the shoulder, and, small though Vogel was, and tall though Kaspar was, Kaspar staggered under the blow. 'Go ahead, and you see Anna whenever you like. All that nonsense . . . go on.'

Kaspar disappeared and returned a little later, a little shame-faced. 'It's father,' he mumbled. 'He says that he can hear tapping under the cellar. It's only in his head, of course.'

'Aye?' Vogel would have liked to tap Haller *on* the head, preferably with a mallet. 'He isn't frightening the women, I hope – or Rudi?'

'No. Anna . . . well . . .' Kaspar did not want to give the impression that he was criticising Frau Vogel. '. . . Anna is keeping them all calm, and Rudi is sound asleep. But, Herr Vogel, my father, you know . . .'

'I know, Kaspar,' Vogel said. 'Well, God made us all as it pleased him. He didn't do much when he made me, come to that.'

'No!' Kaspar slung his musket over his shoulder. 'He made a good man, Herr Vogel. A good, kind, *brave* man.'

'Rubbish. Get along with you.' Vogel pushed Kaspar to the door. 'Go on – and take care.'

'And you. Good night.'

Good night, good night, Vogel turned back to his work. It was his night for compliments, that was for sure, but as he mixed yeast with his dough he was aware of a distant mutter like an angry crowd, and a mutter rising in intensity. It took him a moment or two to realise that it was almost dawn and the muttering was the roar of Turkish cannon bombarding the walls of his city.

Chapter Seventeen

THE PALISADES

DAWN; the cocks began to crow, the Turkish bombardment smashed to a climax, the great mine was exploded and the Janissaries charged and were shot to pieces, and the next wave charged and they were shot to pieces too, and a third charge barely got out of the trenches before they fell back and all the canes and swords of the officers could not get them out again.

All that day a bitter, desultory battle was fought in the craters under the palisades, and all that night, and the next day and night too, finally dying away under a drenching downpour.

In his command post in the Palace Bastion Starhemberg blessed the rain. It meant a respite from the hacking fight on the glacis; time to rest men, relieve them, juggle his troops around the city walls and, taking a calculated risk, to strip the other bastions of cannon and place them on the Lobel and Burg Bastions.

A few lights spluttered on the Austrian side of the outer-wall. Starhemberg tugged at his moustache. The Turks had been given a battering – the bodies outside the palisades were six deep – but still, in one place they had broken into the covered way and could not be dislodged. It was not a hold, a mere finger tip hooked over the palisades, but it was a finger-tip which it was proving hard to lop off. Sooner or later the finger would be joined by another, and then another, widening the gap, then the Turks could descend in the moat. . . .

A company of infantry filed through the bastion. Under a

guttering lantern, Starhemberg watched them pass. They looked steady, unshaken. As if reading his thoughts Colonel Mansfeld, whose regiment was being relieved, said, 'Good men, General.'

Starhemberg nodded. They were. He was not an imaginative man, as little given to flights of fancy as Herr Vogel, but he had a feeling that the privates of the infantry were, in some mysterious way, better men than they had been before the siege began. After all, what were they? Peasant lads without land, town boys without work, joining up for three square meals a day, a uniform, a pittance every week, and the alluring prospect of loot, of course. And yet here, on the walls of Vienna, they were transcending themselves, becoming heroes. Yes, that was not too strong a word. Heroes. Not like the heroes of old, of golden antiquity, fighting in single combat on shining sunlit plains, but in the sweltering gloom of the rat-run of the covered-way heroes just the same. And it was as well that they were.

Mansfeld spoke again. Losses. 'Yes.' Starhemberg was aware of the losses. The daily returns of the garrison were on his desk every morning; a steady drain but not a haemorrhage and with eleven thousand men acceptable, although what Mansfeld said next was not so acceptable.

'I'm concerned about the losses among the officers.'

Starhemberg was concerned, too. There was a heavy casualty rate amongst the officers. Of course that was a source of pride, the officers living up to the highest ideals of the Imperial Army, but they could not be replaced. Not that there was anything to be done about that. Private soldiers could not be expected to fight like lions unless their officers led them properly. 'Well,' Mansfeld slapped his thigh. 'Duty. Good night, Sir.'

'Good night.' Salutes, the rattle of muskets as the guard presented arms. Starhemberg strode away, into the Hofburg.

A meeting. The Burgomaster Liebenberg, Count Caplirs, Rimpler, the Bishop Kollonics. Able men dealing briskly with the city's affairs; grain, water, meat, health, money. The Bishop saying with a half smile that the clergy were disturbed that a Turkish cannon-ball had hit St. Stephen's, damaging the organ

and terrifying the congregation. Rimpler smiling back, an eloquent wave of his Italian hand indicating that although he could,
perhaps, stop the Turks crossing the walls he could not stop their
cannon-balls flying through the air. Liebenberg anxiously enquiring if the rumour that the Turks had found their way into the
sewers was true.

It was a query Starhemberg took seriously. The sewers were
ready-made tunnels into Vienna and the emergence of even a
hundred or so Janissaries emerging in the streets like so many
venomous dwarfs could start a panic during which a gate could
be seized and then – goodnight Vienna. Another question from
the Burgomaster, conscious that when it came to discussing
Imperial affairs a mere burgher, no matter how rich and powerful
in his own right, was guilty of presumption, but nonetheless
enquiring whether, perhaps, there was any news from the
Emperor at Linz.

Caplirs answered; reassuring, help was certainly on the way,
the Saxons and the Bavarians were preparing an army, and the
Franconians, and the King of Poland was about to move from
Warsaw to Cracow to join his army.

A thoughtful silence. Cracow. An eight days journey for one
man mounted on a good horse. How long would it take an entire
army to cover the same distance in reverse, as it were?

Caplirs coughed. 'I am sure that the city will be delighted to
know that the Empress is well and expects her child next month.'

Another thoughtful silence. The health of the Empress,
although, of course a matter of great importance, not being
exactly the most pressing concern of Vienna.

However, 'God be thanked,' said Liebenberg. He dared a last
question. 'Er, can we, ah, expect further Turkish attacks?'

Starhemberg looked coldly at the Burgomaster. 'Yes,' he said. 'I
think we can expect those. That is why they are here.'

The meeting ended as the clock in the Hofburg struck mid-
night, and as the last stroke tolled, the *Serdengceti* filed into the
Turkish assault trenches.

The Serdengceti. Many had heard of them but few had ever

seen them. But they were to be seen now. One thousand of them, standing in the assault trenches like sleepwalkers, rapt, visionary, far from normal human experience; the Serdengceti, literally 'men who had given their heads', given them already to Allah; a suicide squad, volunteers for Paradise, waiting for the dawn, and for the dawn of a new and immortal life.

Vienna slept. Nervous militia men stood guard over the sewers, jumping at shadows, the guard was changed along the gates, the bells tolled and clanked, homeless refugees slept fitfully in dark corners, some of them dying of amoebic dysentery, the rain stopped, a sickly yellow dawn light crept over the eastern horizon, the Turkish cannon began blasting away and, as the birds began their chorus, the Lagunci exploded a new mine. There was a noise like distant thunder, a fountain of muddy earth rose opposite the Burg Bastion and as the last clods fell to earth, screaming 'Ya Islam!' the Serdengceti charged.

In the dark slot of Ottostrasse the windows rattled in Herr Vogel's bakery. Juggling with a hot loaf Vogel paused momentarily, his head cocked. With a mild oath he dropped the loaf and blew on his scorched fingers. He poked his head through the window. There was the familiar barking of the cannon, the splintering crash of cannon-balls on masonry, musketry banging, the crackle of grenades . . . he shook his head, crossed himself, turned and saw his wife in the bakery, still dressed in her nightgown.

'They've started again,' Frau Vogel said. 'It's another attack, isn't it?'

'Sounds like it.' Just as there was none of the old querulousness in Frau Vogel's voice, there was none of the old testiness in Vogel's answer, merely a kind of resignation. Awkwardly he patted his wife's plump shoulder. 'Better get dressed, hey? The customers will be coming soon.'

'Yes,' Frau Vogel went to the door then halted. 'God damn them,' she said. 'God rot them. God curse them to Hell and beyond.'

The first customers came in; the first orders, and the first news, six rolls for Frau Schneider and the Turks had exploded another mine. Two loaves and four rolls for Frau Kappel and there was hand to hand fighting in the covered-way. Eight loaves and twenty rolls for Frau Breitner – extra rations for her since she had three soldiers from Count Neuburg's regiment quartered on her – and General Starhemberg's own cousin, Count Guido was badly wounded, another eight loaves for Frau Theinemann – two soldiers in her house – and Signor Rimpler had been killed . . .

Vogel sweated away, shaking his head in simple wonder. How like an ordinary day it was; the simple routine, baking, serving, and yet instead of the normal neighbourhood gossip there was this litany of battle taking place not a quarter of a mile away where good Austrian men, good Catholics, loyal to the Emperor were being killed, butchered, by . . . by . . . he could not even bring himself to name them.

'God rot them' he shouted, smashing his fist into a mound of dough. 'God rot them and send them to deepest Hell.'

And, according to your point of view, that was where many of the Serdengceti had been despatched in the hours since the attack had begun. They had charged through the welter of mud, into yet another crater, and been met by a wall of fire from the Austrian infantry, quite unshaken by screams; and so, contrary to Herr Vogel's belief, it was the Serdengceti who were being butchered, slaughtered in the mud, still shouting defiance and calling on Allah to witness their sacrifice.

But the gap in the covered-way was a little wider, another finger tip was hooked into the defences, and in the morass the Lagunci were already fortifying the lip of the crater, a new mine shaft was being driven forward, and behind them more Janissaries were ploughing through the blood-soaked rat holes of the glacis. Among them the Twenty-eighth Orta. Corbaci Vasif commanding.

The attack went on all day and half the night and then spluttered out and all the exhortations of the imams, bravely moving into the front line, and all the thunder of the war-drums of the Janissaries, pounding in the rear, could not move the Turkish infantry forward again, and the Aga of the Janissaries called off the battle, pulling back the fighting ortas and replacing them with fresh troops, although the Serdengceti stayed where they were.

Away from the blood, in his silken pavilion, Kara Mustafa glared at his Agas. 'Failed?' he spat. 'Failed!'

The Aga of the Janissaries placed his finger-tips together. 'Not failed, Serasker. We are into the covered-way.'

'The covered-way!' Mustafa's voice was dangerously thick. 'We should have been in the city by now.'

The Aga shrugged in a subtle, Turkish way which made the shrug seem respectful, even deferential. 'Sieges are protracted affairs, Excellency. After all,' he looked up almost slyly. 'It is not like Yusha at Jericho.'

'Jericho?'

'It is in the Book, Serasker. The Israelites blew trumpets outside Jericho and the walls fell down. However, in these times . . .' The Aga sighed as if regretting a laxer age where miracles did not occur – at least outside Vienna. 'Artillery,' he sighed.

Mustafa struck the table. 'The artillery is adequate. I wish to hear no more about it. No more.' He swung around to the Aga of the Lagunci. 'And the mines. Useless!'

The Lagunci touched his breast. 'Serasker, mining is not exact knowledge like astronomy or algebra. We have to feel our way, find the exact consistency of the soil, estimate the correct angle of the shafts, and have good powder – which we do not have –'

Mustafa cut him off sourly. 'More excuses.'

'With the utmost respect, Serasker, not excuses, reasons. And we are learning. The next mines –'

'The next?'

'We are digging now, Serasker. Very best officers . . . very best men . . . personally inspect the gunpowder . . .'

Mustafa waved a moody hand. 'How long?'

'Four, five days, Serasker. A week perhaps.'

'A week!'

'Yes. But as your excellency has often told us, we have plenty of time. We have, do we not?'

Mustafa stared coldly at the Aga but his face was bland, with no trace of mockery. 'Yes,' he said. 'We have plenty of time. Dismiss.'

Ceremoniously, the Agas backed away, leaving their baleful master to stare, savagely, at Vienna and the mocking finger of St. Stephen's, rising above the walls. Like an angry bull, Mustafa's head went down; his implacable will against Vienna's indomitable spirit. Well the Giaours would see.

Accompanied by a train of respectful clerks the camp's Master of Ceremonies approached with the War Diary; flowery rhetoric, inflated claims, praise for the wisdom and omniscience of the Serasker. Mustafa struck it away – instant cringing, bowing, tremors of fear, and, all who could, discreetly moving out of sight as Mustafa stamped into his tent as new troops marched passed the Green Standard, and towards the mutter of the guns.

Lounging by a bivouac, the Twenty-eighth Orta, forty men down, now, watched the new troops go forward with a kind of murderous sympathy.

'Not far to go, wayfarers,' Tedeki bawled with sardonic sympathy. 'Only a thousand paces to Paradise.'

He got a warning nudge in the ribs from Janissary Ghazi, hammered him back with a massive elbow, and looked up into the eyes of an immaculate Odabasi.

The Odabasi had a slender cane which he flicked against his thigh. 'Did I hear you speak, Janissary?' he asked.

Tedeki scratched his groin. 'Why,' he said, 'You might have done. I was encouraging the brothers there.'

'Encouraging?' the cane flicked against a silken thigh.

'That's right. Our Corbaci tells us to do it, encourage the troops. Look forward to Paradise, and all that. Doesn't he?' Tedeki looked around the orta with an air of innocence.

'I see.' The Odabasi nodded. 'Tell me, Janissary. 'How would you *discourage* men?'

'Discourage!' Tedeki scratched himself again vigorously, too vigorously perhaps. 'I wouldn't even know how to do that, *Bey.*'

The cane stopped its ominous flicking. 'Don't call me Bey. You know better than that, don't you?'

Tedeki rolled his eyes. 'Well, Cdabasi, I don't know much, that's for sure. One foot in front of the other and don't ask questions, that's my motto. But I do know one thing.'

'And what might that be?'

'Why,' Tedeki rolled on his side in the sodden, filthy grass. 'Why, if I ever *did* want to discourage a comrade – not that I ever would, of course, but if Shaitan ever put it into my head to do that, which God forbid, then if I saw a nice clean soldier who'd spent the last ten days on easy guard duty then I might – I might show him this, see.' He opened his blouse. 'That might discourage them, hey, Odabasi?'

For a moment the Odabasi stared at the long festering sword slash across Tedeki's chest, then, without a word, strode away.

Janissary Tavasi grinned at Tedeki. 'He'll report you to the Corbaci and then –' he flicked the sole of his foot.

'Maybe.' Tedeki heaved himself to his feet. 'If he ever gets back from there –' jabbing his thumb towards the killing ground –' and if he remembers, and if the Corbaci has nothing better to do than listen to him. Anyway, it's true, isn't it? That is the way to Paradise.'

Unanswerable, certainly the Trautson Gardens led to Paradise, but did it also lead to Vienna? That was the thought running through Timur's head later in the day as, standing at a respectful distance, he listened to Vasif talking with his officers. Odabasi Osman concerned about the state of the men's clothing, Odabasi Maghrebi worried about the number of men down with disease – dysentery mainly – more men down with that than wounds and six dead with it – Vasif, spitting with anger ordering the bastinado for any man found not using a latrine – and finally dismissing the officers with the casual remark that the orta was to be lined up in marching order one hour before dusk.

Osman's jaw dropped. 'We're going in the line again?'

Vasif's gun-barrel eyes focussed on his Odabasi. 'Did you have other plans for the night?' he asked.

'But . . .' Osman spread his hands. 'But Corbaci, we've only just come out of the line.'

'So?'

Osman shrugged. 'The men –'

'The men?' Vasif sounded as surprised as if Osman had said goats or donkeys. 'What have they to do with it?'

To his credit, Osman held his ground. 'Five nights non-stop, Corbaci –'

Vasif clicked his fingers. 'It is nothing to them if we do five years. Dismiss.'

Sombre-faced the officers left. 'Coffee,' Vasif snapped, and turned to his paper work. Timur squatted in a corner of the tent and blew life into the charcoal under Vasif's urn, made cofee, gave it to his Corbaci and was graciously given permission to have one himself. From a corner of the tent, Timur watched Vasif going meticulously through the orta's rolls, so many dead, ticked off – so many wounded, ticked off – so many missing; Janissaries Misri, Nedim, Yunus, Emre –' Vasif's brush halted there for a moment, a real loss, a good Muslim, made a tick, carried on . . .

The Corbaci was a strange man, Vasif thought. For instance just now, he had not told his officers that tonight would be the last time in the trenches for a time because the orta was to be relieved and sent to the north-east of the city. Timur knew that to be so because he had heard the Aga of the Janissaries tell Vasif that morning. A word about that and every man in the orta would have felt better and yet Vasif had kept silent. Yes, a flint-like man, apparently indifferent to suffering or death, propped up by his simple creed; absolute faith in Islam and absolute fidelity to his duty. But suppose that faith and loyalty were not enough? Suppose . . . Timur hardly knew what he supposed and so he drank his coffee having learned one truth about soldiering anyway; take your pleasures when you can and don't think about / what might come next; which was just as well for his peace of mind that drowsy afternoon for at dusk, as the orta sullenly trudged up to the assault trenches the menacing palisades looked different; silhouetted against the sky they had blobs on them, round blobs, like melons.

Some fiendish Christian magic to kill poor Muslims, Timur thought as he slipped and slithered through mud and ordure. It was not until they were in the trench itself that he realized that the melons were heads, Janissaries' heads, impaled, grinning down, and that one of them had belonged to Janissary Emre.

Chapter Eighteen

THE COVERED-WAY

THE Turkish heads grinned down on the murderous lunatic asylum of the glacis. In the covered-way savage, merciless fights took place as the Janissaries stabbed and hacked at the barricades in a desperate attempt to extend their hold on the covered-way, and, beneath the ground the Lagunci drove mine shaft after mine shaft under the counterscarp. Orta after orta was marched forward and thrown into the inferno and, little by little, yard by yard, inch by inch, the city's outer defences were broken down and, as the Sayf al-Islam probed closer to the jugular vein, the Turkish stranglehold was tightened inexorably. Muslim officers were filtered into the suspect vassal armies of Transylvania and Hungary, the patrols of Sipahi sealed off any possible escape routes from Vienna to the outside world.

All day and every day the Turkish bands played wildly and triumphantly outside the Trautson Gardens and Starhemberg ordered his regimental bands to play defiantly back, but for all the brave show the city began a slow slide into squalor and hardship. Rubbish accumulated in the alleyways, filth piled up from the blocked sewers, rats squeaked in the streets and great bloated flies found their way into every house, spreading the gut-draining dysentery. The graveyards were filling up and in the Passerhof hospital the sick and the dying were lying side by side on the floor.

And as the Ottoman grip tightened outside the city, Starhem-

berg tightened his grip inside it. The *Hofbefreiten*, the court servants and officials, were armed, bodies twisted on the gallows on
the Burgplatz – suspected spies or traitors – soldiers were shot for
cowardice and, most ominously of all, the bells of Vienna were
silenced. Only the great bell of St. Stephen's was to be tolled if the
Turks broke into the city.

Across the Danube, in the Vienna woods, the Duke of Lorraine
and his cavalry watched the silent city. It was hard to believe,
Lorraine thought, that he could find out so little about a city not
ten miles away. Occasionally a messenger did get through,
volunteers, disguised as Turks, the garrulous man called
Kolstchitzki, for instance, the other man Seradly, but in any case
they brought little news that was not obvious to any man with
eyes in his head. As far as Lorraine was concerned Vienna might
as well have been on the moon. And he had his own problems,
not least of which was his own daily conference.

Eleven in the morning on the twenty-seventh of July in the
nineteenth day of the siege; Lorraine in his tent, his senior officers
with him, and foreign faces, observers from Saxony and Bavaria,
and a Polish colonel with an unpronounceable name but an
impressive title, dressed in an improbable uniform.

Lorraine sketched in a broad picture; Vienna, of course, still
holding out, the Tartars, alas, roaming the south bank of the
Danube as far as Amstetten, fifty miles to the north, Gyor still
holding out, and Komarom, and the great monastery of Klosterneuburg – which would be an all-important forward base for the
relief of Vienna, but gloomier news from the west where Thokoly
and his rebels were threatening Pressburg, the peasants sullen
and rebellious, sacrilegiously cursing the Church and the priest-
hood for the disasters which they – wrongly, of course, he
hastened to add – had brought upon them and, regretfully, many
towns in Moravia treacherously surrendering to the rebels.

'And what orders from the Emperor?' Herman of Baden,
important, President of the Imperial War Council and, as Lorraine knew very well, despising him for not standing firm at Gyor
before the great retreat.

'No . . . no aggressive orders, Excellency.'

'But –' the Pole, speaking bad German but emphatic for all that. 'Why don't we go attack Turks – zit! Smash them. Hey? Why we not do that? Many men here. Why not Emperor say that?'

Lorraine was not disposed to discuss his Emperor's plans with a Pole with an implausible title but diplomacy demanded an answer, quite apart from the fact that the Pole was an observer for Count Lubomirski who, with three thousand light cavalry was defending his left flank on the River Vah.

'The point is, your . . . your Excellency, the Emperor is organising help from the German states in the Empire. This aid is certainly coming. *Certainly*,' he stressed, as much to reassure himself as the Pole, 'And of course, your own King will be on his way soon. He will, will he not?'

'Ja, most soon. Without doubts.' The Pole spoke as if John Sobieski was about to burst into the camp in the next ten minutes. 'But why not hit Turkishmen now? Big slashing raid. Hey?'

Lorraine suppressed a sigh. Speaking slowly and patiently he said, 'We would find it difficult to cross the Danube, Excellency, and besides, the Emperor thinks it important that we inflict a *crushing* defeat on the Turks. Crushing, and we really need more than cavalry for that. We need infantry and artillery, and when our allies arrive we will certainly have real force. I think that you will understand that – as an experienced soldier,' he added, although as far as he knew the Pole might have spent his life in a monastery.

The Pole nodded, leaned forward, his moustaches bristling. 'Ja, ja. But Duke, what happen if Turkishmen catch Vienna first, hey?'

Ah, what indeed, Lorraine thought, what indeed. However it was important not to show pessimism, especially before the Saxons and Bavarians who had pricked up their ears at the mere suggestion that Vienna might fall. He leaned back, casual in his old grey uniform. 'There is no question of that,' he said firmly. He paused, picking his next words carefully. It was important not to give the allies the impression that Vienna might fall quickly, otherwise their masters might think again about coming to its aid. On the other hand it was equally important to give them a proper sense of urgency that the ever-to-be-damned Turks might capture it. It was, he reflected, not easy being a General. 'I think,' he said, 'I think that I can safely say that Vienna will hold out until we have collected an army which will destroy the Turkish threat for ever. Thank you, gentlemen, and now the Margrave and myself must . . .'

The officers left and Lorraine and Baden put their mutually dissatisfied and discontented heads together to compose a dispatch to their Emperor and to discuss the real, and deadly threat of Thokoly and his rebel Magyars.

The dispatch arrived in Passau the next day and was in the Emperor's hands within hours. He read it carefully and added it to the vast mound of correspondence he had already dealt with that day; letters from Dresden, Munich, Berlin, Warsaw, Madrid, Amsterdam: memoranda from the Exchequer, the Chancery, the Imperial War Council, all scrupulously attended to; then a Solemn Mass, a solemn dinner, a solemn meeting with the Minister of Finance, and a solemn meeting with the Empress, who had a complaint.

'The Countess Von Eckenburg *must* be found better accommodation. She is living in a common tavern. There are soldiers living there, ensigns and sergeants. It is quite intolerable.'

'Yes,' Leopold answered with his invariable courtesy. 'I will mention it but the town is pressed for space.'

An understatement. The little town, pressed between hills and river, was jammed to the last inch with the huge impedimenta of Government which had followed the Emperor in his flight from Vienna, not to mention the vast train of hangers-on who had struggled there. Indeed the Countess Von Eckenburg, whoever she might be, and Leopold had no idea, was lucky to have a room at all.

The Countess disposed of, the Empress moved on to other matters. 'What news from the city?'

'Still holding out, by God's Grace.'

'Amen. And the Circles?'

Leopold's face brightened. From the complex tangle a pattern was appearing. Saxony, Franconia, and Bavaria were making encouraging noises and it was likely that fifty thousand good troops would be available.

'And when will they come?'

Leopold sighed. That was quite another matter. Armies had to be brought together, equipped, fed – and paid, for whatever ties of loyalty and self-interest might, in the end, pull the troops to Vienna one thing was certain; all the kings, princes, electors and dukes were firm on one thing; a down payment, in cash.

'Money.' The Empress was disdainful. 'I thought that the Holy Father was giving you enough.'

'He is,' Leopold agreed. 'But even the Pope has to collect money, borrow it, secure letters of credit . . .'

Leopold had a speculative mind; he was interested in how far away Heaven was, how many angels lived there, and, as he was a music-lover himself, what angelic music was like; and he was interested in politics; in France and Holland, Italy and Spain, for his Empire depended on that interest, and he was extremely interested in money although his grasp on higher finance was as slender as his knowledge of Heaven. These letters of credit, for instance. What were they? Men did not meet and hand over bags of golden thalers to each other, instead these mysterious letters were sent around Europe and, even more mysteriously, other men honoured them, usually, Leopold shuddered a little, usually men in the heretical cities of Amsterdam and London and Geneva.

How strange it all was, Leopold thought, such a complex web, the Circles of the Empire, the Pope in Rome, the far cities of northern Europe, men from Scotland to Baghdad, all orbiting Vienna in circles within circles within circles . . .

His eyes were closing and he pulled himself awake. It would

never do to be discourteous before the Empress and besides there was work to do.

'Work?' The Empress was sharp.

'Yes, my dear. I have my duty.'

'Of course.' The Empress, too, would never deny the call of duty, especially as the duty was the preservation of the Houses of the Habsburgs and Pfalz-Neuburg.

As he left the room Leopold paused. 'It is not all bad news, you know. The Turks have their problems, too. They are short of food and their supply train is vulnerable. If God gives us time then Kara Mustafa may find that he has put his head into a noose.'

'God will give us time,' The Empress said. 'We can be sure of that.'

The Emperor returned to his desk and wrote through the night, giving special instructions to his Governors to take strict measures, including death, to those wicked peasants who, in the grip of the Devil, were attacking priests, but he did not feel tired. God was with him, giving him strength and guiding his hand and his pen. Besides which, he was rather pleased with his remark about Kara Mustafa putting his head into a noose. He did not often make witty remarks and now he wished that he had added another. He could have said that the Polish army would be the knot on the noose. Yes, he wished he had said that and, come to think of it, he would like to say it to King John Sobieski himself. He laid down his pen, took a sip of wine, and wondered what Sobieski was doing at that moment.

In fact, John Sobieski, King John the Third, having had a huge dinner, was having a huge glass of good wine and listening, patiently, to Leopold's envoy who was urging, with all the powers of persuasion at his command, the need for the King to hasten to Vienna.

'Yes,' Sobieski, massive, fleshly, a huge moustache under an aquiline nose, fine flashing eyes, the very model of a king, Sobieski raised a massive, kingly hand. 'Yes, yes, believe me, I understand the need for haste. But there is no point in going to Vienna without an army, a strong army –' He raised his hand again as the Austrian envoy opened his mouth. '– And you must understand that raising an army in Poland is not easy. The distances alone . . .' He sighed, the length of his sigh echoing, as it were, the length of Polish leagues.

The envoy nodded politely. 'Of course, your Majesty. But would it not be possible to move with the forces you do have? Merely the news that you were moving, *you* Sire, would have an enormous effect.'

'Yes it would,' Sobieski said frankly, modesty not being his prime virtue. 'But the essence of the matter is to defeat the Turks utterly. Is that not so?'

'Yes, indeed but –'

The hand again. 'I must wait for the complete union of all my forces. My regular army has to arrive from the south-east. As a soldier, the Duke of Lorraine will agree that there is no substitute for trained troops.'

The envoy was sure that the Duke understood that. He was also sure that the Duke knew perfectly well that Sobieski had no intention of moving unless his force was the largest of the relieving forces. The envoy himself understood it and, indeed, found it quite proper. Kings, even if only elected kings, had to show themselves with proper pomp and power. That, after all, was the whole point of kingship.

The envoy received an affable wave of dismissal and retired, and Sobieski retired also to his bed-chamber and his wife, Queen Maria.

A loving wife, devoted to her husband and her own large family, and determined that they should share in the glory her husband would gain by delivering Vienna and knowing, as well as Sobieski did, that it would never do for one of his generals to get there first and, perhaps, gain that glory for himself.

'And so?' asked Queen Maria.

'And so.' A royal yawn on an heroic scale. 'And so tomorrow we enter Cracow.'

Chapter Nineteen

THE KING

ANOTHER sunrise and in Cracow, that city of marvels, Stefan Zabruski finding another marvel; that other people believed that the earth went around the sun, and not only dirty Jews, oily Italians, sneering French, treacherous Lithuanians, and stuffed Austrians – Stefan had a derogatory adjective for all foreigners – but Poles. Poles of the blood who could trace, or thought that they could trace, their ancestors back for nine hundred years; and even more marvellous, one of them was Vera Soprona.

Stefan had discovered this when he had told Vera the story of Nathan ben Israel, the pedlar and to his utter amazement had heard her answer; 'Ah, les Juifs sont tellement savants, même ceux des regions sauvages,' which, so far as he could understand her, meant that Jews were always knowledgeable, even those from savage regions, which, as Stefan himself came from the same region was hardly complimentary.

Stefan had laughed feebly and lied that he had amazed Pyotr Chelmnitz by saying the very same thing and his face burned again. He seemed to be forever lying to Vera and the more he lied the more he relapsed into a foolish boastfulness, and he suspected that Vera knew this perfectly well and was laughing at him.

But on this sultry day, the twenty-ninth of July in the year of our Lord 1683, there was to be another marvel to take his mind off

his foolishness, for the King himself, with all pomp and cere-
mony, was to enter the city and there was to be a parade or, as the
sophisticates of the city called it in their affected French, a
manoeuvre, nothing too serious, of course, nothing in the nature
of a *drill* – that was the business of the paid soldiers. No, this was
to be a mixture of carnival and pageantry, a ceremonial display of
the armed might of Poland's chivalry.

The parade was to take place early, in the relative cool of the
morning, and by nine Cracow was suffering a traffic jam as the
entire population turned out to see the King.

Sweat, curses, blows and confusion, carriages which had lost a
wheel, baulky horses, despised merchants and labourers being
whipped out of the way, the church bells ringing, and then the
plain where Chelmnitz was waiting in a cart with the precious
Zabruski armour.

To his intense, bitter disappointment, Stefan was not to take
part in the parade, 'Men only', Zabruski had grunted, but
Stefan's disappointment faded as he saw his father mounted on
his war horse. A transformation; Zabruski's squat shape changed
utterly, the death-like helmet, mailed shirt, steel shield flashing
like the sun itself, sabre, lance, battle hammer, menacing and
inhuman, cantering past the line of carriages, dipping lances in
salute. But even the schlactas were dwarfed into insignificance as
the great nobles appeared, lords of forest and steppe, men and
beast, in full armour from head to knee, vast helms, glittering
engraved steel, panther skins on their backs, eagles wings on
their shoulders, the Virgin on their breast plates, lances nineteen
feet long, gigantic horses, trotting across the plain to the sound of
trumpets and drums. Giants, and if Zabruski looked inhuman in
his armour, these looked superhuman, divine beings from
another world, as if their splendour and might, drawn from the
labour of thousands of serfs, justified that labour and made it
right that multitudes should toil for them.

And then the King. Not in armour but robes of state, gold and
silver, a white horse, the gleaming apex of the vast pyramid of
society, himself dazzling, elected but a king, and kingly in his

kingdom, not disappointing even Stefan whose ideas of kings were somewhat confused with pictures of God in heaven and the Archangel Gabriel.

There was another procession, petty gentry, poorer even than the Zabruskis, not even land-owners in their own right, well enough mounted, but without the divinity of armour and armed at best with a sabre, a pistol or two, perhaps a musket, but no one was interested in them. There was perfunctory applause but already the carriages were wheeling around, heading for the city or to country houses, to huge celebratory lunches to be munched through the torrid afternoon.

The Zabruskis had been invited to dine with the Sopronas at their house, ramshackle but rambling and with many servants, an army of idlers it seemed to Stefan as he gave the reins of his horse to one of a horde of ostlers, went through the front door guarded by *two* footmen, had his riding boots polished by a half-drunk boy, and took a glass of wine from a slatternly maid.

The lunch was informal, a *buffet* as the French called it, a wandering, casual meal with innumerable guests. Once, Stefan would have been overwhelmed by such numbers but three months in Cracow had given him a certain amount of poise which he could demonstrate, as when he bowed over Madame Soprona, fat and amiable, kissing her ringed fingers and murmuring, 'enchanté' although the treacherous red invaded his face as she tapped his ear with her fan and said, 'Get along with you, Stefan. You're turning into a regular messieur.'

Stefan wandered from room to room, through the odours of pickles and strawberries, bowing and nodding, looking for Vera, and wandering into a room where his father and Soprona were sitting at a table, drinking hard.

Stefan backed away but was waved in by Soprona. Stefan sat on a divan, took another glass of wine from a shock-headed servant, stretched out his long legs, and listened to the men. The usual talk; of Lubomirski and the cavalry in Austria, how much he was getting – or at least was owed – by the Emperor, the regular army nearly at Cracow, the King wanting to bring cossacks from Zaporozhye . . . Stefan listened idly, his mind on the King and Vera, looking over his glass, catching Soprona's eye and being given a friendly nod and smile.

Stefan smiled diffidently back. Ever since the night of the disastrous ball Soprona had been friendly to him. True, Soprona was not a romantic figure with his hard, shrewd head full of calculations about money, but he had gone out of his way to show small kindnesses to Stefan, giving him a fine Tartar bridle for his horse, and inviting him to stay on the Soprona estate for the winter when the coming campaign was over.

And there was another curious thing – not that Stefan thought the friendliness was curious he was young enough to find that perfectly natural – but more than once Stefan had come across his father and Soprona talking together but, as he approached them, breaking off in an artificial manner. Stefan had an uneasy feeling that he was breaking some mysterious adult code and, in his worst moments, wondered whether they were plotting to leave him behind when the army marched on Vienna although, like the more exalted Leopold, Stefan wondered if it ever would.

Playing cards flipped on the table; already the luncheon was turning into a long, vague, Polish party. Stefan left the room, a process he still found difficult, and strolled through the house. Friends took him by the elbow, talking of the King, the parade, the barbarous Turks, and their own barbarous dreams of glory and blood – other people's blood of course. Normally, Stefan would have been only too glad to join in such talk but over the shoulders of his companions he could see into a drawing room and there, with her mother and a dozen aunts, was Vera Soprona.

But even the new, poised, Stefan was not equal to entering a room under the eyes of the Soprona females; however, there was a verandah and Stefan eased onto it, alone with dreams of bliss and yet able to watch Vera through the tall windows.

Somewhere in the house a serf was playing a balalaika, a long, dreamy melody; the air was heavy with the scent of geraniums and Stefan was heady with the wine and then, as silently as a butterfly, Vera arrived beside him, a posy of marigolds in her white hands.

'Ah, Stefan,' Vera said, 'So you have seen the King.'

'Yes,' Stefan's face as red as the geraniums.

'Did you ever see such a sight?'

Although to impress Vera, Stefan would have been quite ready to say that he had seen pigs flying, he had to admit that he had never, truly, seen such a sight.

'And the nobles,' Vera said, 'Such magnificence.'

'Yes,' Magnificence indeed, Stefan was still blinded by the sight.

'But your father looked splendid, too, Stefan.'

'And so did yours,' Stefan being gallant.

'But the others,' Vera laughed. 'Like pedlars were they not?'

Stefan laughed vigorously, the more so since the gap between the others and his father was so marginal. But, remembering that when the campaign began he would have a horde of uncles and cousins who would be mounted and armed like them, he added, loyally, 'Of course, they are very useful.'

'Useful?' Vera's eyes opened wide. 'In what way, Stefan?'

'Why,' Stefan leaned nonchalantly on the verandah rail. 'Scouting, you know. They find out where the enemy is so that we can charge and smash them.'

'We?' Vera's eyes opened even wider.

'Yes.' Stefan grabbed a glass of wine from a passing servant, stood up as straight as he could and said, sternly, 'The nobles and the schlactas.'

'Ah,' rapt admiration in Vera's voice. 'You are so clever, Stefan.'

Clever! That word, coming from Vera's lips was more melodious to Stefan than any balalaika.

'And brave!' Vera said.

Clever and brave! The words, the wine, the musk of roses and geraniums, and Vera's presence made Stefan's head swim. He did feel clever and brave at that moment. 'Tak!' he said. 'Yes, we learn some things in Ostrova. Yes, and we teach things too. Ask our enemies. Ask them what we teach. And we'll teach the Turks a thing or two at Vienna. I drink to that!' He took a swig of wine and then, recklessly, he raised his glass again. 'And I drink to you, Vera Soprona!'

He drained the glass and, recklessness turning to lunacy, he cried, 'And no one else will ever drink from this glass!' which he hurled into the garden where, alas for romance, and to his utter confusion it bounced harmlessly among the geraniums and, unbroken glinted at him like the sharp and malicious eye of a practical joker.

Stefan stared down in disbelief and then attempted clumsily to climb over the verandah rail only to find his blouse being grasped and himself being hauled back by Madame Soprona.

'That's enough, Stefan.' Madame Soprona's voice had the authority of maturity, and her grasp had the firmness of fifteen stones of formidable flesh.

'The glass,' Stefan mumbled. 'Got to break the glass . . . honour . . .'

'Ah, the glass.' Suppressed laughter in Madame Soprona's voice. 'It's lucky it didn't break. Didn't you know that, Stefan?'

'Lucky?' Stefan blinked.

'Yes. Now go along, a little walk . . .'

Other arms took Stefan by the elbows, friends, a grinning serf, a walk in the garden. Stefan's head clearing as dusk stole in. Lights in the house, a woman's clear voice singing, then time to go home. Farewells, as if none would ever meet again, although they all would the next day and, as Stefan left, Vera darting from the shadows and holding up the cursed, abominable, unbroken glass.

'I will keep it for ever, Stefan,' she cried, and then was gone.

The next day Zabruski sent for Stefan. Chelmnitz brought the message. 'And Pan Soprona is with him,' he added.

'Oh.' Stefan swallowed nervously, thinking of his reckless utterances the previous day. 'Is my father . . . is he . . . ?'

Chelmnitz turned his hand over, this way, that way. 'You know the master.'

'Yes.' Stefan knew his father and his volcanic temper only too well. But there was no escape. He took a deep breath and went into the house. His father was there, bristling behind a table and, lounging in an armchair, was Soprona.

'Father,' Stefan stood before the table, glancing nervously at Soprona who stared impassively back.

Zabruski grunted and waved a meaty hand at Soprona. Stefan made out a few words. 'Land . . . money . . . Vera . . .'

'Vera?' Stefan was bewildered.

'Yes, Vera.' Zabruski scowled. 'Are you stupid? You like her, don't you?'

'Like her?' Stefan who would, or thought he would, have cut out his heart for one kiss from Vera, gave a ghastly smile. 'Er, yes. Yes,' then, remembering his manners, and thinking French was the appropriate language of courtliness, he turned to Soprona and said, 'Votre fille cette une grosse dame,' Whereon, to his amazement, Soprona burst out laughing.

'Stick to Polish Stefan,' Soprona said. 'You've suggested that Vera is a heavyweight. Her mother is but she isn't, hey?'

'No Sir. I didn't mean – I mean I did mean . . .' lost in confusion Stefan gave up.'

'All right, lad.' Soprona grinned. 'Put him out of his misery, Zabruski.'

'Tak.' Zabruski grunted, nodded. 'You and Vera are going to get married.'

Married! After a mile long, wild gallop, Stefan lay on his back in a cherry orchard. He was to be married – and to Vera. The rich, red cherries hung over him in heavy clusters and beyond them the sky arched, vast and dazzling blue, but whatever incomprehensible happenings took place among that heavenly vista they were not, could not, be more incomprehensible or baffling than the news that Zabruski had barked at him. To be married! Not, of course at once, not next month, or even next year, but eventually, in the future. Elucidating Zabruski's barking, Soprona had made it clear; a convenient marriage, estates being brought together, within the great clan of the Lubomirski's the sub clans of the Zabruskis and Sopronas joining and, who knew, perhaps becoming a new clan to rival the greater tribe of which they were a part. And why not? It had happened before, and since Stefan and Vera liked each other it could happen again. Not that it would have mattered too much had Stefan and Vera not liked each other, such whims could not be allowed to decide the fate of property or the destinies of families.

But that was not on Stefan's mind as he lay underneath the cherry trees. He was dreaming of Vera, and of Vienna, for he was going there after all, following his father and his King into the crucible of war, to be refined, tested, the dross burned from him, and to return a fit son of Zabruski, and a fit husband for Vera.

Chapter Twenty

THE GOLDEN EAGLE

HERR Vogel was sitting in the Golden Eagle drinking a stein of beer and listening to Herr Haller who was saying that if God was just, and assuredly He was, and if Herr Vogel was clear-headed, which assuredly *he* was, then one of them, Vogel was not clear which, would ensure that the Hallers would get extra bread, which, while Vogel was not prepared to pre-empt the decisions of the Almighty, he was determed that they would not get.

'No.' he said.

Haller looked regretfully at the stein he had just bought Vogel. 'But we're family,' he said.

'Not yet,' Vogel said firmly.

'Well!' Haller shook his head. 'You mean to sit there and say that you won't let us have a little extra bread?'

'That's right.'

'But think of Kaspar,' Haller said. 'He's risking his life on the walls.'

'He gets extra,' Vogel said.

'I see.' Haller stood up and stalked to the door. 'I only hope that you never need a favour off me,' he said, bitterly, and went out.

Herr Seligmann, the innkeeper leaned over the counter. 'He doesn't look too happy, Jakob.' he said.

Vogel shrugged. 'What a man. Do you know what he's been doing? Standing on the Newgate so that the Turks shoot arrows at him! Then he sells them as souvenirs!'

Seligmann grinned. 'I've heard about it. Mark you, he's not the only one. The troops do it, too.'

Vogel shook his head. It's unbelievable what people will do.'

'Ah, Jakob,' the innkeeper shook *his* head. 'When you've been keeping an inn as long as I have nothing anyone does could surprise you. Mind you, if you'll excuse me saying so, I'm a bit surprised seeing you in here at this time of the day.'

'I can't sleep,' Vogel said.

'The noise keep you awake?'

'No.' Vogel drained his stein. 'It's the silence. The bells I mean. It's funny, really. I've lived in this city all my life and I can't remember a day without hearing the bells. And now they've all stopped. Who would have ever thought that? And who would have ever thought that I'd be rationing bread?' He sighed. 'It's not easy being a baker, these days.'

'I know what you mean.' Seligmann idly wiped the counter. It's the same with everything isn't it? Meat short, fish, vegetables . . . in fact it could happen to me, come to think of it.'

'You?'

'Yes. Here, give me that.' Seligmann leaned over and took Vogel's mug. 'Have this on me. Yes, the beer won't last forever and if we don't get relieved before too long I'll have to start rationing, myself.' He gazed at the portrait of Leopold with an abstracted air. 'But of course I'll look after my regular customers. Know what I mean?'

'I know what you mean.' Vogel downed his beer, stood up and threw a coin on the counter. 'That's for the beer. Good day to you.'

Vogel stumped down Ottostrasse his face set in a determined scowl. So, Seligmann thought that he could do a little blackmail, did he? More beer for more bread; well, as far as he, Vogel was concerned – although he liked his beer as much as any man in Vienna – Seligmann could pour the ale down the nearest drain. That thought cheered him as he entered the bakery but his good humour vanished as he saw his wife and Anna staring stubbornly at each other.

'What's going on?' he growled.

Frau Vogel tossed her head. 'Ask her.'

'Well?' Vogel turned to Anna who had a tray in her hand but, typically, Frau Vogel answered.

'Our soup. She wants to give it to the Grafin.'

Vogel peered at the tray. A bowl of soup and a small roll. 'It won't exactly ruin us, will it?'

'Ruin!' Frau Vogel threw her hands into the air. 'It's food, isn't it? Food.'

'Yes.' Vogel was ready to agree with that. It was certainly food. 'But –'

'Never mind the buts,' Frau Vogel snapped. 'It's *our* food, and it doesn't drop from heaven. Do you know how much food costs now? And how long it takes to get it?'

'Well . . .' Vogel hesitated and turned to Anna.

'She's an old woman, father. Anyway, I'll give her mine.'

'Ach,' Frau Vogel folded her arms pugnaciously. 'She was an old woman before the siege, wasn't she? But did she ever speak to us? Fifteen years she's lived upstairs and never so much as a *guten tag*. A baker's wife wasn't good enough to speak to. I know. But now all the fine ladies have run away, she's dumped on us. I know.'

'Doesn't the priest call?' Vogel asked.

'Yes, but he doesn't bring any food.'

Vogel sighed. He seemed to have spent the whole day talking about food or the lack of it. Under the unrelenting pressure of the Turks the unity of the city was beginning to crack; squabbles over prices, over duties in the militia, over taxes, and now this, a family row over a spoonful of soup and a roll. 'Ach,' he said. 'Give it to her.'

Frau Vogel rattled pots mutinously as Anna went upstairs to the Grafin's rooms. Two of them; faded relics of minor nobility; a portrait of the late Graf von Schwarzbach which looked as if it had been painted by a cross-eyed amateur on a dark night, engravings of the Emperor, the Empress, the Pope, two crucifixes, a statue of the Virgin Mary, a book or two, and the Grafin herself, a withered fragment of the great block of the nobility which laid its dead weight upon the Empire. A black dress, in perpetual mourning for the late Graf, rustling as the Grafin peered into the bowl and a sniff which strongly suggested that the sniffer had known better days, and better food.

Anna watched as a frail hand lifted a trembling spoon to a dry mouth. Faded blue eyes rested on her as the Grafin whispered, 'Where is the wine, girl?'

Anna bobbed in a little courtesy. 'There is no wine, Grafin. I could get some beer.'

'Beer?' the spoon rattled in the bowl. 'Goodness, child, where are you from? Straight from the countryside I expect.' The old head shook in disapproval. 'You girls . . . bring wine from the cellar. Hans will show you . . .'

The old voice mumbled on and Anna stood meekly by her side. The Grafin is losing her memory, she thought, living in some remote time of riches and servants and now here she was, a mere handful of bones covered with yellow skin like a plucked chicken; deserted, forgotten, poor, querulous.

'So hot,' the Grafin broke into Anna's reverie.

'Yes, Grafin.' The heat hung over Vienna like a blanket. 'Should I open the window?'

'The window?' The Grafin made a vague gesture and Anna opened the window with an effort. The rumble of cannon-fire came into the room.

'Thunder,' said the Grafin. 'Yes, there will be a thunderstorm. Tell Hans to cancel the carriage . . .' Her head lolled to one side as she fell asleep.

Anna left the room and went downstairs. Herr Vogel had gone for his nap but Frau Vogel was at the sink and on the table was soup and bread.

'Mother,' Anna took a step towards her mother's formidable back. 'I said that I'd give my soup to the Grafin.'

Frau Vogel swung around, her face sullen. 'And will you give her your supper tonight? And your breakfast tomorrow? And the next day, and the day after that? Will you?'

'But we have lots of food, mother,' Anna said.

'We *haven't* got lots of food.' Frau Vogel's voice was sharp. 'And what we have got is what I've been saving.'

'Saving?'

'Yes.' Frau Vogel sat down at the table and waved Anna to a chair opposite. 'Now listen to me, Anna. These past few weeks I've been a fool –' She held up her hand as Anna tried to speak. 'I've been frightened out of my wits and I still am. Don't interrupt. I say I've been a fool and perhaps I am one. I'm just a baker's wife and that's all, but I'm not all stupid. I've been storing food for months now. Yes, I bought a barrel of salt herrings and your father said I was fool, and I bought those hams, and he said I was a fool then, and all the onions, too. But I was right. When I first heard that the Turks were coming I began storing food.' She leaned back, nodding her head in quiet satisfaction.

'But mother,' Anna said, 'We have enough food for months.'

'I know that,' said Frau Vogel.'

'But . . .'

'Yes,' Frau Vogel nodded again.

'But the Poles are coming,' Anna said.

'Yes.' Frau Vogel leaned forward. 'When did the Turks come? July, wasn't it? And what day is it now? We're into August and where are the Poles? It could be months before they get here – if they ever do.'

'Mother!' Anna put her hand to her mouth.

'Well –' Frau Vogel made a curious, irresolute gesture, as if denying her own words. 'Well, while they are getting here food is going to get shorter than it is now even, and the soldiers will get the pick of that. So I'm not just being a skinflint when –' She gestured to the ceiling.

'And what about her, mother?' Anna showing her mother's trait of single-mindedness.

'Ach!' Frau Vogel gave a resigned shrug. 'We'll feed her I suppose. We can't just let her starve to death.'

A rattle at the door, Rudi coming in, darting across the street from Peter Schreyer's house – darting because there was always the danger of a Turkish cannon-ball ending his short life, although, as the women had said to each other, the children could not be kept in the houses forever. Herr Vogel awakening from his nap, pleased at the newly refound harmony between his wife and daughter, and, against all precedent, before his night's work began, going off for another drink with Sergeant Fischer, quartered with two men on the top floor, who had just finished a day's duty in the Burg Bastion.

'And I don't mind telling you, Herr Vogel, that I'm not sorry,' he said, downing a stein in one draught and wiping a face sooty with musket powder. 'It's like an inferno in the bastion. Of course, I don't need to tell *you* what heat's like.'

'No.' Vogel bought another round of drinks, brushing off Fischer's attempt to pay for them. 'No, you're right there, but I don't have people shooting at me when I'm baking.' He looked into his stein and said, almost furtively, shamefaced, 'I don't suppose there's any sign of them, you know . . . giving up . . .'

Fischer shook his head. 'No sign of it. They just keep coming at us and now they're in the moat . . .'

In the moat. Yes. Even Vogel's hand shook a little as he thought of it. A couple of hundred paces and the Turks would be at the curtain wall, the last defence of the city. 'They're not very far off, are they?' he said.

'Oh,' Fischer shrugged. 'It's further than you might think just looking at it. There are trenches, you know, and pill boxes, spikes, and then there's cross-fire from the bastions, and they have to get past the Ravelin.'

Vogel nodded, eagerly. 'The Ravelin,' he said, thinking of that triangle of masonry in the middle of the moat. 'They won't take that in a hurry, will they?'

'Not in a hurry,' Fischer said.

'You mean. . . ?'

Fischer looked steadily at Vogel. 'Everything can be taken in time, Herr Vogel.'

'But how could they take the Ravelin? I mean, it's solid stone.'

'I daresay that they'll mine it. Give the devil his due, they're good at that.'

'So they could, they actually could break into the city?' Vogel pressed his stein on the table with both hands to stop its give-away clinking.

'They could.' Fischer was stoical, almost matter of fact.

'And what – what –' Vogel forced the words out. '– what happens then, Sergeant?'

Fischer stirred uneasily. 'Best not to think of it.'

'They'll – it will be like Perchtoldsdorf won't it?'

There was no answer this time, no need for one either, or the question, come to that. Everyone in Vienna knew what happened to besieged towns taken by storm, a hundred years of warfare and propaganda had made sure of that.

'Why?' Vogel blurted out, from the depth of his decent, honest heart. 'Why do men behave like that? How can they?'

Fischer shrugged. 'It's a sort of rule of war. If a city is surrounded and refuses to surrender, then when its taken the troops can do what they like for a few days. You know, you're outside a city for weeks, months maybe, your mates are killed, you're living in filth, well, you stop being a human being, and that's the truth. So when you break in . . . well, you know what men are when they're drunk. And what makes a lad become a soldier anyway? The chance of loot, really. After all, what else keeps the lads in the firing line, that or regular pay, and how often does a soldier get that?'

Vogel gave an involuntary twitch. 'I hope that you get regular pay, Sergeant.'

'Us?' Fischer said. 'Yes, I'll say that, regular pay and good pay.'

'So,' conscious that he was moving into a delicate area, Vogel coughed, 'so there's no question of . . . um . . .'

'Of us running away?' Fischer grinned. 'Rest easy there. In any case, there's nowhere to run to and no way to get there.' He paused and cocked an ear as a cannon-ball crashed somewhere. 'Don't know why they do that, waste of powder. But don't worry about the lads. We'll do our duty.'

'But if –' Vogel could not bring himself to say it.

The sergeant stared at the table for a long time then, very quietly, he said, 'Get your girl out, if you can. Sorry.'

He stood up, yawning. 'Time for me to get some sleep.'

'Yes.' Vogel stood up, too. 'Time for me to start work.' He hesitated and then clicked his fingers. 'I'm sorry, Sergeant, I should have asked before. Where are your two men?'

Fischer buckled his grey uniform. 'Hospital. Dysentery. General Starhemberg is down with it, too. Lets hope it doesn't get any worse or there won't be any men left to stop the *verdammt* Turks.'

The bloated, hairy flies drifted across Vienna, deadlier than the Turkish cannon-fire, in the dank alleyways, along the walls and in the bastions, moving lazily in the chasm of the moat, and, in unbelievable clusters along the slaughter-house of the covered-way and into the Ottoman camp, where, because of them, men were dying like flies. All along the great circle of the Turkish army the ranks were thinning, and as man after man after man died, the spirits of those remaining were beginning to ebb; slowly but surely the morale of the army was disintegrating.

Morale was drooping amongst the Twenty-eighth Orta, too. Out of the firing line for a week, on Guard duty, slotted into the Asiatics of the Bey of Diyarbakir opposite the Dominican Bastion. An easy duty, in meadows by the stream of the Wien; no shattering volleys of musket fire, no explosive crackle of grenades, not even the indifferent cough of the solitary cannon Starhemberg had left on the bastion. And yet men were dying there, too, as surely as they were in the evil depth of the moat, where, to discourage the others, the flayed skins of Turkish infantry were being flaunted like ghastly banners.

Standing in line for the noon meal, the news of this reached Vasif's men.

'Well,' Janissary Sivas, one of the new men in the orta, brought from the Buda garrison to fill in the gaps, 'Our turn will come and we'll see how they like it.'

'Will we?' Tedeki spat. 'It's my own skin I'm thinking about.' He held out his dish and looked sullenly at the ladle of rice dumped into it. 'What's this?' he demanded.

'What does it look like?' The cook, bigger even than Tedeki, growled.

'No meat?' Tedeki was incredulous.

'No.' The cook rattled his ladle on the cooking pot. 'And don't pull your face at me, brother. We cook what we're given.' He rattled the ladle again with an air that suggested that he would be perfectly willing to rattle Tedeki's head if necessary and turned away to stir another pot, a cooks' pot, which gave out a pleasant aroma of mutton.

Tedeki squatted with Janissaries Sheyhi and Tavasi, survivors from the old orta and gulped down a mouthful of rice, and even that was barely cooked.

'What an army!' He threw the bowl down in disgust. 'No meat, no firewood, no coffee, and you know what's coming next, don't you?' He glared at Sheyhi and Tavasi. 'The moat, that's what. We'll be dumped down there like dogs to get our heads blown off and the skin ripped from our backs.'

'Well,' Tavasi finished his rice with an effort. 'There's nothing we can do about it.'

'Isn't there though?' Tedeki looked carefully over his shoulder then leaned forward. 'Let me tell you a little thing about that.' His voice dropped into as near a whisper as he could make it and as he whispered Tavasi and Sheyhi looked fearfully over their shoulders, too, and their eyes opened wide.

Under an awning a few yards away, Vasif, studying a rough drawing of the moat and the Ravelin, looked thoughtfully over his spectacles at the three men then clicked his fingers. Like a shadow, Timur appeared.

'Bring Tedeki,' Vasif ordered.

Timur away, returning with Tedeki, squatting in a corner, as Vasif looked coldly at Tedeki, who loomed over him, sweat pouring down his face, shifting from foot to foot.

Vasif took off his spectacles and tapped his chin with them. 'You know the Koran, Janissary Tedeki?'

'The Koran, Corbaci?'

'Yes.'

Tedeki gave an embarrassed grin. 'Well, Corbaci, I know it . . . I mean I know it . . . in a way, that is . . .'

'Good.' Vasif sounded like a schoolmaster complimenting a good pupil. 'Excellent. I know it, too. So we both know that our laws come from the Koran and from the Prophet, peace be on his name. Correct?'

'Oh yes, Corbaci.' Tedeki, whose views on law rested on the assumption that if you weren't caught breaking them then laws did not exist, wagging his head vigorously.

'Excellent.' Vasif put down his spectacles. 'The laws of Islam are just laws. Allah himself, the Lord of all worlds, gave them to us.'

'Yes, Corbaci.' Tedeki gaped at Vasif, bewildered.

'I'm glad that you agree,' Vasif said. 'But let me remind you, Janissary Tedeki, that the Laws of Islam are also severe. You know what that word means?'

'Severe . . . er, yes . . .'

Odabasi Osman ducked his head under the awning and was waved away. Vasif placed a finger on his chin and said, evenly, 'It means, Tedeki, that if I see you whispering to other men then I will have your head off. Understood?'

Tedeki was literally staggered, he took a step back, his face ashen. 'But Corbaci, I was only saying . . . saying . . .'

'Saying what?'

Tedeki rolled his eyes, opened his mouth once or twice, and then, as if inspiration had come from above, said, 'I was saying that we should kill many Giaours, Corbaci!'

'I see.' Vasif nodded. 'I would like you to say that now. But I would like you to say it loudly.'

Tedeki gave a ghastly mockery of a smile which faded before Vasif's bleak stare. 'Kill many Giaours,' he croaked.

'Not good enough,' Vasif said. 'Let the whole camp hear.' Tedeki took a deep breath and in a genuine bull-like bellow roared, 'Kill many Giaours!'

'Much better.' Vasif was approving. 'Now go for a little walk around the camp shouting that until further orders. And make sure that I can hear you – all the time.'

Tedeki's face turned a deep plum-colour, and for a moment Timur thought that he was going to step forward and assault Vasif, but the Corbaci merely said, in his even, unemotional voice, 'I can count up to forty, Janissary Tedeki.'

To Timur's utter astonishment a look of terror crossed Tedeki's face. 'Yes, Corbaci,' he muttered and stumbled from the awning.

Timur blinked at Vasif, and Vasif stared unblinkingly back. From outside came Tedeki's bellow. 'Kill many Giaours! Kill many Giaours!'

Something which might have been a smile touched Vasif's lips. 'Can you count up to forty, Janissary Ven?' he asked.

'Er, yes, Corbaci.'

'Yes.' Vasif replaced his spectacles. 'In your progress to higher rank in the army, assuming that you make it, remember two things.'

'Corbaci?'

'When you see men whispering they are hatching plots against you, and remember to count to forty.'

'I don't understand, Corbaci,' and in fact Timur had no more idea of what Vasif meant than the man in the moon.

'No.' Vasif stood up. 'But you will. You will. Bring me the Odabasis. At the double.'

At the double, here, there, the afternoon enlivened by Tedeki's bellowing and the amazed laughter of the orta until at four in the afternoon, the unit was called to order, shouldered muskets, and marched around the walls, past the Braun Bastion, the Wasserkunst, the Karinthian, through the Trautson Gardens, the trenches, and into the slaughterhouse of the moat.

Chapter Twenty-One

THE MOAT

DOWN into the moat, but down a flight of stairs, solid wooden stairs, lit by flickering oil lamps. An amazing creation. Whistles of admiration from the men and a lightening of spirits. If the engineers could do this under a smashed and shattered counter-scarp then what could they not do? Perhaps the crossing of the moat would not be so difficult, after all, what were a couple of hundred paces more? Even the sourest man in the orta felt a little more cheerful as it filed from the stairs and into a deep, well-shielded trench – until they looked through the loop-holes and saw what awaited them.

Timur looked and was staggered at what he saw. He had imagined a mere stretch of land and then a wall; instead there was a ferocious tangle of stakes and iron bars, mounds of earth, stone parapets and beyond them huge walls, seen from here, from eye level, worm's eye level, as gigantic and unshakeable as mountains. It was, Timur groped for an analogy, it was like being in some colossal street, but a street on fire, with smoke billowing from the windows and then he realized that the windows were not windows but gun-ports, and that the smoke was the smoke from cannon.

Vasif joined him at the loop-hole. 'That is the Burg Bastion,' pointing towards a great blunt triangle of stone, jutting into the moat like the prow of a ship, 'and the wall is what is called a curtain wall. You see it joins up with the Lobel Bastion' – another towering block of masonry – 'And in the middle is the Ravelin' – formidable fortress, looking as deadly as an arrow head.

'But –' Timur could not believe his eyes. It was inconceivable that men could cross the moat and, under the fire from those defences, incredible that mere men could break in to those giant walls.

'We can do it.' Vasif looked sideways at Timur. 'The Ravelin, the bastions, they can all be taken. We mine them. Shake them, shake the Golden Apple tree and the apples will fall to the ground – and then we shall eat them by Shaitan.'

Timur stared at Vasif, amazed. It was rare that Vasif used the name of the Great Satan, rarer still that his voice showed emotion, but there was an icy ferocity in it now, and his blue eyes were glinting like a wild animal's. He means it, Timur thought. He really wants to take the city and destroy it and everyone in it and he is ready to sacrifice us all and himself to make that happen.

Night coming, early in the chasm, tar barrels blazing, the flames licking upwards, yellow and red and as the flames dipped and swayed, shadows moved with them, monstrous, distorted, gigantic; to the left, opposite the Lobel Bastion, an orta charged an Austrian trench and were massacred, trapped in Rimpler's iron maze and shot down by steady volleys from the pill-boxes. Screams and howls in the darkness, hoarse, animal shrieks of hatred and defiance and agony, echoing from the walls of the moat – Paradise or Gehenna, according to which side you were on, but amounting to the same thing, and all the night long the Lagunci pushing trenches forward, foot by foot, and underneath the horrors the mine shafts were driven inexorably forward, under the trenches, under the block-houses, and towards the tip of the Ravelin.

A day and a night in the moat then a shambling relief, a day, exhausted, filthy, in a bivouac then back into purgatory. Time ceasing to have meaning, men, too. The personalities of the orta becoming obliterated, men unrecognizable under layers of filth and blood and gunpowder. Companions of twenty years killed and forgotten within minutes and yet, as the men became sub-human, Vasif became super-human; immune to fatigue, wounds, disease, death itself, he led his orta from bivouac to trench, trench to bivouac, and back again, sparing no one, not himself, nor his men, nor Timur.

Hallucinatory days and nights, and the hallucinations stalking the men into bivouac; men moaning in their sleep, twitching, shouting as the cannon pounded and the muskets cracked, and the pounding turning into a maddening rhythm in Timur's mind; forty, forty, forty, forty. The words became a talisman. As long as he could say forty he would not be killed, mangled, left to rot in the no man's land of the moat. And yet it never occurred to him to ask Vasif what the forty stood for. Indeed he did not want to know what it meant as if the knowledge would take away the power of the spell; forty, forty, forty . . .

There were lucid periods when, given special rations, allowed to wash, rest, sleep for twenty-four hours, like men between bouts of fever, the orta became almost human, capable, even, of curiosity about the enemy, of laughter at some coarse joke. And in one of those lucid moments, looking at the worn, death-like masks of the orta, Timur remembered what Vasif had said once, long ago, in the fort at Osijek, guarding the bridge – the men would be purified, Vasif had said. Purified by fire and war and driven back into Islam. It did not seem true to Timur. The war was purifying no-one. It was turning them into animals – burning away not dross and leaving gold, but burning away the gold and leaving dross, robbing men of their humanity and their souls and leaving them mere animals.

And then the lucidity would go, as if the fever had come back, and like animals the orta was led, driven, back into the moat where they met the Austrians and, like two dogs, each locked the other by the throat.

In the moat half deadly monotony, sealed in the trenches, half terror as the Austrians made sudden attacks, sallies of fifty or a hundred men, shooting at point-blank range, hacking and slashing under a hail of grenades as the Turkish trenches were filled in and the timbers knocked down and burned. Starhemberg himself leading one attack, Count Leslie, General Leslie's brother, killed at his side, Colonel Daun and Colonel Souches leading their regiments, and still the Turks edging forward towards the Ravelin and the curtain wall, and on the eighth day of August the engineers exploding a mine under its tip.

'Ya, Islam!' A wave of Janissaries left their trenches and were met with a withering blast of musketry. Another attack and another volley, the mine having misfired, tearing off a few yards of facing masonry but leaving the Ravelin barely dented. One last charge, one last volley, and the attack was called off and the Turkish troops fell back into their trench under the counterscarp.

In the Burg Bastion, in a chamber reeking with gunpowder, Starhemberg stared unblinkingly at a major from the Ravelin. 'It's all right?'

'Yes.' The major stared unblinkingly back through red-rimmed eyes.

Starhemberg rubbed his chin, unshaven after two days and nights on his feet. 'Losses?' he asked.

'Not too bad. Sixty, maybe. Of course that's only a guess. We've not had time for a proper roll-call yet. God alone knows what they've lost.'

No need to ask who *they* were. There was a pause, an exhausted bone-weary moment of silence. Starhemberg grunted and, in an act of unbelievable condescension for a General and a Count of the Empire towards a professional, paid soldier, and only a major to boot, poured out two glasses of plum brandy.

The major managed a grin as he downed his glass. 'I don't know how they get on without it, sir. Drugs, I suppose. Hashish or whatever they call it. Must be something, the way they keep coming.'

The tramp of feet in the gloomy corridor. Dupigny's regiment moving into the Ravelin. The major rose.

'I'll be off, sir. Thank you.' At the door the major paused. 'Sir, none of my business, but any news of . . . ?'

'The Poles.' Starhemberg tapped his glass thoughtfully. 'On the way, Major. Almost here. Understood?'

'Yes, sir.'

'Quite understood?'

The major hesitated for just a fraction, then, 'Quite understood, sir.'

A salute, the door closing. Starhemberg poured another glass of brandy to still the griping pains in his bowels and looked into the liquid as if it was a magic bowl in which he could see the whole of the world. 'On the way,' he muttered and crossed himself as the light of dawn filtered into the Ravelin.

In *his* bunker, moved well forward of the Trautson Gardens, under fire from the Austrian cannon, there bravely enough to encourage his troops, Kara Mustafa was with his Agas, listening, with more patience now than weeks before, to the Aga of the Lagunci explain why the mine under the Ravelin had failed and accepting it with no more than a mental note that when Vienna had fallen the Aga might be, if not assassinated, then at least exiled to some remote and unpleasant desert.

'And what next?' Swarthy face intent, brooding.

The Aga leaned forward. 'Two mines, Serasker. One under the ravelin and the other under the moat. Huge mines.'

'In the moat?'

'Yes, Serasker. It will blow up a ramp of earth between the counterscarp and the Ravelin itself. The infantry can charge across it from the covered-way and be on the Ravelin before the Giaours know what has happened to them.

'Ah!' Mustafa snapped his fingers. 'A bridge. You will make a bridge.'

'Yes Serasker.'

'Excellent. Excellent.' Mustafa erased his mental note. 'A bridge, yes. And a charge. We take the Ravelin and then the dogs of Austrians come under *our* crossfire. When?'

'Two days, Serasker.'

'Good.' Smiling, charming approval. 'And the infantry?' Smoothly addressing the Aga of the Janissaries.

'The men will be ready, Serasker.'

Simple words, spoken calmly, but with a flicker, a barely perceptible tremor of hesitation behind them, and Mustafa, who, after a lifetime in plots and intricacies of the Ottoman court intrigues, had the sensitivity of a cat, pounced.

'There is some doubt?'

'No, Serasker. The men will do their duty . . . but . . .'

'But what, Aga?' Smiles and charm gone, menace creeping into the bunker with the morning sunshine.

The Aga unmoved by menace. 'In two days we shall have been here almost a month, Serasker.'

'What of it?' Mustafa openly scowling.

'A month is thirty days, Serasker, and when Janissaries reach thirty days at a siege they have been known to count to forty.'

'Forty?' Mustafa held up his hands in unfeigned astonishment. 'What is this? Counting up to forty?'

'It is the law, Serasker. Under the law a Janissary need only stay at a siege for forty days.'

'The law?' Mustafa smashed his fist on the table. 'Bismillah. *I* am the law. *I am the law!* And as God made me and my mother, if any man breaks my law I will nail him to a plank and feed my dogs on him.'

Chapter Twenty-Two

THE RAVELIN

OUT of the moat, out of the grave it seemed to the Twenty-eighth Orta, finally pulled out, exhumed, for a relief and moved around this time to the west of the city, opposite the Scottish gate by the hamlet of Alsergassen. Not much left of Alsergassen now. Every stick taken for firewood, every tree chopped down, every blade of grass eaten by the horses of the cavalry. But still, after the moat, Paradise itself although the food was bad and getting worse.

'Saving it for the poor dogs in the moat,' as Tedeki observed without rancour. 'Well, they're welcome to it. If I could stay here I'd eat cold rice forever. *Raw* cold rice. In fact' – waggishly – 'I'd sooner be here and eat nothing rather than be down there and eat *kebab*. Right, *voyalons*?'

Unanimity among the wayfarers. Anything rather than the moat. 'Amazing, though,' Tedeki poked a finger at Vienna. 'You wouldn't believe there was a war on, would you?'

Sitting by Vasif's tent, Timur Ven was thinking much the same thing. In a way it was unnerving. A walk of a quarter of a mile and the inferno of the moat might as well have been in Istanbul. Beyond the ruined houses and the bare glacis, the walls of Vienna stretched, grey, somnolent, roofs and steeples jutting up behind them, the endless, mocking jangle of the bells silenced, although for what reason Timur could not guess, and not a soul to be seen, not a man, a woman, or dog, although a musket cracked a threat as a group of Tartars edged into the walls a little too close.

Timur rubbed oil on his face, scorched by a grenade. What was going on behind those walls, he wondered. Were the vague, mysterious rumours emanating from the Serasker's headquarters true? Was the city starving, the citizens mutinous, held back from surrendering only by the army, and was the army shattered, exhausted, ready to surrender after one last blow? Were they? Were they? Timur devoutly hoped so. Hoped it all the more since, like the rest of the orta, he was absolutely convinced that, sooner or later, they would be sent back into the graveyard of the moat.

But in fact, behind the deceptively placid walls, in a staggeringly matter-of-fact way the life of the city was going on much as usual; bakers baked, tailors tailored, cobblers patched shoes up, all the various tradesmen of the city tinkered and tapped away, and yet, underneath the humdrum surface, the city was slipping, little by little, down a slope from which there were those who believed it would not, could not climb back. Food was running short, vegetables had disappeared, and fruit, grains were short and prices long, and rising every day. Meat had all but vanished except that little animals were on sale, roof rabbits, they were called, although the day before they had been catching mice and miaowing in a most unrabbit like manner, and with it all amoebic dysentery.

Sullenness in the markets; bitter reproaches from the housewives at profiteering, and imperturbable provision merchants, safe behind their stalls, and particular venom spat at the bakers, and, in the Kohl Market on the Herrengasse, looking for peas, Frau Vogel, with Anna, on an expedition, daring since Frau Vogel had a secret belief that the *verdammt* Turkish gunners had a cannon specially sighted on her, finding out the depth of hatred born against her husband's trade.

Looking at peas and throwing her hands up in horror at the price. 'How much? How much? For peas! You ought to be ashamed. I'll report you to the City Council.'

A murmur of agreement from the other women around the stall, all perfectly ready for Frau Vogel to go to the Council Hall there and then as long as they didn't have to go with her.

'All right.' The stall-holder completely unmoved. 'Go to the Council. I'm not stopping you, am I?'

'I will,' Frau Vogel formidable in anger.

'Carry on,' the stall-holder toyed with a weight. 'And while you're there, Frau, report your husband, too.'

'What?' Frau Vogel swung around. 'What was that?'

'Oh,' the trader gazed innocently at the sky. 'He's a baker, isn't he? Vogel, isn't it?'

Another murmur from the crowd but, amazingly, a hostile murmur. A baker! Sole wielder of the staff of life and, notoriously, the worst profiteers in the city, worse even than the fishermen who at least risked their necks from Turkish marksmen when they ventured on the Danube.

Frau Vogel glared at the crowd and at the trader. 'What of it?' she demanded.

'Well,' the trader put her arms on her hips. 'Well when you're at the Council House report him for putting *his* prices up.'

'You –' Frau Vogel could hardly bring herself to speak and then, in a blinding flash of temper she darted around the stall and cracked the trader on the head with her basket.

A mêlée, blows, unladylike curses, artful hands removing peas and lentils from the stall, market officials separating the women, severe warnings from a militia man, trouble enough fighting the Turks without respectable *Hausfrauen* brawling like common prostitutes, heavy fines next time, go home *now*.

'There,' Frau Vogel, bosom heaving, pale blue eyes dark with rage. 'That's what you get. That's the thanks you get. Your father keeping his prices down and he gets called a profiteer. We'll see what the Bakers' Guild has to say about that.' Turning into Ottostrasse. 'There are laws about –'

But Frau Vogel's views on the law lost as there was a tremendous roar, a huge, ear-splitting double boom, louder than the loudest crack of thunder, as loud as the crack of doom.

Ottostrasse visibly rocked, windows shattered, chimneys swayed, tumbled down, tiles skimmed through the air and, uncannily, dust began to fall and clods of earth and, in an eerie whisper, the church bells tinged and tanged in a muted tintinabulation.

Shaken to her knees, her head bleeding from a flying fragment of brick, Frau Vogel scrabbled at her shopping. 'Oh dear God,' she cried. 'They've come.'

Not come, but coming. The great mines under the moat and at the tip of the Ravelin timed to the moment and in exactly the right place. Gigantic mines, deafening, blinding, thousands of pounds of gunpowder ripping the tip from the Ravelin and heaving up a great mound across the moat, wide enough for fifty men to charge abreast, and, coming through the dust, screaming like demons, led by Serdengceti a thousand Janissaries.

Two hours carnage. The Turks through the shattered parapet and into the first retrenchment, Austrian troops, hacked to pieces as they stumbled among the ruin, blinded and deafened, men from the bastions rushed across to the Ravelin, throwing up desperate, makeshift defences, spiked fences, smashed and jagged timber, bales of wool, sandbags; Starhemberg, stinking on a stretcher, bellowing, threatening, organizing, and the Turks finally held, but held as a man might hold a mastiff by the collar, its slavering teeth inches from his throat, for when the dust cleared, there, on the tip of the Ravelin in the very heart of Vienna's defences, were eight horse-trails.

'Still there?' Herr Vogel to Sergeant Fischer, slumped in a chair in the Vogel's parlour, downing a quart of beer, a jagged slash across his forehead, powder burns on his lips.

'Still there.' Fischer shook his head. 'And they'll take some shifting, if you ask me. Sorry to hear about your wife, by the way.'

'Ach –' Vogel waved his hand. 'It's only a scratch, thank God. A bit of a headache. She's over at the Breitners with Anna. Frau Breitner is very good with herbs, making her willow tea, or something.' He peered a little closer at Fischer's face. 'You look as if you could do with something yourself, Sergeant.'

'This?' Fischer touched his forehead. 'A scratch. Chip of flying stone. That's the trouble with these old walls. They're faced with masonry instead of earth so if a cannon-ball hits them you get these bits flying about.'

'As dangerous as a musket shot,' Vogel observed.

'Have to contradict you there.' Fischer took another mighty swig of beer. 'Musket balls . . . soft lead. When they hit they splatter out. Bad news, Herr Vogel. Like today.'

'It *is* bad news then?' Vogel hesitated. 'I mean really bad.'

'I've got to admit it,' Fischer said.

'But,' Vogel groped for words. 'But why don't the cannon on the bastions just . . . just blast them off the Ravelin?'

'It's not that easy.' Without protest Fischer let Vogel fill his mug again. 'See, it's what I was just saying. The walls are old-fashioned and the bastions, well, there's not room to handle the cannon properly and anyway, we can't just sweep the Ravelin with artillery. The Turks are only on the tip of it. Our lads are up there, too. God help them.'

'Amen to that.' Vogel crossed himself piously, gravely. The Turks would take some shifting, Fischer had said. What would happen if they weren't shifted? Mother of God, what would happen if the Turks did the shifting? It was a question he didn't want to ask, was afraid to ask, but the words were in his throat and about to tumble out when the front door clacked open.

'That'll be the wife.' Vogel heaved himself to his feet. 'Don't move, Sergeant. She'll want to have a word, I'm sure. You know what – well!' as the parlour door opened, 'Kaspar – and Frau Haller –' His jaw dropped as Frau Haller burst into hysterical tears. 'Now, then Frau Haller, it was only a knock on the head. She's across the road right now.'

'It's not that, Herr Vogel.' Kaspar stepped forward, his open face unusually grave. 'It's father.'

'Father?'

'He's gone.'

'Gone? Gone where?' Vogel was mystified but his mystification turned to total astonishment as Kaspar handed over a scrap of paper.

'He left this, Herr Vogel.'

Vogel peered at the paper, holding it up to the lamp; sprawled, almost illegible, incoherent, blotted. 'He says he's gone for help,' he said. 'What does it mean?'

Kaspar shuffled his feet, profoundly embarrassed. 'You know, Herr Vogel, he . . . he's been getting a bit strange . . . strange lately . . . er . . .'

Vogel thought that Haller had never been anything *but* strange but he nodded understandingly. 'Yes, I have noticed that he, that he wasn't himself. But this –' He waved the paper as Frau Haller began sobbing again. 'Gone to get help?'

'He's been talking about Passau, a lot,' Kasper said. 'About the Emperor. Saying that the Emperor doesn't know how badly off we are. He said someone ought to go and tell him, the Emperor.'

Vogel shook his head and handed the paper over to Fischer. 'What do you make of it, Sergeant?'

Fischer shrugged his burly shoulders. 'If he knows the city he might get out – bribe a guard or two or get through a sewer. Messengers do get out, you know, but outside . . .'

Outside! Outside the grey walls, that familiar perimeter holding at bay the terrors of the night. Inconceivable that Haller with his long nose and shambling legs should be wandering about in the darkness where the Janissaries patrolled with their slashing swords – and the Tartars . . .

'It's incredible. Simply incredible.' Vogel could not bring himself to believe that it was not some extraordinary practical joke. 'After all,' he said, 'Refugees are trying to get *into* the city. And to go to Passau!'

Frau Haller burst into tears again. Herr Vogel dosed her with his precious plum brandy, Kaspar brought Frau Vogel and Anna from the Breitners, in their wake, much to Vogel's annoyance, the Breitners themselves, crowding into his parlour and being perfectly willing to sit there and drink plum brandy, too.

High drama in Ottostrasse! Frau Haller veering between wild accusations that Haller had deserted her – left her to the horrors of the Turks – saved his own skin – and, as the plum brandy got to work, painting a noble picture of her husband risking – giving – his life to save Vienna; the Breitners agreeing impartially with both statements as they knocked back free drinks, Kaspar vainly trying to silence his mother, saying bluntly that his father's mind was deranged and enraging her the more, Frau Vogel vainly trying to bring the conversation around to her cut head, Sergeant Fischer, with the prospect of meeting the Turks the next day himself, silent in a corner, Herr Vogel truly dumbfounded, and then Anna, in a quiet, self-effacing way, saying to Fischer:

'Herr Sergeant, there are a lot of other soldiers outside, aren't there? I mean not Turkish?'

'Oh yes, Fraulein. Transylvanians, Wallachians . . .'

'And they're not, I mean not really cruel like the Turks, are they?'

Fischer, whose views on the human race were somewhat bleaker than Anna's, and who had seen what Transylvanians and Wallachians could do, seized on the comforting idea. After all, anything to stop the *verdammt* screeching of the hag whose husband, obviously, and in Fischer's eyes quite sensibly, tried to clear out while the going was good. He slapped his thigh. 'Quite right, Fraulein. I'll bet he got out through the Carinthian Gate, that's where the Protestants are. If he winds up there he'll be all right. That's it. Safe as houses.'

In their hearts, not one person present believed this for a moment but the straw grasped at, Frau Haller's tears staunched, the Breitners ushered out, Kaspar, with a meaning look at Herr Vogel taking his mother home, Fischer to bed. The Vogel's left, sitting around their table.

'Well,' Vogel looked a little ruefully at his brandy bottle. 'Might as well finish it off.'

Two large drinks and one small one. Frau Vogel gingerly shook her head. 'What do you make of that?'

Vogel breathed through his nose like a horse. 'It's got to him, I suppose. Highly-strung. He always was like a cat on hot bricks and the strain of this,' – no need to explain what this was –' people crack up . . .'

'He's a coward.' A flat statement from Frau Vogel.

Vogel stirred uneasily. 'A coward, you know – running away, it must have crossed everyone's mind.'

'It didn't cross yours.'

'No.' Vogel had to agree. It never had crossed his mind but he felt an obscure, groping doubt even as he agreed. Why, really, had he stayed? Had he put worldly possessions above life? The stuffed heron, the lamp, the dresser? And had the little life he led in the dark street with its familiar round dulled him, robbed himself of something which Haller, for all his folly and gossip and nervous leaping about had maintained; imagination, fantasy, curiosity? Haller had always liked a good tale, romances, stories of far off lands. He actually believed that somewhere in the world there were men whose eyes were in their bellies and whose heads grew underneath their arms – not that he was alone in that.

'Ah well,' he sighed and stood up. 'Time for work. You get to bed, rest your head. You too, Anna. That was clever about the Christians out there. It quietened Frau Haller, anyway.'

Anna's beautiful violet eyes rested on him gravely. 'Do you think it's true, father?'

'I don't know. That's the truth. I just don't know.'

A little later. The house silent, sleeping, Vienna sleeping, but uneasily like a trapped animal, twitching restlessly in its sleep, opening lambent eyes and spitting defiance before falling back into torpor. Herr Vogel pounding his dough and shaking his head. 'It's true,' he thought. 'Perfectly true. I just don't know anything any more.'

Two more days ticking away. Savage fighting on the Ravelin, another mine exploded on the counterscarp opposite the Burg Bastion, the Janissaries gnawing forward opposite the Lobel Bastion, no news of Herr Haller, no news of the Poles, no news of the Emperor; the fifteenth of August, thirty-one days of siege.

At Alsergassen, by the Scottish Gate, Vasif facing his men, a scroll in his hand. 'Holiday over.' A dry, clipped voice from puffed lips where a musket butt had smashed him in the mouth. 'A message from the Serasker' – opening the scroll – 'The Emperor of Austria is dead. Vienna has the plague. There are food riots. The city has few soldiers left and they are short of ammunition. One last heave and Vienna is ours.'

A dismal, sceptical silence then Janissary Maghrebi raised a hand and got a nod from Vasif.

'Corbaci, er . . . how does the Serasker know about, about these riots and shortages?'

Vasif looked coldly at Mahgrebi. 'Special information. March.'

The orta marched; gloomy faces, reluctant feet, round the counterscarp of the Molker Bastion, the Lobel Bastion, into the Trautson Gardens, the orchard unharmed for the delectation of the Serasker – and two men nailed to boards; Janissaries; lounging by the bodies'; executioners, fat, greasy, grinning as the orta trudged forward to the smoke and roar of the guns.

In Cracow, kneeling before another man nailed to planks, John Sobieski at Solemn High Mass in the cathedral church. Behind him the nobility of Poland, Counts, Schlactas, Gentry, graded accorded to rank, Lubomirskis, Potockis, Sopronas, Zabruskis, the crucified Christ staring down on them and they, praying for intercession in battle, looking devoutly up at him.

Prayers to God the Father, God the Son, and God the Holy Ghost, and, on this day of Assumption of Our Lady into Heaven, special prayers to the Mother of God. 'Defend us from the swords of the Turks. Save us from the arrows of the Tartars. From plague and pestilence and death, preserve us, and bless and sanctify *our* swords and lances. Amen, amen, amen.'

And, blessed and sanctified, to the blare of trumpets and the thunder of drums, the King and his army left Cracow and, at last, headed for Vienna.

Chapter Twenty-Three

THE MAGIC HILL

A MAJESTIC army led by majesty. Sobieski every inch a king, although, as Stefan thought once or twice, there were rather a lot of inches. In fact, not to put too fine a point on it, the King was distinctly fat, but his double chin and huge belly were carried well, with pride and imperious elan. The Queen, too, in her carriage, looked every inch a queen, the more so as, like the Empress Eleanora, she had been pregnant, but, in her carriage, looking a fit consort for John Sobieski.

And so a majestic procession but a slow one, wending its way from Cracow at a snail's pace along the valley of the Vistula for twenty miles or so and taking two days about it. And then, to Stefan's utter astonishment, the King and half the army turned north, away from Vienna, and to his utter bewilderment he found that neither he nor his father were going with Sobieski.

That piece of news was given to him on a pleasant morning as he and Chelmnitz, and two Zabruski serfs were sitting by their cart on a meadow by the river. A pleasant morning, and pleasant to be living this gypsy life, the cart with grain and armour in it, the serfs to fetch and carry and cook, Chelmnitz to look after all, but the idyll momentarily shattered as Zabruski leaned heavily against the cart and broke the news.

'But what are we going to do?' Stefan dismayed at the prospect of spending the next weeks camping in the meadow, and even more dismayed at the thought of returning to Cracow and Vera

Soprona having done nothing more warlike than taken part in a glorified parade.

'It's all right.' Zabruski growled, but his growl was almost amiable. The army is being split into two columns, that's all. The King is going north to Tarnowskie to collect the Cossacks and the Lithuanians and to join up with Field Hetman Jablonowski and the regular army. We're going direct with Field Hetman Sienowski. We're all going to meet again at in the south, in Moravia.'

Stefan, raw though he was, could see the sense in that. Two columns meant easier foraging, and speed, too, but he was disappointed. Not to ride with the King . . . not to share in the shining Imperial glory . . . not to be able to regale Vera with stories of courtly splendour. . . .

His dismay showed on his face and Zabruski, as shrewd as ever, saw it. 'We're better off,' he grunted. 'A real fighting column, not a procession. Take that lot' – jabbing a huge thumb at the nobles – 'Jablonowski is waiting for the King, the King waits for the Queen, and the Queen waits for the nobles.' He laughed, not without humour. 'No, let them drag about. We'll meet again anyway.'

With that Stefan had to be content, the King departing north, himself, his father, Chelmnitz, the cart and the serfs striking south through the wooded hills of Moravia.

A strange journey. Fifteen thousand men and horses wandering forward, gnawing the land bare; tattered infantry stripping orchards, small meadows in the wooded hills swept clean for fodder, sullen villages watching the army straggle past without jubilation, not as the supporters of a great crusading army, but as victims of an occupying horde.

News filtering through from Field Hetman Sienawski; the King had reached, Tarnowskie – the Queen had left for Warsaw – the cossacks and the Lithuanians had not shown up but the King had started south on a parallel course making triumphal entries into this town and that town – Gliwice, Opava, Olomouc, creeping slowly, slowly, slowly, but surely, to the great rendezvous.

And news of other armies. The Saxons, seven thousand crack

infantry, four thousand cavalry moving through Prague and up the valley of the Elbe, the Franconians and Bavarians moving down the banks of the Danube; from out of the maze of treaties, obligations, threats, bribes, entreaties, treacheries, interests balanced against interests a clear pattern emerging at last: three routes to Vienna, three armies marching to its relief, a clear recognition that the city could not be allowed to fall, and, among all the haggling over payment for troops, payment for food, payment for ammunition, one overriding, overwhelming question looming. Would Vienna still be standing when the Christian armies arrived?

And as the sodden, soggy days of August passed the city did still stand. Battered and pounded, short of food, short of water, short of medicine, and growing short of men it stood, shaken and rended, but inviolate, held in Starhemberg's unyielding grip.

Unyielding Starhemberg, implacable Kara Mustafa. Will against will, steel slashing at flint, showers of sparks glinting momentarily, men, wave after wave, dying and gone forever.

Kara Mustafa bravely moving forward into the trenches giving rewards, and punishments; promotions, demotions, executions, gifts of land and money, summoning more troops, stripping his lines of communication in a desperate gamble where the prize was the Golden Apple and the stakes were the lives of thousands of men.

The Aga of the Janissaries pointing out the losses to his Serasker, Kara Mustafa nodding in agreement, understanding, almost gentle.

'Yes, of course. But we are nearly there. Once we have cleared the Ravelin . . . you agree, do you not?'

'I agree, Serasker. But first it has to be cleared.'

An ominous little note the Ravelin. Mustafa looked at the great plan of the moat, and that triangle between the bastions. It was almost inconceivable that it was still half-held by the Austrians. Two weeks pounding, blasting, hand-to-hand fighting over a few yards and still it held out. The Magic Hill the Janissaries called it because men went on to it and vanished.

An aide murmured into the Serasker's ear, 'Increased Austrian artillery fire . . . His Excellency should retire for the sake of the army . . .'

Reluctantly Mustafa allowed himself to be guided by reason. If he was killed then the entire campaign would come to nothing. Out of the command bunker, officers bowing, Mustafa graciously bowing back, one of the officers catching his eye, a colonel of the Janissaries with blue eyes. Mustafa paused, remembering him, the Devshirme. Weeks ago, years ago it seemed, he had reprimanded the Colonel in some way, although he could not remember how, or even why. But the man was still alive, and wounded, too, a bandage around his forehead. A valuable man, more valuable now than then as Janissaries fell like autumn leaves. A time to be magnanimous. Mustafa touched his breast.

'You have been wounded, Corbaci?'

Vasif bowed. 'A scratch, Serasker.'

'You have seen some fighting, though?' Mustafa sounded sympathetic, as if the fighting had nothing to do with him but was a kind of natural catastrophe which Vasif had had to endure.

'Some fighting, Serasker. Yes.'

'And rest –' Mustafa solicitous, almost tender. 'You have had rest? And your orta?'

'Yes, Serasker.'

'And now?'

'The Ravelin, Serasker.'

'So. One last heave, hey, Corbaci?'

'As Allah wills.'

The sharp answers stirred Mustafa's memory. It had been such abrupt fatalism which had angered him the previous time. But they did not anger him now. Rather they made him feel respect for the unyielding man before him and agreement with his views. After all, in the end, it was as Allah willed, and it was as well that the Ottoman troops should believe that. They needed some belief to drive them forward against the Austrians. And then he remembered that there had been . . . he searched his memory –

'You had a youth, a young Janissary?'

'Yes, Serasker.'

'Is he . . . ?'

'Still alive? Yes.'

'And he has fought?'

'Yes, Serasker.' The faintest of smiles crossed Vasif's lips. 'He has been, shielded a little. But only a little.'

Mustafa shook his head admiringly. 'So young and he has been through that. I will reward him. Certainly I will reward him. Send him to me.'

'Now, Serasker?' The smile had gone from Vasif's face. 'He is with the men on the covered-way. It would not be good for discipline to send him out of the line before an attack.'

'Of course, of course.' Mustafa had no interest in when he saw the youth. 'Just as you think fit, Corbaci. Allah go with you.'

'And with you, Serasker.' Kara Mustafa making his grand and ceremonial exit, Vasif making his own, simple, unobtrusive exit, too – in the opposite direction. Up through the trenches, on to the covered-way – a few hundred yards, a few minutes' trudge, and the burial ground of thousands of men destroyed there in the past five weeks. His orta was in a trench, what was left of it, half-stirring as he entered, looking at him with lack-lustre eyes, listening to him incuriously, as if what he had to say was of no concern of their's, but was addressed to some other men. Vasif was not surprised. Men went through stages in a long battle; excitement first, mingled with fear, of course, but the excitement overcoming the fear, then came simple fear without the excitement. That was when they might break – go insane, run away, find their heads under the executioner's sword, and then came battle fatigue where men no longer thought or feared but moved like sleepwalkers, indifferent to their fate, dulled by the sight of death. When men reached that stage it was time for a rest. A real rest. Vasif made a promise to himself to see they got it, those who survived the next attack.

He moved down the trench, having a word here and there; with Tedeki – indestructible, even his chest had healed – Sheyhi and Tavesi, Odabasi Osman, Janissary Ven.

Vasif peered intently at Timur. Strange that the lad should seem the least affected by the strain of battle. It was youth, he supposed, and yet he had seen young men break at the first sound of a musket shot. But the lad had good stuff in him. He leaned forward to say a word to Timur, to mention the Serasker's words but his voice was drowned by the roar of a battery of Turkish cannon a few yards to the rear, blasting point-blank at the Burg Bastion. With a shrug he turned, raised his hand, and led his men on to the Magic Hill.

A familiar route, fifty yards into eternity, across the mound of earth – through it, rather, for even there, incredibly enough, under the gaping mouths of the Austrian guns, the engineers had dug trenches, boarded them, covered them – and into the rubble of the Ravelin.

It was like being in the rubble of a collapsed house; great jumbled blocks of masonry, baulks of timber lying at crazy angles, craters half filled with muddy, stinking water, dark, sinister holes which led down into the gun platforms of the Ravelin, where, in the darkness, men hacked and jabbed at shapes they could barely see.

The orta crept – crawled forward like rats, or spiders, or lizards, but not like men; face down, belly down, edging towards the base of the triangle.

It was a small world, as desolate as the moon, and a world without meaning in any normal sense; liquid fell from heaven, but it was boiling pitch, objects sprouted from the ground, but they were iron spikes, creatures with arms and legs and minds crouched behind barricades not ten yards away but they were faceless monsters. All order dissolved. The orta ceased to be a unit; men in twos or threes crouched in craters, jabbing and poking with spears and swords through gaps in the Austrian defences, edging forward a yard perhaps, being driven back a foot, howling and shrieking but their howls and screams lost in the din of battle so that they looked like madmen, their mouths opening and closing soundlessly.

At Vasif's heels, Timur, creeping on his belly, Tedeki and Maghrebi on *his* heels, edged forward through the shattered Austrian trenches, his world reduced to a few inches of smashed masonry, mud, bits of bodies, and then, a muffled boom and before Vasif a crack appeared in the masonry. The crack widened, gaped blackly like the mouth of a corpse. Vasif jerked his arm frantically and scrambled into the hole.

Amazingly, or so it seemed to Timur, he too went willingly into the hole, Tedeki and a handful of Janissaries following him. Suffocating dust, a lurid glow from burning timbers, men coughing and cursing as they scrambled forward meeting a confused, impenetrable barrier of timber baulks. The men scrabbled at the timbers with their bare hands, Timur with them and finding under a beam, trapped by one leg, a man.

Timur stared down almost in disbelief. A man! An Austrian! It was as strange and as mysterious as finding a bird down in that inferno. And the man was alive, struggling to free himself. A big man, his face blackened with powder burns, as dark as Timur's; an Austrian, a Giaour, and it suddenly occurred to Timur that in forty days at the siege he had never before seen the face of his enemy. He had seen vague shapes, stabbing behind the barricades on the counterscarp or in the gloom of the covered-way, dark figures charging from the trenches at night, but never before had he seen the enemy face to face, as a man seeing another man, and now he was seeing him, here in this entrance to Gehenna, lit by the orange light of flaming wood, and it was a face like any other, the face of a man and not a beast or a devil, and his impulse was to pull the man free from the flames. And he almost did that. He took the man by the collar of his blue coat and then a voice roared into his ear; Vasif snarling an order – 'Kill him. Kill him.'

And Timur did, driving his sword into the man, turning his face away as he did so and then there was another boom, another mine going off somewhere in the depths, the ground shook and the beams gave way and one of them slammed against the side of his head.

He was vaguely aware of what happened next. Being dragged by the heels, moaning a protest that he was a good Muslim, believing that he was being taken by djinns down into Gehenna to roast in the fires of Hell forever, of being sick, cursed at, vomiting again, and then he went into the darkness, too.

He awoke sometime later, dimly aware of lights, a splitting headache, vomited, and collapsed again. The next time he came around his head felt as though there were an axe buried in it, but he had stopped vomiting. Someone had wiped his face and opened his blouse and he was lying on a mat under a rough and ready awning. There was even an earthenware jar full of water next to him. By Turkish standards he was being well cared for. He raised his head feebly and looked around him. Other mats, other men, the unmistakeable sour-sweet smell of blood, other smells, flies, moans, a shriek or two. He drank some water and slept. When he awoke it was dusk, and it was raining heavily. Already the rain was finding its way under the awning and forming in rivulets on the ground. Two men, not Ottoman, were carrying a body out, stopping at the edge of the rough tent and heaving the body out into the rain. As they repassed Timur he called to them. They stopped, cringing. 'Water.' Timur pointed to his pot. 'Water!' angrily, making a sipping gesture.

'Ah!' One of the men, tall, terrified, with a long nose, whip marks across his back, sweating with more than the heat, darted off and came back with a jug, filling Timur's pot, grinning nervously, twitching with fear. Timur drank and put the pot down. The man filled it again and backed away. A slave, lucky to be alive, luckier still to be working in the hospital, luckier than the Ottoman soldiers.

Timur retched a little, spat out bile, turned and found Tedeki looming over him.

'All right?' Tedeki looked as though he should have been on the mat.

'Yes. Think so.' The truth was that Timur did not know whether he was all right or not. 'Am I?'

Tedeki gave an unexpected grin. 'If you don't know –' he shrugged. 'I'll find out.' He shambled off and, eventually came back with a man in a bloodsoaked tunic. A doctor, Turkish style. The man casually heaved Timur over, felt his bones, nodded.

'All right.'

'I can take him?' Tedeki asked.

The doctor held out the palms of his hands in the indifferent Turkish gesture and walked away. Tedeki heaved Timur up.

'Better out of here,' he said. 'It's only a place to die in. Lucky they didn't cut your legs off by mistake. Come on. Corbaci wants you.'

One huge arm around Timur he propelled him into the dusk. Timur walked for a few yards then collapsed, legs going in opposite directions.

'I'm all right,' he said. 'All right. Just dizzy. Rest a minute.'

'Dok.' Tedeki released him and stood, unconcerned in the rain, as Timur slid to the ground.

'What happened?' Timur on all-fours, his voice somewhat muffled.

'Chunk of stone. Fell right on your head.' Tedeki squatted, booming into Timur's ear. 'The Corbaci dragged you out, and me. *Ibn Kelb*! Son of a dog, I thought that he was going crazy. He told Sivas to see you back and said that he'd have his head off if he didn't. I never knew the Corbaci had so much feeling in him. That was after you killed the Austrian.'

'Killed the Austrian?'

'Don't you remember?' Tedeki dropped to his hands and knees like a huge dog and twisted his neck, peering into Timur's face. 'A big sergeant, trapped in some timber. You skewered him. Right in.'

'Oh yes.' Timur remembered, remembered dimly, as in a dream, the man, the clang of battle, dust . . . the first Austrian he had ever clearly seen, and the first he knew for certain that he had killed. 'Yes,' he said. 'I remember,' although he wished that he didn't.

'Right.' Tedeki heaved Timur to his feet. 'Better not keep the Corbaci waiting.'

They stumbled on through the camp, ankle deep in mud and worse, 'And only this morning,' Timur murmured to himself.

'What?' Tedeki bent a huge, bruised, and hairy ear.

'Only this morning,' Timur's voice was as wobbly as his legs. 'That Austrian.'

Tedeki laughed. 'This morning? You've been out cold for two days. Why do you think I'm down here?'

Vasif; amazingly spruce, best uniform, white hat, sword, blue eyes glinting from a scarred and battered face, observing Timur dispassionately, turning to Tedeki. 'Wash him, please. Get that blood off his head. You –' to Timur. 'Then change. There's a clean uniform in my tent. Quick.'

A quick, painful but affable scrub from Tedeki, a change, before Vasif again and being handed his own sword, brown with blood.

'Don't clean that,' Vasif said. 'Follow me.'

Mystified, bewildered indeed, Timur followed, groggily but fairly upright, past the usual paraphernalia of the camp, and into the Trautson Gardens, into undamaged orchards, a garden, Paradise after the shambles outside, and before the presence of the Serasker himself.

'Janissary Ven.' Vasif waved a hand and stood back a pace.

A brown hand waving, yellow silk rustling as Timur bowed. A whispered greeting and a question; 'This is the sword?'

'Yes, Serasker.' Vasif's sharp voice.

'So. Stand up, stand up boy – Janissary.' Kara Mustafa smiled graciously. 'We have met before, Janissary. Then your sword was unbloodied but now you have seen battle, served Islam and the Sultan and the Empire. Done your duty.' Mustafa snapped his fingers, a servant scurried forward – a new uniform, finest Damascus silk, a sword, hilt inlaid with gold, money. . . . 'A reward,' Mustafa said, 'For bravery'.

Timur muttered inarticulate thanks; first a gold coin, now a gold sword, it occurred to him that if the siege went on much longer he would be the richest Janissary in the army. But Mustafa had not finished;

'. . . Bravery, but a man, a young man, can be brave enough, do more than his share . . . would Timur like to stay in the Headquarters . . . use could be found for him . . .'

It took Timur a moment or two to grasp what he was being offered. A place next to Kara Mustafa; luxury in the camp, no danger of death or mutilation, limitless prospects for promotion, wealth, ease, power . . . a prospect more tempting than any apple, no matter how golden. Mustafa smiled at him, his aides, immaculate smiled with him, but from the corner of his eye Timur could see Vasif, straight as an arrow, uncorrupted, incorruptible, and behind him, Tedeki, huge and shambling, stupid, perhaps, but the bravest of the brave, unnoticed and unrewarded, and there was the rest of the orta, men of simple beliefs, grumblers, complainers, stoics, humourists, but all of whom had marched to the guns, following their Corbaci and the yellow and red forked standard.

Taking a deep breath, Timur made his immortal decision. 'If the Serasker permits, I would sooner stay with the orta.'

'Bismillah.' A kind of wonder crossed Mustafa's face. 'It is your decision? Yours alone?'

'Yes, Serasker.' Timur raised his head. 'Mine alone.'

'Then let it be so.' Mustafa was crisp, decisive, slapping his hands, the audience over. 'May God be with you.'

Vasif and Timur returned to Vasif's tent. There Vasif turned to Timur whose back itched a little as he wondered whether – as when once before he had refused a gift from the Serasker, and one less than his life – he would feel a rattan stick across it. But Vasif merely nodded. 'You might make a Janissary yet,' he said.

Chapter Twenty-Four

THE BEAR CAGE

AND while Timur Ven was being made into a Janissary, a true Janissary, a soldier without fear or pity, other men were being turned into non-janissaries, into non-men as the Magic Hill swallowed them up. And Austrian infantry were being turned into non-men, too, as it swallowed them up also. A remorseless, endless drain; man after man, company after company, as long as the galleries from the bastion remained open, they filed into the Ravelin – the Bear Cage they called it – and their taste of Hell. Souches' regiment, Serenyi's, Sherffenberg's, Wurttemberg's, Dupigny's dragoons, into the Ravelin, and, like the Janissaries, vanishing as though they had never been.

Tawny skinned clerks added up the Ottoman dead, pallid clerks totted up the Austrian dead. Meticulous columns of ink replaced columns of living men. The daily totals of the dead stretched out digit by digit as the armies dwindled and in Vienna the numbers shrank steadily from twelve thousand to eleven thousand to ten . . . nine . . . eight . . . an inexorable count-down to extinction as huge mines were exploded and, apparently inexhaustible, wave after wave of Turkish infantry rose from the old covered-way and came, shrieking, into the attack.

Heavy, drenching rain, and the smell of corruption hanging over the moat and the city; and not only the smell of the newly dead but the dead of old Vienna, too, receiving an earlier resurrection than they might have anticpated, as the graveyards were reopened.

That sour stench was upsetting Herr Vogel as he sat drinking a beer in The Swan – having resolutely given up the The Golden Eagle. It was not merely the smell, Vienna had grown used to that, but the thought of Wenzel's grave being disturbed by strangers, by unceremonious and callous grave diggers. Vogel had seen them once in the old Augustinian grave-yard throwing bones about and laughing.

He moved uneasily. It was a bad thought to have, and, really, he had worse worries he reminded himself. His wife was sick, sweating with a fever, Rudi was peaky, running, too often, to the choked privy, the Turks were closing in . . . one of the random texts he had heard from the pulpit had been haunting him for days; 'Let the dead bury the dead.' He had never understood that before but he thought that he understood it now, and it was right of course – the living should look to the living. Yes, that was right, he braced himself murmuring, 'Let the dead bury the dead.'

'What was that Herr Vogel?' the innkeeper leaned ingratiatingly over the counter.

'Nothing.' Vogel was abrupt to the point of rudeness, downed his beer and was about to leave when the door opened and Kaspar came in.

Vogel started but Kaspar held out a reassuring hand. 'It's all right, Herr Vogel. I've just come from your house. Everything is all right.'

'Ah,' Vogel sank back and raised two fingers at the innkeeper. 'It's come to a state, hasn't it? You see someone and the first thing you think of is bad news. Of course' – showing his hard-headed realism – 'Nowadays it usually *is* bad news.'

Two steins appeared and Kaspar took a drink. 'I'm sorry Frau Vogel isn't well.'

Vogel raised his stein. 'We had a doctor in.' He gave a short, bitter laugh. 'It's amazing. You spend all day trying to find a doctor, tell him your wife's got fever, bribe him to come round, and when he does he takes one look says, that's right, she's got the fever, and clears off. Anyway, he says it's not the . . . the plague.'

'No. That's one thing, Herr Vogel,' Kaspar, more worn-looking than a few weeks previously, nodded encouragingly. 'There's no plague in the city.'

'Thank God. Thank God Almighty for it.' Despite himself Vogel's eyes watered. 'Sorry,' he growled. 'It's just that I was thinking about . . . well, you can guess.' He brushed his eyes angrily. 'Ach, a bit of strain I suppose. Working all night, and then in the militia half the day. I even missed the roll call this week. First time since the Siege began. How long is that? Fifty days or thereabouts. Seems more like a lifetime.' He sighed. 'And no news of your father?'

'No.'

Vogel forced a smile. 'You know what they say, Kaspar. No news is good news, and I'll tell you, if I had to bet on any man on earth turning up safe and sound it would be him. Tell your mother I said so. And you keep out of harm's way, too.'

'I'll try.' Kaspar nodded, his face grave. 'I ought to tell you, Herr Vogel. Tomorrow we're going to start work on the Spaniard.'

'The Spaniard!' Vogel almost dropped his stein. 'But –' He found it hard to believe his ears. The Spaniard was the name the Viennese gave to a ramshackle medieval wall behind the Burg Bastion.

'It's true.' Kaspar was deeply serious. 'It's in case the Turks capture the Ravelin. And there's something else I think I ought to tell you.' He leaned forward and dropped his voice to a whisper. 'There's talk that the City Council wants to surrender.'

'What? What?' Vogel gaped. 'Where did you hear that for God's sake?'

Kaspar had the grace to blush a little. 'Well, you know that relative of ours who works in the Hofburg? Yes, I know' – as Vogel groaned – 'I know, but he does get to hear things and he says that there are some Councillors who think we could get terms from the Turks. They say we can't go on like this. There's no news from the Emperor – there's no news from anywhere come to that – but Count Kunitz – you know? He smuggled a letter in that says the Turks are as badly off as we are and they might make a deal.'

'Over my dead body.' Vogel slammed down his stein. 'I'd rather rot in hell.'

'Me too,' Kaspar said. 'But I thought that you ought to know.' He finished his drink and stood up. 'I've got to go. Mother . . .'

'I'm going, too.' Vogel paid for the drinks and the two men left the tavern. Immediately they were surrounded by a horde of beggars, refugees, in rags, hardly strong enough to stand, skeletal hands outstretched.

Vogel threw a few coins at them. Almost shame-faced he muttered, 'Someone's got to do it.'

'Like someone gives them bread.' Kaspar laughed. '*Gute Nacht.*'

'*Nacht.*' Vogel swung away, found Ottostrasse, walked down it into his house and found Anna, arms akimbo, and an unshaven captain and two armed men facing her.

'What the Devil!' Vogel elbowed past the soldiers.

'They charged in,' Anna said.

'Charged in?' Vogel glowered at the men, blue murder in his eyes, a stocky, ferocious sight, except that he did not perturb the captain who looked as if he had spent his life facing men with real murder in their eyes.

'Vogel?' he asked. 'Jakob Vogel? Baker? Of this address?'

'Yes,' Vogel bellowed. 'Jakob Vogel, baker, of this address. What of it? And what do you mean charging in here?'

'Didn't charge – walked. You're supposed to be in the Bakers' militia aren't you?'

'*Supposed* – I *am* in the militia. There's my musket.' Vogel pointed to that museum piece.

'Oh yes,' the captain looked casually at a list in his hand. 'Then why haven't you been reporting for duty?'

Vogel was staggered. 'Not reporting? I'm the only damned baker in Vienna who's never missed a parade. Ask our Guild Master.'

'We have. That's why we're here. You haven't been on a parade for five days.'

'Oh.' The wind was taken out of Vogel. 'Er, yes, that's true. But my wife has been ill.'

'Is that right?' the Captain said in a tone of voice which suggested that he had heard that tale before. 'It wouldn't have anything to do with the militia being moved on to the bastions would it?'

'No it wouldn't,' Vogel snapped. 'And look here Captain whatever your name is –'

'Busch.' The captain yawned. 'Souches' regiment.'

'All right. Captain Busch. I've got a wife ill, my son is sick, I've got to run a bakery –'

'And you've got to parade,' Busch said. 'And if you don't you'll get taken for a walk on the Burgplatz and be shot.'

'Shot?' Vogel was incredulous. 'Shot?'

'That's right,' Busch said. 'Orders of General Starhemberg. And don't give me all this stuff about running a bakery. We know all about bakers.'

'How dare you!' Anna stepped forward, her violet eyes dark with temper. 'How dare you talk to my father like that.'

Busch half-turned. 'Keep out of this Fraulein. It's none of your business.'

'Not my business?' Anna's hands were like claws. 'You come in here and say that you're going to shoot my father and you say that it's not my business? He's the finest baker in Vienna. Ask anyone. He was the first to volunteer for the militia and he's hardly raised his prices at all and you dare to say that he's no good!'

Anna's voice trembled but with anger, not fear. She's changing, Vogel thought. She's becoming a woman. She's like her mother.

'Get out. Go on, out!' Anna pointed dramatically and, since there was only one, unnecessarily, to the door.

223

Busch shifted a little uneasily. 'We're only doing our duty, Fraulein.'

Anna was scornful. 'I thought your duty was on the bastions.'

Busch's face changed abruptly, as though he had suddenly grown twenty years older. 'We've done that, Fraulein,' he said, very quietly. 'Two weeks in the Bear Cage.'

'And before that a month on the Lobel.' One of the other soldiers, lounging perilously close to the stuffed heron.

'And we're going back.' The third soldier. 'Where will you be going, Herr Baker?'

Vogel raised a weary hand. 'You're doing your duty,' he said. 'I can only do mine as well as I can.'

'They're *paid* to do their duty.' Anna, utterly unrepentant.

'My God!' Vogel raised his eyes to the ceiling. She's turned into her mother. And despite everything, despite Turks, sickness, overwork, the threat that he might be shot, he burst out laughing. 'Have a drink,' he said 'Anna, get out the plum brandy. You will have a drink, gentlemen?'

Yes, the soldiers would have a drink. They sat down as Anna, mutinously, brought out the brandy.

'Excuse me a moment.' Vogel went upstairs to the big bedroom. Frau Vogel was asleep, fretful, feverish, but sleeping, and Rudi, too, in his little cupboard. Vogel crossed himself devoutly and went back downstairs. He joined the soldiers at the table, poured himself a drink and raised his glass in salute.

'Did you mean it, Captain?' he asked.

'About shooting you?' Busch grinned, a friendly, battered sort of grin. 'Oh, yes. Orders are orders. But I think we'll let you off. I didn't mean to frighten the young lady, though.'

'You didn't frighten *me*.' Anna sharp but not, Vogel thought, totally displeased at being the sole woman in the room, smoothing the table cloth and giving the soldier who had disarranged it a piercing glare.

'Well,' Vogel said. 'They might not have frightened you, Anna, but they damned well frightened me. No offence lads.'

None taken. The men only too ready to stretch out their legs, drink good brandy, and eat good bread; amiable, affable, looking strangely youthful without their big cocked hats, politely doffed. And then the windows gave an ominous rattle.

Busch cocked an ear. 'Another,' he said, casually. No need ask another what. Another mine under the Ravelin. 'By the way.' Busch fished out his list. 'Don't want to sound nosy, but who else lives in this house?'

'Quite all right, Captain.' Vogel pushed the bottle round. 'There's just us, and then the Grafin von Schwarzbach – oh, and three soldiers in the attic.'

Busch stared a little groggily at his list. 'Sergeant Fischer, Corporal Hannebeck, Corporal Muller. Right?'

'Right. And good men they are too. We've not seen them for a few days but I'll tell you, they're a sight better than those vagabonds who used to live up there.'

'Glad to hear it.' Busch finished his drink. 'Right lads. Time to go. Much obliged to you Herr Vogel, Fraulein. *Gute Nacht.*'

Good night, good night, the rattle of muskets and swords, and Vogel found that Busch had him held discreetly by the shirt and was pulling him to the door. His heart pounding Vogel yielded to the tug and followed the men to the door, and was pulled a little further. Busch leaned forward, speaking quietly. 'Herr Vogel – didn't want to upset the fraulein again . . .'

'What is it?' Vogel was near to fainting.

'It's just that you'll have three new lads in tomorrow. The others are dead.'

'Dead?' Vogel couldn't believe his ears.

'That's right. In the Ravelin. The bears gobbled them up. Nacht.'

The men marched down Ottostrasse, and Vogel leaned against the wall of his bakery. He felt a deep sorrow, the big, solid and enduring sergeant gone, and the corporals. How strange that he should feel so distressed. He had only known the men for a few weeks, and he had not seen much of them at that, and yet he felt a sense of personal loss. What had Busch called the Ravelin? The Bear Cage, and the men had been gobbled up by the bears. Not a nice way of putting it but, Vogel supposed, the troops grew callous, found words which made light of horrors which would otherwise be too unendurable to talk about.

It was almost dark now. Across the street Herr Breitner began to test a violin, a scale and then a simple melody, a light, charming air. Vogel shook his head, a few hundred yards away in the red glare of cannon, men being slaughtered, and in here, in the friendly little street, the clear notes of the violin. It seemed wrong, and yet it seemed right. Life had to go on. Let the dead bury their dead. Yes. He turned and went inside.

The table was cleared, the glasses washed and put away, the bottle back in the cupboard, Anna sitting in her chair, a look on her face Vogel knew very well, having seen it on her mother's face a thousand times or so; a sharp, authoritative expression which was the prelude to some rebuke or other; which he got.

'You should go to the Council tomorrow and complain about those soldiers. The very idea! Coming in here like that, threatening you!'

'Now, now,' Vogel put on his apron, ready for the night's work. 'They didn't really mean any harm. They weren't to know that I wasn't a dodger – there's plenty of them. It was my fault anyway, I should have told the Guild Master. And when you've gone through what those lads face, well,' he shrugged.

Anna gave a disbelieving, and disapproving 'tut' and rocked slightly in her chair. Despite himself, Vogel grinned. He had seen his wife do that a thousand times, too, and his wife's mother, come to that. Odd, really. Generations came and went, like the grass in the fields, and yet the new generations sprang up, all different and yet all the same. He wondered if Sergeant Fischer had left children. He hoped so although he did not believe it. He opened his mouth, about to tell Anna of the death of the soldiers, then decided against it. Tomorrow would be time enough. Sufficient unto the day was the evil thereof. He gave himself a little shake. What was the matter with him? Endless random scraps from the Bible running through his head. If he wasn't careful he would end up like the old women who spent half their time mumbling away in St. Luke's. In any case, dearly though he loved Anna, *he* was the master in his house and *he* would decide what to do, although, looking at the new Anna, he was rather glad that she was going to get married when this *verdammt* siege was over. The combination of her and her mother might be rather formidable.

He went into the bakery and set to work, breaking his heart as, to conserve his dwindling stocks, he made loaves just that much smaller than they should be, and with just that little less yeast . . . and then, as full dark came upon the city, an orange glow lit up Ottostrasse.

'What the?' He dropped his dough and bustled out. Another red glow, a fiery train of sparks arcing into the sky. Breitner joined him, a fiddle still under his arm. 'What's going on?'

'Don't know.' Vogel walked briskly up Ottostrasse and was challenged by a guard on the night patrol.

'Me, Vogel, baker – what's happening?'

The guard spat in the gutter. 'Rockets. They're sending rockets up from St. Stephen's. Asking for help, as you might say. And Mother of God, we need it.'

Chapter Twenty-Five

THE PLAIN OF TULLN

THE rockets soared from St. Stephen's tall steeple night after night; fiery desperate signals, but the stars in their silent courses gave as much response as the outside world, and if the angels and archangels of Heaven itself saw them, or heard the prayers which accompanied them on their sparkling way, they gave no sign; even the shooting stars being blotted out by clouds.

Darkness beyond the Turkish lines; not a glimpse of Lorraine's cavalry; not a man, not a horse, not a picket or a scout moving across the Danube and, as the last days of August ticked away, the rockets went up utterly unheeded.

Unheeded that is except by the Ottoman host. Kara Mustafa in his vast camp clapping his hands with glee and every man in the army with him, any soldier with even half an eye able to recognize signs of desperation when they saw them, and the Keeper of the War Diary able to write with certitude, 'Now may the Almighty Lord of Heaven obliterate the infidels utterly from the face of the Earth.'

Which the servants of that Almighty Lord of Heaven did their best to do. In the gardens of the Neue Favorita Palace, captives by the hundreds and by the thousand were beheaded, and on the Ravelin butchery of another sort took place.

Only the base of the Ravelin was still held by the Austrians, but while it was held the city could stand firm; bastions protecting the Ravelin, the Ravelin protecting the bastions and the block-houses in the moat, and all three protecting the fragile, the vulnerable, but the precious curtain-wall. On the Ravelin, as the rockets soared and the Turkish bands played, a company of Starhemberg's own regiment, Captain Heisterman commanding. The company weary to the bone; bloody, filthy, stinking, although, behind a barrier of solid timber from the Emperor's own theatre, unyielding but, above the reek of the unburied dead sniffing something else. A sergeant worming his way to Captain Heisterman.

'Sir. Sir!' A musket ball whined past the sergeant's ear. 'Sir, the barricade is on fire!'

On fire with a vengeance; half the company trapped in the flames, the Twenty-eighth Orta blasting down those who tried to claw their way free, a mine, almost merciful in its effect, bringing down the face of the Burg Bastion, its deafening blast obliterating the screams of the dying. And yet Heisterman and his remnant held out throughout the night, and the morning, for what reasons only they and God Almighty knew, until, as an impassive clock in the Burgplatz said two o'clock in the afternoon of the second of September, Starhemberg ordered them to retreat and surrender the Ravelin.

Heisterman and his survivors fell back, fighting to the last, and as the horse-tail standards fluttered, were flaunted on the Ravelin, along the curtain wall and on the bastions troops caught each other's eye and sent the unspoken message, 'the beginning of the end' as the Magic Hill worked its last and most potent spell.

As Heisterman's scorched, battered, and bleeding remnant shambled onto the Burg Bastion, Stefan Zabruski was in a meadow, leaning against a wheel of the Zabruski waggon watching Pyotr Chelmnitz and two Zabruski serfs hovering over a fire. It was a pleasant meadow, deep with grass and the last flowers of summer; gentians, deep purple, pale-blue harebells, red willow herb – the first sign of autumn. Swifts and swallows skimmed across the meadow, ready for *their* journey south and the scent of pine needles freshened the sultry air.

Stefan yawned and rubbed his thighs, a little sore after ten days in the saddle riding down from Cracow. Chelmnitz and the serfs finished their alchemy over the fire and came to him. Chelmnitz handed over a wooden platter; bread, boiled lentils, and an extraordinary corpse.

Stefan looked at the corpse. 'What's this?'

One of the serfs, Grigor, leaned forward. 'It's an owl, Pan.'

'An owl?'

'Yes, Pan,' Grigor grinned amiably. 'I knocked it down from a tree this morning.'

Stefan pushed the owl on to Grigor's plate. 'You have it.'

'Thank you, Pan.' Grigor bolted the meat down before Chelmnitz could demand it. The master had strange tastes but it was a stroke of good fortune for him. He gnawed at the owl, spat out a bone, and said, 'Pan, where are we?'

It was a good question. The trouble was that Stefan had no good answer. For the past two weeks Field Hetman Sienawski had led his divison of the army through the valleys of Moravia in a leisurely, sauntering, summer amble; up hill and down dale, the men looting and robbing in an amiable enough fashion; the valleys becoming wider, deeper, more fertile, the farms richer, richer than Stefan had ever dreamed of, the language changing from Polish and Slovak to German, the peasants altering from sullen aquiescence to defiance and then, without explanation, in what Stefan was beginning to learn was the inexplicable habit of armies, they had halted and had been camped in this meadow for three days. All Stefan really knew was that they had left Poland, and Vera Soprona, and that they were eating owls.

Grigor sucked the owl's claw, 'Where is the Master, Pan?'

Another question Stefan found hard to answer. His father had ridden off with Soprona and the other schlactas a day or so before but where they had gone to he had no idea.

'Well, Pan –' Grigor tucked his hand up his ragged sleeve so that only the owl's claw showed and suddenly scratched his fellow serf's neck. 'Hooo!' he called and burst out laughing as the serf jumped. Stefan laughed, too, and Chelminitz.

'Ah, Pan,' Grigor leaned on his back. 'It's all one anyway' – and then his laughter died away – 'The Master,' he said.

Zabruski returning, riding his second-best horse, dismounting, clicking his fingers for a flask of Moravian wine, grunting, snuffling, settling down, passing the wine around quite unselfconsciously, treating Chelmnitz and the serfs as he might treat his house-dogs, tit-bits one moment, kicks the next.

'Get ready to move out,' he said, addressing Stefan. 'Tomorrow. Pyotr, you and these' – jerking his head at the serfs –' stay here.'

Stefan blinked. Was that all? It seemed so, since his father showed no sign of saying more. 'Er . . .' he gave a little, unnecessary cough. 'Grigor doesn't know where we are,' he said, as if this was the most amazing demonstration of ignorance since – he thought of himself and Nathan the pedlar and blushed.

Zabruski stared at Grigor. 'Does it matter to you?'

'No, Master.' Grigor grinned disarmingly.

Zabruski swatted away a fly and peered around through his piggy eye. 'I've been to a conference,' he said. 'At a place called Stetteldorf.'

'A conference?' Stefan leaned forward. 'And were you at it, Father?'

Zabruski gave a rare, ironic grin. 'It was a conference of kings.'

'Of Kings master?' Grigor, gaping, even the sour Chelmnitz impressed.

'Kings, yes, or something like them.' 'Zabruski stirred scorched bones with his boot. 'What in God's name are those?'

'An owl, master,' Grigor said.

Zabruski kicked the bones again. 'I've eaten worse,' he said. He blew out his pink cheeks. 'Aye, kings, or something like them, the Elector of Saxony, the Duke of Lorraine, a Count . . . Count Waldeck from Franconia, some Bavarian called Degenfeld – and John Sobieski.'

Sobieski! Stefan swelled a little, even the cynical flogger Chelm-

nitz straightened his slouching back, even the serfs looked
up.

'And the Emperor?' Stefan asked. 'Was he there?'

'No.' Zabruski gave a crooked grin. 'He's stuck somewhere up
the Danube. The right place, too. Who wants him around?'

'Oh.' If his father said so then Stefan was ready to agree, but he
was deeply disappointed. Kings, even Kings of Poland were all
very well, and Electors – whatever they might be – and Barons
and Counts, but an Emperor – the name had a certain ring to
it . . .

'It's what they call precedence,' Zabruski said. 'Who comes
first. Who commands the army. If the Emperor comes he has to
take charge, and he's no soldier.'

Stefan could grasp that. Most important, precedence, rank,
title, birth, who came first in the great social order, ordained by
God Almighty since Adam; man over the beasts, super-men over
sub-men; Chelmnitz over the serfs, himself over Chelmnitz, his
father over him, Lubomirski over the Zabruskis, and the King
over all, although, as Stefan was beginning to understand, that
convenient system did not always work; after all, it was the serfs
who knew how to find food, Chelmnitz who knew how to drive
the oxen, Hetman Sienawski who knew how to bring an army
from Poland to here – wherever that was – asking, and receiving
for once, an answer.

'We're near a place called Tulln,' Zabruski said. 'It's just across
the Danube. They've built a bridge there. We cross tomorrow and
march downstream and attack the Turks.'

'How far is that, Father,' Stefan blurted out the question.

'Twenty miles or so.'

Stefan blinked. Twenty miles! It was hard to believe. After the
months of waiting and travelling, Vienna, that great city was a
mere cock's stride away. Why, tomorrow they could be riding in
triumph through it. Saying so and receiving a sardonic answer
from his father – 'You've got a lot to learn about armies.'

A lot to learn, and Stefan began learning it the next day as Field
Hetman Sienawski's column was mustered and put into some

sort of order of march, filtering slowly through a forest on to a ride hacked out by fifteen hundred men which led down to the Danube and the bridge of Tulln. A rough and ready ordering, taking all that day and all the next day, too, in a drenching downpour which turned the clearing into a quagmire where horses sank fetlock deep, exhausted but flogged forward by men as exhausted. And that was only the beginning. As Sienawski's column reached the bridge of Tulln, Sobieski's troops were arriving, too, fighting for a place across the swollen Danube, almost, as it did occur to Stefan, as if they were fighting to join the ranks of the dead – and there were plenty of those – bloated bodies bobbing downstream, victims of the Tartar raids up the river.

The fourth of September; the Polish host spared ten minutes for prayers to St. Marcellus, his name day, a blistering sun came out through the clouds, blazing down on the army, and the bridge, and on the woods and the hills and on Vienna.

That city a slimy purgatory and the moat a stinking Hell Sweat pouring from General Count Starhemberg as he juggled his men from post to post; sixty-four posts to be watched and defended and less than six thousand men left for duty and a half of those barely fit to stand, let alone face the Turks.

In the Burg Bastion, Colonel Souches having a furious row with his Quartermaster over a shortage of water for his men; on the Spaniard, Kaspar Haller, stripped to the waist, slaving away; in Ottostrasse, Anna mopping her mother and Rudi; in the Bakers' Guild Hall, Herr Vogel demanding, but not getting, a certificate of exemption from militia duty and then, at two o'clock, another gigantic explosion shook the city as a mine exploded under the Burg Bastion and horse-tails and pennants came through the dust.

Two hours of battle, Starhemberg himself leading the counterattack. The Austrian infantry standing on the bastion so close-packed that the dead could not fall to the ground but were held upright by the ranks of the living. Point-blank cannon fire, swarms of Turkish arrows so dense they darkened the sky, Dupigny's dragoons charging forward, sealing the gap and driving the Janissaries back into the moat.

Four hundred Austrian dead, and they the bravest of the brave; the Ottoman dead uncountable and uncounted, but they came again the next day, *Allah* on their lips and murder in their hearts, clawing over the shattered masonry, blasted by case-shot and crashing volleys of musketry, skewered on pikes and bayonets but as night drew its curtain on the fifth of September, and as faces from half the world stared with sightless eyes at the unheeding stars, and as the rockets fizzed from St. Stephen's, the forces of the Sultan were on the bastion, and they were there to stay.

The Ravelin taken, the Burg Bastion half Turkish. Kara Mustafa gave an order and, surrounded by his Albanian bodyguard, his band struck up, the long Turkish trumpets wailing derisively, kettle drums pounding, gongs reverberating . . .

On the curtain wall, where once, Herr Haller had frightened Anna Vogel, back on active duty, and, after his brush with Anna and other Viennese women, not unhappy to be so, Captain Busch rubbed his scrubby chin with calloused hands and shook his head. 'Make's you wonder, doesn't it?' he said to his sergeant.

'Sir?'

'I said it makes you wonder. Listen to that?'

An obedient soul the sergeant listened to the Turkish bands but, not being of a reflective frame of mind, merely shrugged. 'Sounds like a lot of scalded cats to me, Sir.'

Busch grinned his friendly, chipped grin. 'Does to me, too,' he admitted. 'Must be something in it though. Look at the way they've come at us this past two days – two months, come to that.'

'Ja, they've got guts, Sir.' A ready admission from a man who knew what charging cannon meant.

'Yes.' Busch scratched a yellow-green ulcer on his hand. 'They've got guts right enough. I wonder what makes them tick, hey? I just wonder.'

Kara Mustafa himself could not have answered that question, nor could Corbaci Vasif, nor his Odabasis, nor Timur, nor Tedeki, nor any man in the Ottoman army. Certainly it was no longer the fear of an officer's sword in the back, or an executioner's sword across the neck. Those threats had long since lost their menace. By now the Turkish troops were immune from the fear of death as men might be immunised from disease. They no longer wondered whether they were going to die, or when, or how, since they knew that they were as certain to die as they were that the sun would rise the next day – if Allah allowed them to see it.

Watching his orta as they shuffled back into the trenches, Vasif was satisfied. Once, weeks before, he had thought of the stages men went through in battle; excitement, fear, fatigue, then the destruction of nerve which left men futile. But there was a state beyond that where warriors walked, as it were, through a gauze curtain which had separated them from the infinite and each step took them to the knowledge that they were close to God, close to Allah, the Lord of the Worlds, and ready to await the ghostly camels which would take them to Paradise and all its charms.

And so, as God made the sun rise on the sixth of September, and the orta rose with it, Vasif was satisfied, and especially as he saw Timur Ven bowing in his prayers – seventeen years by human counting, seven times seventeen by human experience – purified, refined, by suffering as he had been promised long ago in Osijek, by the great bridge over the Drava. But there were other bridges, Vasif thought as he, too, knelt and bowed, one of a hundred million, from Vienna to Java, from Timbuctoo to the Crimea; yes, other bridges which crossed not mere rivers, idiotic barriers dividing men from men, but bridges which led from this mortal and corrupt world to the very gates of the immortal and incorruptible world beyond worlds. Thinking that as the orta stood and Timur, holding his golden sword and himself as thin as a Toledo blade, marched back to the firing line.

As the Twenty-eighth Orta marched, Stefan, on his fine horse, next to his father, was moving down to the bridge at Tulln. As became a King, Sobieski crossed first, followed by the nobility, the pontoon bridge swaying precariously under the weight of the armour, then the schlactas, and then the infantry of the Standing Army, so ragged that Sobieski felt obliged to say that they had left their best uniforms behind, expecting to be better clad from the spoils of the victory to come. Lorraine smiled politely but hoped, deeply and sincerely, that the performance of the infantry would be better than their appearance.

But across the bridge at last and onto the plain of Tulln, the great and final rendezvous; Saxons, Bavarians, Franconians, Poles and – the wonder of the world, volunteers from all Europe; princes from Hanover, Brunswick, Hesse, Sweden, Italy, Scotland and Ireland – even an English nobleman, the Lord Lansdowne – and, astonishingly, men from France, but over all, fifty-two years old, obese, fat bulging over the saddle of his horse, John Sobieski, apart from the Emperor languishing on his barge, the undisputed leader of the army, writing out the order of battle with his own, majestic hand.

The Order of Battle; simple really, filtering down through Hetmans and generals and colonels, to Zabruski. A field officer standing among a group of schlacta, a rough map in his hand, and explaining the tactics.

'Here are we' – a jab at the map –' and here is Vienna. Between us is forest what the Austrians call the Wienerwald, the Vienna woods. Rough country, hills and forest but nothing that Poles can't get through.'

A growl of agreement, nothing on God's earth that could stop a Polish army.

'So *kolega* – comrades – the Saxons and the Bavarians are going to march along the banks of the Danube. The Austrians will march in the centre, and here.' A finger made a wide detour on the map. 'Here, on the right of the line – us.'

A growl of pleasure, the right of the line being the place of honour in battle.

'Now.' The officer peered closer at his map. 'There is a little valley called the Weidling valley. Further orders when we get there. Austrian foresters are going to guide us through the forest. So, *kolega*, move as the generals say and may God and the Virgin of Czestochowa guard you from evil.'

Amen to that, and Amen again, as the Polish army moved across the plain behind the German troops. An unwieldy man-oeuvre, as awkward as shuffling a pack of cards with one hand but as the day progressed Stefan began to see logic of the apparently random and chaotic movements; close on a hundred thousand men had to be pushed and prodded into order, each army in its proper place and in its correct divisons; infantry, cavalry, artillery, supplies, although, as evening came and rations were given out, it was dawning on Stefan that although great armies might move on horses, both horses and men needed food, and the fact that the Polish waggons had been left across the Danube became of more importance to him than the sight of men in armour, and he would have cheerfully swapped Sobieski's sword for a leg of lamb.

But in the end, as stars broke through the rain-cloud, the great shift of position had taken place and the armies stretched across the plain, facing the Vienna woods, Vienna itself, and the army of the Sultan of the Ottoman Empire.

Chapter Twenty-Six

THE CURTAIN WALL

As half-Europe wheeled and manoeuvred across the plain of Tulln, half Asia hurled itself again at the citadel of Christendom. Having smashed at the Burg Bastion, Kara Mustafa, like a boxer switching from his right hand to his left, attacked the Lobel Bastion and at noon exactly, as the garrison of Vienna expected to hear the familiar call to prayer from the Ottoman camp, the never-ceasing Lagunci exploded two mines under the Lobel Bastion.

Huge mines, half-demolishing the antiquated structure, the stonework like shrapnel mowing down the Austrian infantry, scores of men suffocated, inside the casemates and horse tails coming again through the dust.

More hours of fighting, savagery, courage, the first wave of Janissaries beaten back, and a second until, under the blazing sun, the fighting died down as suddenly as it had begun, but when the dust settled it was clear that the last of the city's defences were virtually useless.

'What are we to do?' Lord Mayor Liebenberg, sick, dying, propped up in his bed talking to Starhemberg.

'Do?' Starhemberg shrugged as if the question was ridiculous. 'What do you think we're going to do. Carry on as before.'

'But the bastions . . . shattered . . .' Liebenberg was almost too weak to get the words from his mouth. 'If they get through . . .'

'We'll fight them street by street. House by house. Room by

room if necessary. Every man armed – every woman, come to that.'

'And no news from the Emperor?'

'No news.' Starhemberg flat, emphatic, unmoved. 'No news at all.'

No news, but every soul in Vienna knowing perfectly well what the assault on the Lobel Bastion meant.

'It's the end, isn't it?' Frau Vogel, still a little sickly, but on her feet again, sat in the parlour of the little bakery. 'One more attack and they'll be in.'

'No, no,' Herr Vogel attempted to be reassuring, but his words sounded hollow in his own ears. 'The walls are still standing, and the soldiers –'

Frau Vogel raised a finger and pointed it to the ceiling. Vogel understood perfectly well the significance of that gesture. His wife was not pointing to the Grafin, still keeping her fragile hold on life, but to the attics where new troops had taken over Fischer's quarters.

'I know,' Vogel muttered. And he did know. The soldiers, a corporal and two privates were more like walking scarecrows than men. 'But the Turks are no better,' he said.

'How do you know?'

'Well . . .' Really Vogel had no answer to that and it suddenly dawned on him that, incredible though it seemed, in two months he had not seen a single Turk. On, a militia post where he spent his afternoon duty he could see tents, horses, men, but a soldier had told him that they were Transylvanians, Christians.

Anna in her new-found maturity admitted to family councils, had never seen a Turk, either, in fact she had not even seen the Transylvanians, but Kaspar had. 'He says that they're starving,' she said.

'So are we.' Frau Vogel stating the worst, and not far from the truth, either the herrings long since finished, and the lentils and the peas.

'Not starving, Mother.' Vogel tried a feeble smile. 'We've got bread.'

'And how long can we live on that?'

'Oh, we can manage on it for a long time. Bread is a very good food you know. People don't really know how good bread is when it's made properly. Why –' He stopped and grinned sheepishly. 'Once a baker always a baker,' he said, 'Anyway, we've enough to last us until the relief gets here.'

'And when will that be?'

'Oh,' Vogel affected a hearty confidence. 'Soon. Quite soon. You'll see, mother. They'll be here before you know it.'

'They'll never come.'

'Don't you believe that.' Vogel shook himself, stood up and took his musket. 'Must be off. Militia.'

'And where are you going?' Frau Vogel asked.

'The usual place. On the Carinthian gate. Nice and quiet there, ha ha. The Transylvanians, you know. They wave to us. It's true,' he said. 'Yes' – red in the face – 'Why, it's safer there than here.'

'You're going on the bastions, aren't you?' Frau Vogel spoke with unnatural calm.

'No . . .' Vogel's voice died away. He was not a good liar.

'Frau Breitner told me.' Frau Vogel nodded. 'She told me last night.'

'Well she told you wrong.' Vogel slapped the table. 'We're not on the bastions at all. We're, well, we're on the Burgplatz, I don't deny that, but we're out of harm's way. We're just a last –' He stopped and looked at his worn shoes.

'Last resort.' Frau Vogel said.

No answer to that. Vogel kissed his wife and Anna, another innovation of the siege, kissed Rudi, pale and thin in his little cupboard bed, and went out to do his duty.

Vogel's footsteps echoed down the little street. A voice cried '*Tag*,' then silence. Frau Vogel plucked at the table cloth.

'It's the end,' she said. 'The end. Dear God, what's to become of us?'

Anna stood up and took her mother by the elbow. 'Come along mother. You have to rest.'

'Rest?'

'Yes.' Anna said 'Time to lie down.'

'I can't. No.' Tears trickled down Frau Vogels white cheeks.

'Yes you can.' Anna was soothing. 'A nice lie down. Remember what the Doctor said. Come along now.'

'Lie down' – Frau Vogel's voice rose – 'And have the Turks find me in my bed . . .'

'Now mother,' Anna was firm. 'They won't do any such thing. Come along now.' Wheedling and cajoling she got her mother to her feet. 'Hush now, you mustn't frighten Rudi.'

The trickle became a silent flood. 'Rudi –' a long, stifled wail.

'Sssh, shush,' Anna patted her mother on the back. 'It's going to be all right. Now, now,' taking her to the door, leading her upstairs, 'Lie down now, father will take care of us, and Kaspar.' Mopping her forehead with vinegar. 'Sleep. Sleep. Rest and sleep . . .'

Frau Vogel closed her eyes, murmured something indistinct, slipped away into a merciful slumber. Anna stared down at her for a moment or two then carefully tip-toed into her own bedroom. Rudi was asleep, whimpering some childish name. Anna looked down upon him, too, for a little while, then went downstairs into the bakery. She opened the big drawer where her father kept his tools and took out Vogel's huge, razor-sharp knife, went into the parlour and sat down facing the door, the knife in her hand, waiting as the sultry afternoon wore away.

A thunderstorm at about four sent the militia behind the bastions scurrying for cover, more for the sake of their gunpowder than for themselves, and silenced the Turkish cannon blasting from the old counterscarp. Starhemberg and his colonel drew up the defence roster for the coming night, a hundred or so dead bodies were flung into the open graves of the Paserhof cemetery, Starhemberg, his colonels and engineers walked the streets leading from the Burgplatz, and, behind the Spaniard, worked out how much chain would be needed to blockade the streets, and the last of the day's wounded died in the moat.

A fiery sunset, the sky an ominous red; night, rockets fizzed up from St. Stephen's and along the walls the infantry stood to, peering out into the darkness of the moat, and beyond the moat the Turkish infantry lined up for another attack.

Opposite the Lobel Bastion Vasif faced his men. Only forty left of the one hundred and eighty who had marched so boldly across the Drava three months ago, only half a company mustered anyway, the Odabasi making a token gesture of a salute and murmuring, 'Ninety men present, Corbaci. All others accounted for.'

'So,' Vasif nodded and took a step forward. Unless directly ordered to he rarely addressed his men directly and was contemptuous of those colonels who did, regarding them as merely currying favour. He obeyed his orders unquestioningly and he expected to be obeyed in the same way. Allah would decide the rights and wrongs at the Day of Judgement. But there were times, and there were times, and this, he thought, was one of them.

'*Voyalons*, wayfarers, you have been told before that Vienna is ready to fall. Now I tell you – *I* – that it is. Those rockets are cries for help. Tonight –' He stopped and flicked his thigh. 'Janissary Tedeki. Tedeki!'

'Corbaci,' Tedeki was staring into the night, a puzzled frown on his amiably murderous face.

'Don't think, Tedeki,' Vasif said coldly. 'Listen.'

'Yes, Corbaci, but I thought I saw – there's another!' He stretched out a huge hand. 'Look, Corbaci.'

Almost despite himself Vasif turned and looked to the west, into the impenetrable darkness of the Wienerwald. Absolutely nothing to be seen there, only the huge bulk of the Kahlenburg ridge, darker even than the sky. 'I wonder if the man's gone off his head,' he thought, not without pity – and then, and then his face changed;

'Allah!' he said.

Shouts and cries echoed down Ottostrasse, a fist hammered on the door of Herr Vogel's bakery, and a voice bellowed, 'Vogel – Vogel, come out, quick!'

In the parlour Frau Vogel screamed.

'Right. Right!' Vogel strode into the parlour and took down his musket.

Anna and Frau Vogel stared at him. 'They're here, aren't they?' said Frau Vogel. Her voice oddly enough was calm, level, unflinching.

'Sounds like it.' Vogel said. He looked for the last time at his little parlour, the heron, the lamp, his pots and pans, the crucifix . . . 'Leave all this,' he snapped. 'Get as much bread as you can carry. Get the Hallers and go to St. Stephens.'

The door pounded again, there were shrieks from the street, shrieks and howls.

'Right!' Vogel roared, opened the door, and found Herr Breitner on the step.

'They've come! They've come!' Breitner, his hands flung high, dancing hysterically, the street full of people, shouting, roaring, hysterically.

'Right!' Vogel gave a bellow loud enough to stir the great bell of St. Stephen's. 'Get your musket. All of you!'

And then, incredibly, Breitner began laughing. 'You don't understand,' he bellowed back. '*Our* armies have come! We're saved, Herr Vogel. Saved!'

Fires on the Kahlenberg, Colonel Heisler and 600 dragoons riding through the dusk to answer Vienna's calls for help. The first troops of the allies, volunteers sent forward by the Duke of Lorraine, and coming up behind them the relieving army, but coming slowly, creeping across the plain of Tulln at a snail's pace; wrangles over precedence, command, routes, supplies, the Duke of Lorraine in his old grey coat, self-effacing and by his plain straightforward simplicity finding compromises which satisfied the pride of princes and the ambitions of kings.

An agonisingly slow movement then across the burned and looted plain, Germans to the left, Poles swinging to the right, and with every laborious step forward the hills of the Wienerwald looming larger; larger indeed than the Poles had bargained for, and hardened soldiers with a lifetime in their profession looking at the barrier thoughtfully as they reached the next rendezvous, on the little river Weidling at the base of the forest.

Fifteen miles away, in his great encampment, Kara Mustafa and his Agas were looking at the hills equally thoughtfully as they listened to a Tartar scout sent in by Murad Ghiraj.

'Eighty thousand men? Forty thousand cavalry? And two hundred cannon?'

'Yes, Serasker. Many men, many guns, many horse – Sipahi.'

'Ah!' Mustafa snatched at the word. Sipahi – heavy cavalry, huge horses carrying a giant weight of armour. 'They will take some moving,' he murmured, 'and some feeding too. And the cannon . . .'

'Very bad for cannon –' The scout waved an eloquent hand at the mountains.

'So,' Mustafa looked around at his generals, an unspoken question but one which did not need putting into words; that question was really the posing of a choice: to withdraw the army from the city, swing west and with their full might face the enemy on the mountains, or to make a final onslaught on Vienna.

Mustafa had no doubt whatever about his answer. Vienna was his. He knew it in his bones, in the very heart of his grasping, ambitious being. One more shake of that heretical tree and the Golden Apple would fall down into his grasp and he would have triumphed where even Suleiman the Magnificent had failed. He pointed to the Aga of the Engineers. 'Can we break through the Curtain Wall?'

'But certainly, Serasker.' The Aga was confident that his men could break the walls of Hell if required.

'How long?'

'Two, three days, no more. We have mine shafts almost against the wall now.'

Three days. Mustafa had a bitter taste in his mouth. Seventy two hours between him and the ultimate Turkish victory. 'Very well.' He made *his* immortal decision. 'We carry on with the siege.'

He raised his hand as an almost inaudible murmur of disbelief – discontent – ran around his commanders. 'We can hold the enemy off in the mountains, inshallah, and with the city ours we can turn on them with all our forces and destroy them utterly. Utterly. What a victory will be ours then!'

He peered around. Beys, Beylerbeyis, Pashas, Agas, and saw only apprehension. What a victory indeed might be ours, the veiled eyes and lowered faces seemed to suggest – and what a defeat; a gigantic army marching on them and an undefeated fortress to their rear. One Aga bold enough to make a suggestion, *echo* a suggestion, covering *his* rear, too. 'Ibrahim Pasha, Serasker.'

'What of him?' Mustafa was viciously sharp, having deliberately kept the old man from the conference.

'Merely, Serasker, I think his view is that we should leave a minimum of men here and take the whole army to face the enemy. Shatter them, and what is left for Vienna?'

Profound sense in that remark. The observation of a fighting man. Even Kara Mustafa could see that and yet, and yet, he slapped his knee. 'In the name of God we can do both.'

No further argument once the Serasker had spoken and by the afternoon, in a brilliant tour-de-force of organization, the Ottoman plans were made and being carried out; Sari Hussain, that elegant prince from Syria, the grim old Ibrahim, and Kara Mehmed Pasha were moving away from Vienna to the base of the Kahlenburg mountain with thirty thousand cavalry.

On the walls of Vienna, from St. Stephen's tower, and from every conceivable vantage point, the Viennese watched the movement of the host of cavalry.

'They're going – they're going!' Total strangers hugging each other in the street, dancing and capering, laughing – and crying, Lord Mayor Liebenberg hearing the news too, whispered into his ear, as he took the Last Rites and died.

The sound of a city celebrating reached the ears of Starhemberg in a room overlooking the Burgplatz and the shattered bastions, as he, too, watched the Turkish cavalry move at lightning speed towards the mountains. A young ensign with him shook his head in disbelief. 'They are going, Sir. They are.' Turning and his overjoyed smile vanishing as he saw Starhemberg's implacable face.

'Cavalry,' Starhemberg said. 'By God, he's going to try it.'

'Try it, Sir?'

'Try and do both – hold off the Duke and take the city too. He's left the Janissaries. My God.'

'But Sir,' the ensign was aghast. 'Surely it's finished. We're relieved.'

'We'll be relieved when the Duke and Sobieski get here and not before. Where is Major Rosstaucher?'

Major Rosstaucher sent for, brought, standing stiffly to attention as Starhemberg gave him precise orders. 'Now Liebenberg is dead I am placing you in charge of all the burgher companies. Drum-head court martial for any man not doing his duty. Chain the streets, barricades, any houses marked down by me, turn out the owners and get troops in there. Understood?'

Understood. Rosstaucher looking like the sort of man perfectly ready to shoot the whole of Vienna if ordered. Starhemberg went back to the window, and nodded towards the Wienerwald. 'It can take a day riding over that. How long will it take to bring an army across it? Hey?'

The same thought was going through the mind of the Duke of Lorraine, John Sobieski, the Elector of Saxony, their generals and hetmans, field officers and men, down to the humblest poor bloody infantryman, and it was going through the mind of Stefan Zabruski, hungry, cold, wet, waiting, the interminable wait of a soldier, and as the eastern sky darkened looking at the black bulk of the Wienerwald grow ever more menacingly dark and ominous with every passing minute, and, a lad used to pork and pike for his breakfast, not cheered either by being given, after a few hours uneasy, shivering sleep, a chunk of bread, and even less cheered when, as he munched his bread and his horse ground away at a handful of oats, to hear two infantrymen, looking more like refugees from some natural disaster saying, as they passed, 'Jesu Maria, they don't want troops to get over that lot. They ought to get a herd of goats.' Laughing with gallows humour as they slouched away.

But the sun burned away the morning mists, trumpets sounded, Zabruski rode back from a meeting with the Hetman. 'Up there' – pointing to the hills – 'Us first, then the infantry, then the guns. *And stay with me*'.

Stefan swung onto his horse, bonier now than it had been, like Stefan himself; but mounted, sword in scabbard, pistols across his saddle, his spirits rose, rising with his elevation, as it were. All around him the murmur and clamour of the army, as far as the eye could see banners and standards raised, long, reverberating calls, orders, a posse of light horsemen cantering into the woods, and then a field officer waving an imperious hand and the schlactas moving forward.

Ah! Stefan's heart leaped. Now, at last, the knighthood of Poland, invincible and unconquerable, wending their way on the last crusade. What tales he would have to tell Vera Soprona, what trophies he would lay at her feet, what airs he would demonstrate among those unfortunate youths who had never known hardship – or battle. Aiee, as he rode behind his father he felt an exultation, a transfiguration from that gauche, half-idiotic youth who, only a year ago, had flushed with rage at the remark of a pedlar.

But an hour later the exultation had gone, and the transformation was a different kind, as, dismounted, sweating, mud-spattered, he dragged his horse up a slimy trail; one pace forward, two back, the horse slithering, jerking its head, eyes rolling, the bridle tugging his arms until he felt that they were being pulled from their sockets.

Within two hours, having travelled half a mile, he had lost his father. He had stopped, exhausted, one of a column of a thousand cavalry and been driven off the track by a major, a giant and a professional, his armour strapped across his horse. 'Off the track, by Jesus. Off the track –' A slash of a stick across Stefan's horse to make the point.

'Mother of God.' Stefan collapsed under a tree. Mosquitoes and flies swarmed around him, stinging, biting, his pale face, reddened by the sun, a mass of lumps, hungry, thirsty, and, if the truth be told, not far from tears.

Joined by another Pole, short, stocky, cheerful, resting his horse, giving Stefan a mouthful of water from a flask and laughing when he found out that Stefan did not have one. 'You'll learn,' he said. 'Take your time, anyway. If you have to stop – why, stop. Get out of the way, take a rest, and give your horse one as well, you'll need it whenever we get out of these God-damned hills. And don't worry, they can't start without us.'

A friendly wave as Stefan lurched to his feet and filtered into the line of cavalry. A hundred slippery feet to a crest, a slither down into a ravine, and then another ridge, worse than the previous one. Rain, heat, mosquitoes, biting flies, the stink of horses, curses, blows at times, and, now and then, the crack of a musket as a merciful trooper shot a horse with a broken leg, and by night on the tenth of September, as Stefan plunged down into a tiny hamlet on a brook, the Polish vanguard had advanced two miles, and the artillery had not got as far even as that.

Stefan collapsed by the brook but, with an enormous effort, and remembering the stocky man in the forest, watered his horse, found some branches with leaves on, and made a token effort to feed it. As he was doing so a man came up to him, a provost major, hard as nails. He looked Stefan over. 'Zabruski?' he asked.

'Yes.'

'Your father's been asking for you. He's upstream.'

It was a piece of news Stefan would have been glad not to have received that night, as all he wished to do was stay there for the next several months, but he dragged himself up and stumbled along the little valley and found his father.

Zabruski took one look at his son. 'Here.' He passed Stefan a bottle of vodka. Two swigs of that on an empty stomach and Stefan's weariness melted away. In fact he was ready to set off for Vienna there and then but Zabruski casually kicked his legs from under him.

'Lie down. Get some sleep. We've a hard day's work tomorrow.' Zabruski drank some vodka himself and looked thoughtfully at Stefan. 'Maybe you ought to stay behind,' he said.

'No!' A cry almost of pain from Stefan. Stay behind! After coming so far . . . it was like a sentence of death. To return and say that after a journey of four hundred miles his body had given way on the last lap. It was inconceivable.

'Well,' Zabruski uncharacteristically hesitated. 'We'll see tomorrow.'

Another mouthful of old bread, another swig of vodka, curtains for Stefan, sleeping the sleep of the dead, one of thousands, and tens of thousands sprawled across the Vienna woods in a huge, straggling and uncoordinated line, stretching from the great and unconquered monastery of Klosterneuburg on the Danube to Mount Tulbing, ten miles to the south.

And another day's purgatory to come. In dense cloud the Polish army dragged its way over another ridge, and another interminable ridge, going down, as exhausting as going up, as horses lost their footing and crashed down on panicky men but by noon the advance guard had reached the valley of the Weidling and by late afternoon, as the rest of the troops straggled in, something like a coherent line had been established. And there was food, fresh bread at least, sent down valley from the Danube, some proof at least that someone, somewhere, knew, in a groping sort of way what was happening, although, after the past two days, Stefan took some persuading of that. But news filtered down through the vague command of the Polish army. Soprona himself finding Zabruski and Stefan and, sprawled in a meadow, explaining in a hazy manner, what was happening.

'Lorraine and the King are at Weidling down the river. Making plans.'

Zabruski gave a barking laugh. 'Plans for what for Jesus Christ's sake?'

'For that.' Soprona jabbed a thumb across the stream. Another ridge, pine covered, ominous, looming over them like a black cloud.

'And what's over that,' Zabruski growled.

'Oh,' Soprona was elaborately casual. 'Vienna.'

'Vienna?' Stefan stared at the ridge. 'Vienna?'

Soprona spat. 'That's what they say, Stefan. Its the end of the road.

The end of the road. After the past week Stefan found it hard to believe: the road had seemed to have so many endings; Tulln, Konigstetten, the entry into the Wienerwald, and each ending had merely been the start of another interminable, dragging stage of an endless journey. He stared again at the forbidding ridge. 'Really?' he asked. 'Really?'

'Yes.' Soprona said. 'Really.'

There was a stir along the banks of the stream, men standing, the chink of bridles, the clatter of armour. A field officer picked his way down to the Zabruskis and Soprona.

'If you please, your Honours, be ready to move.'

Stefan stood up, raised a hand. 'What is the name of that mountain?'

The officer glanced over his shoulder. 'What the devil does it matter?'

As Stefan was beginning that last step to fame and glory, Sobieski was with Lorraine in the ruins of the old monastery of St. Joseph, actually on the Kahlenberg seized the night before in a lightning attack by volunteer Italians. Already the Saxons and Austrian infantry were moving steadily forward, forming a solid line. Good troops, well clothed, well armed, steady, disciplined, and, since they were close to the Danube and the great base of Klosterneuburg, well fed, too.

An impressive sight and one of which Lorraine was, with

reason, proud in his modest, matter of fact way; sitting on a stone as simple as a burgher on an afternoon stroll, pointing down to where, surrounded by Ottoman tents, and half-hidden by the smoke from ten thousand campfires, Vienna lay, still inviolate, and not two and a half miles distance.

But Sobieski, magnificent in silks and furs and jewels, although dutifully interested in the city he had come to save, was staring, instead and aghast at the foreground. 'Mother of God!' he cried. 'What's this?'

Lorraine coughed, drily, 'Er, yes your Majesty. The ground is a little broken.'

'Broken!' Sobieski was incredulous. 'It's worse than we've come through.' A point in that, too. More hills ahead, ridges, crests, ravines before the land levelled. 'Christ Almighty and his Mother!' Sobieski's huge jowls trembled. 'What good is cavalry here?'

Lorraine was soothing. 'We have scouted it, your Majesty. Believe me it looks worse than it is.'

'It couldn't be worse than it looks.' Sobieski said bitterly, wrathfully, for Kings could afford to be wrathful. He swung his huge bulk around, on his left the Danube, on his right the ridge of the Kahlenberg, then other lumpy forest tangled hills; Hermann-skogel, Dreimarkstein, Grunberg, Rosskopf, five miles of barrier before the land fell away towards the Vienna River. 'I must move to my right. Beyond that, '– Sobieski pointed to the farthest hill – 'What is it called?'

Lorraine consulted an aide, the aide consulted a map. 'Ross-kopf, your Majesty.'

'Rosskopf, then. Swing my cavalry around it onto the plain and attack along that river.'

'Yes. Yes.' Lorraine nodded thoughtfully. 'Of course it would take time.'

'Time,' Sobieski shrugged, 'After half a year what are a few days more?'

'Well, nothing I suppose, Sire. Of course,' thoughtfully, 'The city could fall. . . .'

A dismissive wave. 'It can hold a few days longer.'

'Perhaps – certainly, if your Majesty says so, but . . .' Lorraine stroked his chin. 'The Elector, Count Waldeck, General Herman –'

Sobieski scowled. 'Let me remind you General, *I* am commander of this army.'

'Without doubt, your Majesty.' Lorraine gave a fair imitation of shock. 'But there is always a possibility of troops being drawn into battle – if the Turks attack us, and suppose that happened and the Turks broke. . . ?'

A pregnant pause as that seed of doubt germinated in Sobieski's mind. It was undoubtedly true that troops could be sucked into a battle, whether their generals wished them to or not, and suppose that did happen, and suppose the Turks did break, and suppose, suppose the Germans and Austrians relieved the city while he, Sobieski, the hammer of Europe and commander-in-chief was wandering around that god-forsaken valley . . .

Lorraine straightened his legs. 'I always thought that your Majesty's plan was an excellent one,' he said. 'Most excellent. We hold the Turks here and your cavalry – your incomparable cavalry, storm from the hills and crush the main force.' He gave his dry cough. 'There are three valleys. It occurred to me that your Majesty might divide your cavalry into three brigades and reform on the plain. As you can see, you would be directly opposite the Turkenschanz.'

'The Turkenschanz?'

'The headquarters, your Majesty. The headquarters of the Grand Vizier.'

Sobieski pondered, his massive brow wrinkled, the fate of Empires in huge hands, vanity, cupidity, true heroism and the future of his own country weighed in the balance, true valour and honour tipping the balance – and after all, as Lorraine had rightly said, the plan was his, and so would be the glory, depending only, of course, on the execution. He took one last look at the hideous tangle of hill and forest before him. Faintly he heard the irregular crackle of musket fire – Lorraine's scouts clashing with the first Turkish pickets, the battle beginning, as battles often did, regardless of the wishes or desires of the high command. Men being sucked into battle. So. He heaved his corpulent frame upright. 'What is the name of this hill?' he asked.

'The Kahlenberg, your Majesty.'

'The Kahlenberg.' Sobieski hesitated one last time then waved his hand. 'Let us go forward,' he said.

Chapter Twenty-Seven

12 SEPTEMBER 1683

DAWN on the twelfth day of September. Under the curtain wall the tireless Lagunci hacked out the last of the great mine chambers. Above them, the guard changed on the Burgplatz, Souches' regiment taking over from Serenyi's; one man grunting and going down as a musket shot from a Turkish sharp-shooter caught him between the eyes, Turkish cannon on the old covered-way sweeping the bastions with a steady, unremitting fire.

Behind The Spaniard, Starhemberg, a group of aides at his heels, left his headquarters, answered the salute of a motley mob of the cobblers' and bakers' militia and strode down the Karntner-gasse and into St. Stephen's.

The church was full; Sunday and a High Mass, Bishop Kollo-nics of the iron hand and iron heart celebrating it. Starhemberg ducked and crossed himself, swung left, and climbed the tower of the steeple. Under the silent bells he put a telescope to his eye and trained it on the Kahlenberg.

Tiny blobs of colour; the red and white tents of Sari Hussain and Ibrahim Pasha, and beyond them, moving down the moun-tain, men in Saxon grey and blue, other men in the royal white of Austria, puffs of smoke eddying from cannon on the crest of the ridge, cavalry moving; a silent battle, tiny figures moving to and fro like toy soldiers in a child's game. Starhemberg clapped his telescope shut and looked up, once, at the bells, permitted himself a rare, grim smile, then went back down the steps to his duty.

On the Kahlenberg itself the blue and white troops pressed forward; the army in order and obeying orders. Swinging like a door pivoting on its hinges, pushing the Ottoman troops off the mountain and away from the Danube.

From his vantage point on the ridge, Lorraine, steady and casual, sent out orders. Heisler and his dragoons to take the village of Kahlenbergdorf, Count Leslie to get his cannon onto the Nussberg, Herman of Baden to capture the village of Nuss-dorf, the Saxons to support the Grana Regiment, being pushed back by a savage attack.

All in order, all correct. That was the theory, the practice was different. On the broken slopes of the ridge whole regiments disappeared from view, dispersed into companies, companies broke up into platoons fighting desperate little battles of their own in ravines and gullies, along stone walls, in vineyards, around isolated cottages, hacking and chopping their way for-ward from ridge to valley, valley to ridge.

The sun came out; blistering heat, men dropped with exhaus-tion, horses foundered, but by noon the Ottoman troops had been pushed off the left of the mountain, and Lorraine had a firm, connected line ready for the next advance. Almost by mutual consent the fighting died down and then, on the right of the line, on the far crest of the Kahlenberg, armour glinted and glittered. The Poles had arrived.

Under a canopy in his vast encampment, Kara Mustafa, sip-ping sherbert saw the glitter, as ominous as distant lightning on a summer's day. He talked, briefly, to his Agas, nodded agreement gave orders, and within the half hour an incredulous Vienna saw a stirring in the Ottoman encirclement. Cavalry began to trot away, heading for the Kahlenberg and following them were infantry, men in tall white hats and swinging curved swords – among them the Twenty-eighth Orta of the Corps of Janissaries; Corbaci Vasif commanding.

As the Janissaries marched forward the Polish line moved

forward, too. Three columns, sliding over the crest of the ridge with the slow inevitability of a glacier. Down the ridge, through scrub and thorn and vineyards, the way blasted clear by skirmishers and General Katski's cannon, and onto the Michaelerburg.

Riding stirrup to stirrup with his father in Sienawski's column Stefan heard above the din of fighting a strange noise, a roaring coming from his left; the Habsburg troops, seeing their allies arrive at last, cheering themselves hoarse across a shallow ravine, and the advance was halted. A thousand Janissaries in the vineyards of Potzleinsdorf, fighting to the last man, and every man having to be driven out before the slow advance could begin again. On the far right, Hetman Jablonowski brushed aside a feeble Tartar attack, and in the centre Sobieski led his column down into the Alsbach valley. Another blazing fight at the mouth of the valley, two hours bloody battle against a solid line of Janissaries; the Voivode of Cracow leading a suicidal charge, crashing through the Turkish first line and being butchered by the second; the Starost of Halicz his nephew losing his head to a slash from a Sipahi, the Crown Grand Treasurer killed with him, other nobles falling, a ferocious Turkish counter-attack driving the Poles back, threatening the entire army but themselves held and driven back in turn by four steady battalions of German infantry; retreating to a slight ridge between Weinhaus and Ottakring, giving up the valley and so the entire Polish force coming at last onto level ground.

A time to halt, to realign the cavalry, and a time for decision. On the left, Lorraine conferred with his generals. It had been a hard-fought day, the men were tired, Lorraine was tired; should he call it a day, rest the army and give the final blow the next day?

He took off his old cocked hat, brushed it casually with his sleeve, stuck it back on his head and put the question. 'Now or tomorrow?'

'Ach,' General Goltz, a Saxon, grey-headed, weary, wiped his face. 'What time is it?'

Equably, Lorraine fished out his watch, looked at it, shook it, put it against his ear, gave it another glance. 'About four o'clock.'

'So.' Goltz heaved himself up. 'Let's finish it. I'm an old man and I'd like to sleep in a proper bed tonight.'

'Well said.' Lorraine stood up, too, unimpressive in his old grey coat. 'What are we waiting for? *Allons, marchons* – Let's go.'

A wave of the hand, Christian infantry in squares moving across the plain shattering the Turkish resistance; twenty paces forward – Volley! Twenty paces forward – Volley! Nothing to it, really and the infantry quite ready to march like that all the way to Istanbul if required.

The musketry rippled along the Allied front, reaching the ears of Sobieski who was having a brief conference with *his* generals and coming to the same conclusion as Lorraine. 'Order the line of battle,' he commanded. 'It is time to make an end.'

Stefan was standing by his horse. 'I have done it,' he thought. 'I have seen battle.' Men had fired at him and he had fired back. Now he could truly say that he was a man, a warrior, a Polish warrior; and yet the afternoon had been merely a confused blur; a series of vague, disconnected memories; an Hussar dismounting to relieve himself, a dog, caught in a hail of cross-fire running around in circles and barking hysterically, a figure in red who might have been a Turk . . . In truth his memories of the interminable, dragging journey through the Wienerwald were more vivid and more real. Not that he had any intention of telling Vera Soprona that.

'Stefan.' His father calling him. 'Up.'

Stefan bent, took Zabruski's foot and heaved as his father swung over the saddle. 'We're going to attack, now.' Zabruski said.

'A real attack? A charge?'

'Yes.' Zabruski stared down, a curious, enigmatical expression on his face. 'I –' he began, then cut that sentence short. 'Stay with me,' he growled. 'Understand?'

'Yes, father.'

'So.' Again that curious expression crossed the shadowed face. 'God with you.'

'And with you, father,' Stefan answered as he kissed Zabruski's gauntleted hand.

Field officers cantered down the line giving orders and the password – the war-cry *'Jesus Maria Ratui'*. Twenty thousand horsemen moving into the formation for the charge; Sobieski's own tactics, a square of heavy cavalry, a square of light cavalry, heavy, light, alternating in a checkerboard formation, the squares of heavy cavalry forward of the light.

The hetmans rode forward to take their places, and then Sobieski; blue silk over his armour, Prince Jacob, aged fourteen, at his side, a herald, a knight bearing the King's standard, great nobles forming the train. And then Sobieski rode forward a little with his son and raised his hand and his gigantic battle-hammer.

As the King raised his hand, by one of the curious tricks of fate which can be played upon a battle-field, a silence fell; the musket-fire died away, the cannon stopped its roar. The King lowered his hand and without a backward glance began walking his horse forward and with an eerie rattle, twenty thousand lances were lowered as his cavalry walked their horses forward with him.

On a spur of the Kahlenberg the German infantry stared down, entranced. A young private in the Grana regiment turned to his Captain. 'Have you ever seen anything like that before, Sir?'

'No,' the Captain shook his head. 'No, I never did. And take a good look, because you'll never see its like again.'

Never again. The last of Polish chivalry. The last fully armoured knights of Europe walking forward, picking their way through a little broken ground, dressing the line, and then Sobieski spurred his horse into a slow trot, the cavalry trotting too, the great war-horses needing time to reach a gallop but even so the pounding of their hooves shaking the earth.

A half mile away the Ottoman troops were marshalled on the slight ridge. Cavalry, a cannon or two, the infantry, and behind them the Turkish camp.

In the centre of the line, Vasif walked along his orta, as cool as though on parade, talking to his men. 'Fire on the volley. Open ranks and let them through. Slash the horses' legs. Don't be afraid to go down. The horses don't like treading on bodies and the knights can't reach down to strike you.'

At the end of the line he reached Timur and paused. What he said was surprising. 'You've grown.'

'Corbaci?'

'You've grown taller.' The blue eyes rested on Timur for a moment, then, 'Go to the rear.'

'Corbaci?' Timur was astounded.

'Go to the rear.'

'But Corbaci –'

'No buts. That is a direct order. If you refuse I will have your head off now. Go to the rear. Go to the Serasker and guard the Standard of Islam. Rejoin me as ordered.'

A direct order and irrefutable. 'Corbaci.' Timur touched his breast and left the line, walking into the great warren of the Serasker's camp.

Vasif turned, not sparing Timur another glance. The sun was dipping to the west, low enough to make Vasif raise his hand to his eyes. There was a cloud of dust at the base of the dark bulk of the Kahlenberg, and in the dust there were sparks, glints of light, like fireflies at dusk.

More glints, more sparks, sunlight glittering on steel tipped lances, and slowly, slowly from the dust came huge shapes, towering figures silhouettes in black as they moved into the sun; eagle wings and leopard pelts, plumes which nodded to the slow trot of gigantic horses, and lances swaying, dipping and falling forward like a forest being felled.

Somewhere to Vasif's left a light cannon gave a futile bark and from the corner of his eye he saw a Janissary break from the line to be chopped down before he had taken two steps, by Tedeki.

'Good man,' Vasif thought. 'Good man.'

Sounds were coming from the dust now. Hoarse cries, commands, yells, the whinnying of horses, and the beat of their hooves upon the earth like the roll of drums at a funeral.

Across the plain, his sabre out, Stefan was fighting to hold back his horse as the heavy cavalry built up speed. A long way from Ostrova, a long way from Cracow, Vera Soprona forgotten as the canter moved inexorably into a gallop and the cavalry turned into battering rams of steel.

'Mother of God!' Stefan's horse stumbled and he wrenched savagely on the bit, bloody saliva spattering him as he brought the horse's head round. He raked the horses flanks with his spurs and battered his way back to his place in the squadron, by his father.

The formation was breaking a little now; knights on better horses moving ahead, the light cavalry losing it's cohesion, but the whole enormous force was swinging into a tremendous triangle with the King and his banner at the apex.

Vasif saw the banner with its red cross, and the King's deadly helm, plume streaming behind it, and he felt the earth vibrate beneath his feet.

'Fire,' he ordered, and as the ragged crash of musketry died away he unsheathed his curved sword and stepped forward.

'Allah Akbar!' he cried. 'God is Great,' and swung his sword.

Timur actually was looking for the standard. He was still looking for it when the Polish cavalry crashed into the Turkish line.

He actually heard the splintering of lances as the first wave of cavalry smashed into the Sipahi. When he turned he saw that the Twenty-eighth Orta had gone, swept into oblivion, and men and horses like giants were into the camp. The camp itself was disintegrating, drenched with cannon-fire musketry from the sides. Timur fell back by the executioners' tent, seeing the Serasker himself, lance in hand, charging forward and being dragged back by his Albanian bodyguards and then, through the dust and against the setting sun, he saw a man on a horse; not an armoured knight, light cavalry the rider swinging a sabre.

Quite deliberately Timur slung his sword over his shoulder and raised his musket, ready primed and loaded. He squinted carefully along the barrel. He could see the horseman quite clearly, a young face flushed with triumph. Mouth open shouting some triumphant war-cry. A Giaour, a Christian, a heretic, an enemy. Timur pressed the trigger of his gun and blew away Stefan's head. A moment later Zabruski's lance took Timur in the ribs under his right arm and skewered him to the ground.

The battle lasted another hour or so. Men killed each other, the ghostly camels came for Vasif, Osman, Tedeki, Ghiraj, and for the soul of young Timur Ven. Kara Mustafa escaped, crossing the Vienna River, and led the remnant of his army south. He was not pursued. By half past five of the clock it was all over; the fighting had ended and the looting had begun. On the Burg Bastion Starhemberg turned to Major Rosstaucher. 'Now sound the bells,' he ordered.

Epilogue

HERR Jakob Vogel tugged irritably at his collar. It was high and tight and he hated wearing it, as he did his best, stiff brown coat, and he wore them only when he had to, on Sundays and Feastdays.

'Give me a tug.' Frau Vogel, somewhat enmeshed in *her* finery, a gown, snuff coloured as became a respectable tradesman's wife but with what seemed to Vogel to be an improbable number of strings. He tugged here and there and Frau Vogel's shape altered in a mysterious fashion.

'Are you ready.'

Vogel picked up his hat. '*I've* been ready for two hours,' he said. 'Are *you* ready?'

Frau Vogel peered at herself in a speckled mirror. 'Yes.'

'Thank the Lord for that,' Vogel said. He went to the bedroom door and called up the stairs, 'Kaspar!'

'Ready.' Kaspar shouted back from the attics where he and Anna were living until their new house in St. Ulrich was finished.

On the third floor a door opened and the Grafin von Schwarz-bach peered out disapprovingly. 'If we could have a little less noise Herr Vogel, I have important guests.'

'Yes, yes,' Vogel turned away. Important guests! A few scraps of the aristocracy who had been blown back into Vienna like withered leaves. Amazing how the old birds had survived, but they had and back they were; Grafs and Grafins, Barons and

Baronesses . . . but that was the nature of things the natural order ordained by God, and the pyramid of rank, with the Emperor at the pinnacle and landless peasants at the bottom had remained unshaken by the Great Siege. Not that Vogel minded. As long as he had his little bakery and all his family were well, the social pyramid could stand forever. In fact he rather hoped that it would.

Down the stairs the front door opened; voices, Johann down from Amstetten greeting the Hallers, Frau *and* Herr, Haller having miraculously reappeared, as Anna had once said, being taken prisoner by the Transylvanians and not the Turks and so surviving the great slaughter of prisoners during the last week of the Siege.

'Go and meet them,' Frau Vogel, making last minute adjustments to her hair.

Vogel sighed and went down into the parlour. 'Ah! Compliments of the season, Herr Vogel.' Haller togged up in his Sunday best, blocking off the stove and drinking a glass of spiced wine. 'I was just telling Johann here about my escape.'

Vogel groaned inwardly. He had been hearing about the escape for three months. He really wanted to bellow that Haller had panicked and deserted his wife, but what was the use? Haller had persuaded himself that he was a hero – he had even written to the Emperor asking for a medal – and he had succeeded in persuading half Vienna the same thing. Certainly Frau Haller believed it and what good would it do persuading her otherwise?

'Yes, the Transylvanians were good to me,' Haller droned on. 'Christians you see. They left a cross in the woods. You've seen it, Herr Vogel.'

Yes, Vogel had seen it. The whole of Vienna had seen the huge cross with its strange apology. But Vogel was sick of hearing about the Siege. He wanted to forget and the endless squabbles which had followed; arguments over who had saved the city, Sobieski and the Poles or Lorraine and the Germans. Had Leopold been a coward or a wise statesman? It was over and done with. Not that what he felt would make any difference. He knew in his heart that he was doomed to hear Haller's fantasies until one or other of them died.

'Well!' Haller broke off his droning narrative as Frau Vogel came into the room with Rudi, followed by Kaspar in a neat brown coat and Anna in moss green, a little pregnant now. A glass of wine all round and Vogel looked at the company; his wife, Johann, Rudi who, as a special treat, had been taken to see the ostrich, Kaspar and Anna, the Hallers, ach! They were all one kin, one family, simple burgherlike folk and they had come through it all – survived – and besides it was not the day for ill-will, even towards Haller. He raised his glass in a toast; 'Good health to all here,' he said as the bell of St. Luke's chimed its summons.

The bells were ringing across Europe; in Vienna, Warsaw, and in Cracow where Madame Soprona was ringing a bell too.

A slatternly housemaid answered the bell and gave a weird apology for a curtsy.

'Tell Vera it is time to go to church,' Madame Soprona said.

The housemaid ambled off and the coachman tapped on the window. Madame Soprona gestured and the coachman opened the window and poked his head into the room.

'Nearly ready,' Madame Soprona said. 'Nearly. Girls!'

'Aye Mistress,' The coachman sighed heavily and gazed wistfully at the table under the window.

'If you can reach,' Madame Soprona said.

The coachman could. A long arm stretched out and poured a glass of vodka. 'Your health, Mistress,' he said, 'And here's to our Saviour.'

Madame Soprona laughed in her amiable way. 'Does it take you long to dress?'

'Me Mistress?' The Coachman scratched his head. 'Not long,' he said, truthfully, since when he went to bed he took little off anyway. With an air of amazing absent-mindedness he poured out another vodka. 'Any more news from the Master?'

'Back for the New Year. God and the weather willing.'

'Pan Zabruski, too?'

'Him too.'

'And that lad of his, Mistress, the one who didn't have a horse. We won't be seeing him again.'

It was not a question and Madame Soprona didn't answer it. The door opened, the coachman vanished, Vera entered, elegant in furs, sable around her white neck, looking wistful.

'None of that.' The steel in Madame Soprona showed. 'No moping.'

'No Mama. It's just that . . .'

'Just that, never mind.' Madame Soprona heaved herself to her feet. 'Stefan's gone and grieving won't bring him back. Thank the good Lord that your father and Zabruski came through it all. Not that I'm not sorry for the lad's mother and I'll say a prayer for Stefan and her in church, but he always looked delicate to me. His brother is twice the lad. A fine strapping boy. We'll have him over next spring and see how you get on. You'd like that, wouldn't you?'

Vera smiled her dazzling smile, with only a tooth or two missing. 'Yes Mamma,' she said as they left for church.

One hundred and eighty miles away, in Buda, a bell or two rang out also. In the Beylerbeyi's palace Kara Mustafa heard them ring. The day of the birth of the prophet Isa, Christmas day the Giaours called it which was why the bells were ringing.

A few flakes of snow drifted past the window, over a year since he had spoken to Kunitz and Caprara in Edirne. A long time, and an even longer journey, all the way to the accursed Vienna, and all the way back to Buda. Mustafa shuddered at the mere thought of the retreat, harried by the enemy, defeat after defeat, the masssacre on the bridge at Parkany, the fall of Esztergom, indeed it was only by the miraculous intervention of Allah that any of the army had survived at all. But it had survived, as he had written to the Sultan. The trouble was that his enemies in Istanbul were doing their best to bring him down, and he had enemies in plenty. True he had got rid of many. Old Ibrahim Pasha, he had been strangled with a bow-string, and a dozen other pashas with him but even he, Kara Mustafa, Grand Vizier, Serasker Lord of all he surveyed, even he could not strangle the whole of the Ottoman Empire.

Nearing noon, a muezzin's call rang out, answering the Christian's bells. Mustafa stood up, turning to face Mecca and as he did so the doors of the Audience Chamber opened and three men came in. But not ordinary men; the High Chamberlain of the Empire, the Marshal of the Court, and another, who was very large.

The Marshall bowed respectfully and handed over a scroll of parchment. Mustafa unrolled it, knowing before he read it what it contained and a glance at the beautiful script merely confirming it – the Imperial Seal, the Sacred Standard, the keys of the Kaaba, the Holy temple of Mecca, all to be graciously delivered to the Sultan's trusted servants and, in return, they were to entrust the soul of Kara Mustafa to the grace of the Ever Merciful Lord.

'So.' Mustafa nodded. 'You will allow me a moment or two. He finished his prayers, saying them, perhaps, more devoutly than ever before, and asked for his prayer mat to be taken away. 'Now,' he said, thoughtfully lifting his beard as the third man walked towards him with a silken bow string.

It did not take long. The High Chamberlain took a thoughtful look down. 'Send his head to the Sultan,' he ordered.

The executioner's knife went to work, and as it did so, in Vienna the bells rang out and the Vogel's and the Hallers left St. Luke's and above their heads, freshly painted and gilded in honour of the Austrian victory, the little knight with the red cross on his white mantle rode from his niche and, triumphantly, shook his sword on high.

Historical Ironies

A little more than one hundred years after King John Sobieski's great charge on 12 September 1683, Poland had ceased to exist.

The Ottoman Empire lasted, virtually without change, for another 231 years.

The Ravelin, where so many men died, was grassed over and in the nineteenth century the citizens of Vienna could stroll out and listen to Johann Strauss give open air concerts on it.

In 1934 Vienna heard gun-fire again as the great blocks of workers flats, built on the site of the old city walls, the model for Europe and the stronghold of the Austrian Social-Democratic Party, were shelled by the right-wing Government. The minister of the interior who authorized the shelling was a certain Prince Rudiger von Starhemberg.

Author's Note

The Siege of Vienna was a crucial action in the history of Europe, and in the conflict between the cultures of Islam and Christianity. Necessarily, when dealing with an event so complex I have had to simplify matters and ignore others. Readers who might like to know more about the Siege should read, 'The Siege of Vienna', by John Stoye, and 'Double Eagle and Crescent', by Thomas M. Barker. To both these books (among many others) I am deeply indebted. As to this novel, I can only say in the words of the seventeenth century Turkish poet Ziya Pasha;

> 'The things I've chosen are a drop, no more.
> The undiminished sea stil crowds the shore.'

P.C.